A Small Town Summer

Book 4: Love in Harmony Valley Series

Melinda Curtis

Franny Beth Books

This is a work of fiction. Names, characters, places, and incidents are products of the author's imagination or are used fictitiously and are not to be construed as real. Any resemblance to actual events, locales, organizations or persons, living or dead, is entirely coincidental.

First Edition: Copyright @2015 by Melinda Curtis

Second Edition: Copyright @2023 by Melinda Curtis

All rights reserved. No part of this book may be reproduced in any form or by any electronic or mechanical means, including information storage and retrieval systems, systems, without written permission from the author, except for the use of brief quotations in a book review.

Chapter One

"Accept my apology, Sugar Lips?" Gage Jamero was up to his elbows in trouble with his latest lady love.

Well, at least one elbow.

Sugar Lips's contraction built like a blood pressure cuff around Gage's right biceps. His face heated, his fingers numbed, his body felt as if it was wrapped in a too-tight bandage.

"Breathe easy, honey." Gage tried to follow his own advice. During his internship and residency, he'd gained quite a reputation as a horse whisperer when it came to peevish, pregnant horses. Since then, he'd soothed countless mares and saved many foals trapped in utero by breach positions, like this one was. But this foal, sired by a Kentucky Derby winner, was the equivalent of a million dollar baby.

On the floor of a hay-lined stall, sprawled on his back, his legs half across Sugar Lips's chestnut flanks, Gage sweated through the mare's next contraction. He hadn't been this nervous about his performance since he choked while asking his lab partner out in the twelfth grade. Saving this foal would make or break his fledgling career.

He'd graduated. He'd passed his licensing exam, both in California and Kentucky. He had a job offer in Lexington. All he was waiting for was his predecessor's retirement. Until then, he was working for lucrative per-delivery fees from the Thomason Equine Hospital, a facility in Davis which was also an open classroom to local university vet students. They received notification when a procedure or delivery was imminent at Thomason and were able to observe through specially installed viewing windows. Today they were witnessing Gage, one of their own a year ago, on the main stage.

He'd never been requested to deliver such a valuable foal before. If he screwed this up—and there were many ways to fail here—it would be a blow to his young career. He might even lose the job in Kentucky.

As if sensing what was at stake, the student onlookers and support staff in the hallway of the birthing center fell into a hushed silence, much like the gallery at a golf tournament before a pro-golfer shot for birdie and the win. And just like that pro-golfer, Gage knew he had supporters and detractors. No one wanted anything bad to happen to the mare and her foal, but everyone was hungry for the spotlight he'd recently claimed.

The contraction faded and Gage regained use of his fingers, pressing them harder against the flat of the foal's forehead, pushing it farther back into the mare's uterus. He shifted more weight onto his shoulders and the mare's haunches. Extending his arm, he found the foal's front leg and eased it forward without snagging the umbilical cord until he had two delicate hooves in his grasp.

"Here we go, Sugar Lips," he crooned, much too aware that his back was at the mare's mercy should she kick.

The mare's wet flanks heaved as if this breath would be her last. She was young and this was her first pregnancy. She'd spent much of her pre-labor huffing, glaring and kicking at Gage, blaming him for her condition. So far he'd been extremely lucky in avoiding injury, but luck only lasted so long when idiots were present.

"Dr. Jamero?" The question echoed through the birthing stall.

Sugar Lips coldcocked Gage in the kidney with one powerful hoof.

Pain sucked Gage's legs and torso into a stiff ball. He almost lost his grip on the foal. It was a sign of how spent the mare was that she didn't kick him repeatedly. It was a sign of good fortune that this position allowed him greater mobility to shift when delivery was at hand. He'd have to remember that. File for use later.

Because Sugar Lips's uterus tensed once more. It was go-time.

Moments later, Gage lay panting in the hay cradling the trembling key to his dreams. Sugar Lips lifted her head to see what all the fuss was about, whinnying when she saw her newborn.

Gage's chest swelled with pride. This was what he loved about being a veterinarian—facing difficult challenges, saving a life, making a connection with a beautiful creature that communicated primarily with body language.

Some boneheads started clapping. Gage curled protectively around the foal being careful not to tear the umbilical cord. He glared at the lone student who was still applauding until the onlooker stopped. Steady hands transferred the newborn to the ground and checked the vitals of both mare and foal.

Dr. Leo Faraji, a colleague and the man Gage had beaten out for the Kentucky job, helped him to his feet. "Need a doctor, doctor?" he asked in his singsong accent.

"Never." Knowing he looked as if he was the only survivor in a horror movie, covered as he was in blood and birth fluids, Gage drew himself up to his full six-two height, pretending Sugar Lips hadn't nearly deflated his kidney.

"Someone wanted me?" he asked. And then he smiled.

His mother always said his smile could charm a tantrumy two-year-old into eating vegetables. Since Nick had died, Gage saw it more as a first line of defense. He smiled and people assumed he was okay. Now he used it because he wasn't going to let these clean, white-coated, wanna-be veterinarians see how nauseous and spent he was.

Someone sucked in a breath, as if awestruck.

That was a more god-like reaction than he'd been hoping for, but as veiled praise went, Gage would take it.

"Yeah, um, Dr. Jamero? There's some guy on the phone for you." It was the center's new student assistant. She hadn't been around long enough for Gage to learn her name, test her knowledge, or teach her barn etiquette. "He's been on hold awhile now." She handed him a pink note.

Gage's smile didn't break as he reached for the message, dripping the mare's afterbirth onto the girl's hand.

Accidentally, of course.

"Ew." She hopped back, shaking the fluid from her fingers.

"Sorry." Gage checked the stained pink pad and read the name—Dr. Wentworth. His smile faded as he sped from the stall, his steps purposeful and steady, despite the pain radiating in his midsection.

Dr. Wentworth had nurtured Gage's interest in animals since he was a kid. Whenever he called, Gage quickly responded.

Gage's family had been small town cattle ranchers. Their home had been situated in the middle of a neighborhood street on the edge of Harmony Valley, one without sidewalks or streetlights. Their backyard led out to acres and acres of grazing land. Doc's family had been their next door neighbors and were always bringing home stray animals in need of care. Gage had gravitated toward Doc and his patients. He'd set broken legs and viewed medical procedures before he'd earned his driver's license.

Minutes later, Gage had ditched the messy smock he'd been wearing and grabbed the office phone. Today was one heck-of-a good day. He couldn't wait to share the news of the healthy foal with Dr. Wentworth. "What can I do for you?"

"Turn on your cell phone, for one." The gruff voice, loaded with the attitude of a seasoned hound dog, brought back fond memories of the things Gage liked best about Harmony Valley—its people. "Whoever heard of a doctor nowadays without a phone or a beeper strapped to his waist, Gage?"

"I'll turn on my cell as soon as we hang up." Gage's phone was in his backpack in the corner of the sparsely furnished office beneath a picture of Secretariat draped in red roses.

The old vet wasted no time on pleasantries. "I wanted to be the first to offer you a chance to buy into a practice—mine. Here in Harmony Valley."

"Wow." Gage's knees buckled and his butt dropped onto the metal desktop. Practice back home? That wasn't happening. Harmony Valley was filled with bittersweet memories. Not to mention it was wine country now. No racing thoroughbreds or horse breeding farms in the entire off-the-beaten-path valley. "Uh, thanks b—"

"The folks in Harmony Valley sure do have a lot of respect for you. We need a vet."

"But—"

"Don't interrupt. Did leaving town wipe away all your manners?"

"No, sir." It had just reinforced the view that life outside Harmony Valley had more to offer and less heartache.

"Now. Where was I?"

"You were talking about good manners," Gage suggested helpfully.

"My father—" Doc began in a sweeping tone "—would have said you're being impertinent. I called to talk business, Doctor Jamero. It's true, I've had to let much of my practice go in recent years, although I do still treat Bea Larkin's milk goats."

Gage's shoulders sagged beneath the weight of the old man's expectations. "Well, you see—"

"There you go again." There was a snap in his voice that indicated the cantankerous old dog was about to bite. "Just because an old man takes a breath doesn't mean he's finished speaking."

Gage wisely refrained from any jokes about Dr. Wentworth's age, old dogs, and new tricks.

"What I'm trying to say is that we'd make a good team. I can mentor you, like I used to." The old man drew an audible breath, as if he'd spoken too quickly. "Young people are slowly moving back here. They'll be having kids, adopting dogs, and getting hamsters and all kinds of creatures who'll need a vet. Don't tell me you can't come back. Why, Shelby moved in with me yesterday. I'm sure she called you along with the other volunteers they've rounded up to help harvest grapes this Friday night. The winery she's working wasn't able to schedule a harvesting crew last minute, so they are gathering the troops."

This was news to Gage. Shelby hadn't called. She'd stopped calling over a year ago.

Secretariat stared down on him with a gaze that had never backed away from a challenge. Of course, Secretariat had his choice of women.

If Gage's career decision was racehorses versus some old woman's shaggy milk goats; the excitement of the training yard, breeding stables and track versus the slow paced life in small town Harmony Valley; or a life where no one knew his past versus a life where everyone knew why he had a scar on his right temple...

It didn't matter how many pros and cons Gage thought of, the life of a racehorse veterinarian was the one he desired. It was the one he'd choose every time he was asked.

So it made no sense that he didn't reject Dr. Wentworth's offer outright, other than to show his respect and spare the old man's feelings.

Because Gage refused to acknowledge that Shelby Hawkley—Doc's granddaughter—had anything to do with his return to Harmony Valley.

Shelby Hawkley knew what it was like to go from fulfilled and happy to broken and sad, knew how fast it could happen, knew how it came at you from your blind side.

It could happen in a blink. It could stop your breath. It could break your heart.

It being disaster. It changing her life forever.

Just moments ago, she'd been happy, secure in the knowledge that things were looking up. And then she'd blinked.

"If there's an earthquake now, there'll be trouble." Shelby stood in the middle of a narrow trail carved through her grandfather's living room, willing herself not to blink.

Thirty or so five-foot-tall stacks of books, journals, periodicals, and magazines occupied the space. It looked like crowded Manhattan skyscrapers, minus the straight-gridded streets. Her grandfather had created twisted paths, one of which ended at the television, leaving just enough room for him to sit on the hearth and watch the news.

"Don't move and everything will be all right," her grandfather replied, non-plussed. Doctor Warren Wentworth sat cross-legged, all sharp, bony angles, his hair a dry white mop. He looked like he'd been lost on this trail for too long and had missed too many dinners.

"Grandpa, we've got to move. Now." Before she bumped something, and their surroundings tumbled upon them. There'd been a time when she thought she and her loved ones were impervious to disaster. That period was long past.

Her grandfather turned off the TV, unfurled his limbs and rose, wobbling slightly.

Shelby reached for him, careful to keep her elbows within the confines of the path, hyperaware that she was prone to stumble if she didn't keep her attention firmly on the floor. "How did this happen? This...this...book maze."

He harrumphed. "Don't overreact, hot shot. This is my library. I'm exploring the stacks. Didn't you once tell me I wasn't very adventurous?"

"Grandma said that." Keeping her tone matter-of-fact, Shelby began backing toward safety, towing him gingerly along with her.

"It's called the adventure of life." Grandpa's breath smelled of coffee. He couldn't have been sitting on the hearth for long. "What fun would life be if it was a wide, straight road and you knew the ending?"

"What fun would it be if all this fell down on us?" His bones were old and fragile. "If this collapses...I'm just saying...I'm done with surprises and hospitals." Morgues and funeral homes.

"You're still grieving, love. I understand." He squeezed her hands. "I miss your grandmother terribly."

Grandma Ruby and Shelby's husband, Nick, had died within a week of one another nearly two years ago. Shelby and her grandfather had leaned on each other through those difficult first few weeks. As only children from a long line of only children, the pair didn't have a lot of family to rely on.

Shelby sighed. She wasn't still grieving. She wasn't still lost. But she was cautious. She couldn't say the same about her grandfather. This was a trip, fall, and fire hazard. "Tell me the rest of the house isn't like this."

"Young lady, if it is, it's none of your business." Grandpa spoke in grandiose tones, as if he was a knighted explorer being led out of a newly discovered jungle instead of a retired veterinarian being led out of his living room in the small remote California town of Harmony Valley.

"I take that for a yes."

"That is a no."

Their footsteps were muted by the worn avacado shag. One more turn. One more twist.

"Where's Mushu?" Her grandmother's ancient cocker spaniel.

"That dog's been spending a lot of time in the backyard."

Shelby couldn't blame her. One misplaced wag of the dog's tail and she'd be history. The house needed disaster-proofing.

Shelby navigated the fork toward the kitchen, refusing to dwell on how bony her grandfather's hands were. She could only tackle one problem at a time. "And Gaipan? Did you chase her outside, too?" The old Siamese was probably upset that she couldn't sit on the back of the couch and dream of pouncing on the birds in the front yard. The couch was littered with books, haphazardly stacked, ready to tumble.

"Gaipan doesn't like me. Never has," Grandpa said in an endearing voice, as if he respected the cat's right to like or dislike her owners. "She stays outside mostly, except when she's hungry."

They reached the kitchen, which was blessedly stack-free and optimistically yellow, just as her grandmother had been. Goldenrod Formica. Daisy patterned linoleum. Canary-yellow walls. The September afternoon sun angled through the windows facing the backyard.

This feels like home.

And the view outside...

Mushu lay on the grass in the shade of a peach tree, a black and gray ball of curly fur. Beyond the fence, the Jameros' empty pastures rolled up toward Parish Hill, a large outcropping of granite that thrust into the clear blue sky.

Some things never change.

Parish Hill. The sun-drenched kitchen. The fields of brown summer grass.

But the fields were empty.

Shelby's heart panged.

The Jameros had left town, like the majority of residents after the grain mill exploded and jobs disappeared, until the once quaint and charismatic town of Harmony Valley was quiet and quirky. Not exactly the thriving, supportive community of her youth, but a community Shelby longed for nonetheless. And one that was growing again in dribs and drabs.

Shelby released her grandfather and sat on a walnut ladder-back chair. The room was uncluttered. Shelby didn't count her grandmother's collection of animal salt-and-pepper shakers lining the kitchen counter and grouped in the center of the kitchen table. They'd been there as long as she could remember.

"Do you ever hear from the Jameros?" She couldn't keep herself from adding, "Or from Dead Gage?"

"Don't call him that." Her grandfather gripped the chair next to hers. "He's not dead."

"He's dead to me." Had been since the day of Nick's funeral. Since then, Gage hadn't answered any of her calls or pokes on social media.

She picked up the bumblebee saltshaker, wiping dust off the curves of its black and yellow body. She added cleaning to her list of to-do's, along with living room decluttering.

"If Gage really was dead to you, you wouldn't ask about him." Grandpa traversed the length of the kitchen and back as though he was aboard a ship deck, pitching and rolling with each step. "Might be you'd pick up the phone and give him a call."

Having too many of her calls to Gage roll to voicemail, Shelby ignored that invitation. "When did you start to wobble like that? Where's Grandma's cane?" Shelby stretched a hand toward him.

He tottered backward. "I don't need a cane."

"You don't need to fall." She extended a hand again, but he swatted her away.

"Give a man some room."

"I would, but look what you did with the living room," she said drily, giving up for now. "My question is, why? Why is your living room a library?"

"I'm writing a paper on the non-invasive assessment of equine musculature recovery post-delivery." Grandpa sat next to her. Since he'd retired, he'd written many papers. As titles went, this one was almost decipherable. Almost. After a moment, he caved to her questioning look, giving her an explanation. "How a mare's muscles regain their tone after delivering a foal."

"And you need all those books and magazines for that?" Shelby knew her expression conveyed incredulity.

Nick used to take one look at that expression, and capitulate with an endearing, "*Babe.*"

On the other hand, Gage, her former best friend, used to take one look at Shelby and say, "*Barnacles.*" That was his way of saying they were each sticking to their own opinion and would agree to disagree.

Dead Gage...

Shelby rolled her shoulders back. She was getting distracted. "You didn't answer me, Grandpa. You can't need every one of those books and magazines."

"Of course, not." Her grandfather turned in his chair to glance back through the archway toward the living room. "The stacks by the piano were for the paper I did on canine word retention. The stacks by the fireplace were for the paper I did on bovine stimulus-response. The stacks—"

"Hold up." Shelby raised a hand. "There are stacks in there from papers you've already written?"

He faced her, nodding gravely while rubbing his white stubbled chin.

"Submitted for publication?"

Another nod.

"Been published?"

He shrugged. "Mostly."

"So we can get rid of those."

"No, no, no. What if someone challenges my findings? I may need to write a rebuttal or be asked to write a companion piece." He drew himself up in bony regalness. "I have a system. Don't touch a thing."

"You do remember I'm here to stay with you through harvest?" She'd landed a job as the cellar master at the new, local winery.

Grape harvest at Harmony Valley Vineyards started soon. She'd be working ten hours or more a day from now until the holidays, managing the various containers and equipment where the grapes would ferment, plus making clean transfers as the wine moved from crusher to tank to barrel to bottle. Once this was under way, as well as launching construction of a wine cellar, she'd have time to find a place of her own. By then, she'd know if she could stand being back in the town where she'd fallen in love with Nick or if she'd need to continue looking to find a place where daily life didn't make her melancholy.

"Of course, I remember why you've come home," Grandpa said.

"And you do remember I'm not that graceful." That was putting it mildly.

"You fell no more than other kids growing up." Grandpa tapped his temple with a thin, age-spotted finger. "I remember details, Shelby. I'm not senile."

"We need to find a place to put your inactive research, so I won't—" and her grandfather wouldn't "—come in late at night when my reflexes are shot and knock everything down." Given how he walked, it was a miracle the stacks hadn't toppled already.

"I like my library where it is. You can come in the kitchen door." Her grandfather had a barnacle expression of his own, reminding her why his nickname was War.

Shelby realized she'd have to raise the stakes. "You know, Grandma Ruby wouldn't approve."

"Maybe not," he allowed. "But she'd understand. You'll come through the kitchen door."

Chapter Two

"Shelby, I heard you were back in town." Mayor Larry claimed one of her hands with both of his and gave it a vigorous shake. The unlikely politician—a former hippy who still sported a waist-length ponytail, albeit gray—had been in office for decades. He'd shown up on Friday night at the winery for the volunteer harvesting. "How've you been? Cut your hair, I see."

"I'm doing well." *Now*. Shelby's hand was pumped like an old water well handle. She smiled at the old man's enthusiasm. A few of the volunteers had arrived for the night harvest, including the mayor. It felt wonderful to receive friendly greetings and reflect upon shared histories, to hear warm welcomes and *how've you beens*. "I cut my hair a few years ago. Unlike you," she teased.

"At my age, I'm lucky to have hair." The mayor released her hand and smoothed his long ponytail. And then he reached into a cloth bag on his shoulder, shaking out a purple and yellow tie-dyed T-shirt. "You'll be registering to vote, of course. How about a shirt?"

"Oh…" The T-shirt had the Harmony Valley Vineyards' logo silk-screened on it—a running horse on a weather vane. "I didn't bring any money with me." She'd walked over from her grandfather's house.

"Don't make it sound as though she has to buy one, Larry. It's free." Christine Alexander, Shelby's boss and head winemaker, plucked the shirt from the mayor's fingers and gave it to Shelby. Her long blond hair was pulled into a high ponytail that swung from a hole in a navy green baseball cap. "We bought enough shirts for all our workers and volunteers. And you made a tidy profit, Larry." Christine softened her words with a kiss to Larry's cheek.

While Christine and Larry set about distributing T-shirts, Shelby took a moment to take in her surroundings. She'd only been working at the winery a week, and still couldn't get over the charm of the place. The white two-story farmhouse had been renovated into an elegant tasting room on the first floor with open office space above. To the right, the winery's main building had been constructed over the original barn's footprint, and housed wine processing equipment along with some expensive wine barrels. It was a very small operation set in the middle of a beautiful vineyard. If done right, the wine would be exquisite. After Christine worked her winemaking magic, it was Shelby's job to make sure the wine aged to perfection.

The sun was going down, bathing everything in a golden glow even as a cool breeze from the nearby Pacific ocean picked up.

Shelby began turning on the tall, propane heaters that would keep the workers warm during breaks. What had begun as an impossible challenge was turning into a positive. The winery had been unable to entice a professional harvesting team to work on such a small job in this isolated, northeastern border town of Sonoma County. A bit of networking had resulted in former residents being recruited to help. Twenty acres of Chardonnay grapes. Less than an eighth square mile to cover. Together they could be done by dawn. In another few weeks, if the weather remained mild, the final acres with Cabernet Sauvignon grapes would be ready to harvest, and the request for volunteers would go out again.

"I was wondering when I'd get to see you." Agnes Villanova came to stand next to Shelby. She'd been a friend of Shelby's grandmother. Her big heart came in a petite package. She was barely five feet tall, and one of the town's most active citizens. She wore a red stocking cap over her short gray hair and a bright green sweatshirt. At first glance, she looked like a beardless garden gnome.

Shelby leaned over to give her a hug. "I've been meaning to come by."

"You young people are always so busy." Agnes moved closer to Christine and slid her arm around her granddaughter's waist. "First you move home, and we think we'll see you more often, and then you work just as hard as you did before you moved here. So we still never see you."

"The grapes wait for no one, Nana." Christine pressed a purple T-shirt into her hands.

"Nor the wine," Shelby added, exchanging a smile with her boss.

"There's Ryan. Yoo-hoo!" Agnes waved to the young assistant winemaker. "You ladies go easy on him tonight."

"Go easy on him? He's a grown man. A paid employee." Christine's words were clipped as if this argument was oft repeated. "Don't baby him, Nana."

"Ah, but he's so sweet." Agnes's expression turned sly. "Until I have great-grandchildren, who can I dote on?"

Christine rolled her eyes.

Just then, Shelby noticed someone shuffling in her direction. It was Hiro Takata, or Old Man Takata as everyone in her generation called him, the town's former undertaker.

The nip in the air suddenly permeated her bones. She hadn't seen the old man since Nick's funeral.

"My dear." The old man came close enough to reach for her hand. "It's good to see you back and doing well." The same soothing voice. The same gentle, compassionate handhold.

She'd clung to anyone who reached out to her that day.

Shelby swallowed thickly. Even though she considered herself recovered from Nick's death, there were still moments, like this one, that caught her by surprise.

Old Man Takata used his grip to reel himself to her side. He grunted as he strained to straighten hunched shoulders and lift the kindly aging face of his Japanese ancestors to her. "Where's your grandfather? Did War skip out on the excitement?" Cigar smoke drifted to her along with his words.

"He's at home, hip deep in research." Shelby couldn't get Grandpa to promise to stay out of his stacks while she was gone. She'd worry about him all night.

Old Man Takata smiled. "Are you by any chance a bowler?"

Slade, one of the winery owners, appeared before them. He was knock-your-socks-off handsome, a former Wall Street whiz, and Christine's fiancé. "Shelby won't be bowling for your team, Hiro. If she bowls for anyone, it's the winery." Slade gave Shelby a brief once-over, like a coach checking out a new recruit. "The winery bowls in a league in Cloverdale. Do you bowl, Shelby?"

Bowling? Athletics? That spelled disaster. "I don't bowl unless pumpkin bowling for the Harvest Queen crown counts?"

"Ah." The old man laughed. "It's coming back to me. You have a wonky release. Don't you remember, Slade? Her pumpkin nearly took out a spectator."

Just Gage.

Shelby contained a sigh.

"Slade, you may have her. Now, find me a seat under one of those heaters." Old Man Takata released Shelby, but didn't move away. "Let me know if you need company visiting Nick's grave."

Shelby's breath caught.

How did he know I haven't been able to go alone?

She managed a nod.

Needing a moment, Shelby faded away from the gathering crowd, retreating to the banks of the Harmony River on the edge of the vineyard. She drew her green army jacket around herself as the water drifted past with slow swirls that caught the last rays of the day.

The first time Shelby had moved to Harmony Valley was more than eight years ago. She'd learned quickly she could rely on two things—the steady flow of the river, and Gage Jamero. He had the smile of a heartbreaker and the smarts of a Rhodes Scholar. But most endearingly, he was kind and tongue-tied.

He'd introduced her to his best friend, Nick Hawkley. Nick was handsome and had a way of putting people at ease. She'd felt as if she'd known him forever. Nick had asked her out and that was that. She'd gained a love, and a best friend in less than a week. It only took one day to lose both.

She hadn't visited this part of the river since she'd been in high school. Memories came rushing back, along with bittersweet emotion. The trouble with being a relatively new widow were all the "firsts." The first night she'd slept in their bed after Nick died. The first time she'd passed by the church where they'd been married. The first holidays without him at her side.

Firsts were gut-clenching, cold moments. They clogged her throat, flooded her eyes, and cut off her breath. It took time to process them. To acknowledge the innocence, to accept things would never be the same again, and to release the melancholy.

Yeah...the melancholy.

She'd once floated around this picturesque river bend on a raft with Nick and Gage. They'd been talking about college options—although they all knew they'd end up at the same university. They were that close. Then Gage had announced he wasn't coming back to Harmony Valley after graduation.

Because of the scars of her parents' nomadic, career-driven lifestyle, Shelby had been doggedly against Gage moving elsewhere. She'd lived in six cities by the time she was sixteen while her parents climbed corporate ladders in the advertising world. Always the new girl, always on the outside.

"You have no idea what it's like to be someplace else. Nobody knows you like they do here. Harmony Valley cares about their neighbors." She'd pounded the yellow raft's inflatable sides. "We're all coming back here. Nick's going to be mayor. I'm going to teach science. And you, Gage?" She'd shot him her most imperial look. "You'll take over Grandpa's practice."

"Come on, Shelby. At eighteen nobody knows what they really want to do or where they'll end up," Gage had scoffed. "You think you love...some...some thing, but it's just a phase. I loved chicken nuggets when I was four. Now I love sushi. I don't know what I'm going to love ten years from now, but I do know I'm not coming back here. I want to go someplace where people don't know my life's history, including all the stuff I want to forget."

Nick had been unusually silent.

She hadn't understood Gage's sentiment when they were kids. But after Nick's death, Shelby knew exactly how Gage had felt. She hadn't wanted to return either, not because she didn't love Harmony Valley, but because she couldn't handle the town's grief for Nick along with her own.

So instead, she'd taken a job at a winery at the foot of the Sierras, where no one knew her. She worked hard and kept to herself. Ice cream was her best friend. Nick's pillow her midnight confidante. She was lonely, but loneliness was a guarantee that her heart would never be torn apart again.

Then a few months ago, her car had broken down on a stretch of less-traveled highway north of Sacramento. It was dark and deserted. She'd had no one to call for help. Her parents were working at an ad agency overseas. She hadn't talked to them in several weeks. In a blink, she'd realized her life was an empty shell. Those things she'd craved growing up? Close friends, being part of a community, the feeling of permanence? She had none.

The next day, she'd heard about the Harmony Valley Vineyards job posting from her grandfather. She'd decided a compromise needed to be made.

A small shaggy, mostly black dog ran by her, drawing her attention back to the present. Behind the dog was a panting, ginger-headed young boy.

"Hi, Shelby! I get to stay up late tonight picking grapes." Truman, the seven year-old nephew of Flynn, one of the winery's owners, raced past, disappearing into a row of grapevines behind her.

A few seconds later, Slade's ten year-old daughters burst out of another row. They were dark haired, identical twins, although they dressed nothing alike.

"Did you see Truman?" one asked as she gasped for breath and fanned her face. She wore a pair of overalls and a blue hoodie.

Her twin, similarly red-cheeked and breathless, scanned the area. She wore pink leggings and a black sweater.

"You can't catch me," Truman taunted from deep within a row. His laughter danced over rustling grape leaves.

The girls raced after him, leaving Shelby with a lightened heart. It was good to see children back in town, good to see the kind of friendships she'd had the year she'd lived here.

In the distance, cars rumbled over the winery's gravel driveway. Her Harmony Valley past was returning. *Without Nick's optimism and humor. Without Gage's wit and blinding smile.*

"Shelby? Where are you?" Christine called from the farmhouse porch several hundred feet away. "It's almost time to start."

"Coming." Shelby walked through rows of bushy grapevines dotted with the occasional browning leaf. The sky softened to twilight gray as several vehicles shut off and headlights dimmed. The nip of evening breathed over the vineyard. Soon the temperature would drop, and the only light would come from portable metal booms as they harvested the Chardonnay grapes that would make up the first vintage of Harmony Valley Vineyards wine.

Christine gestured for Shelby to join her on the porch, next to Ryan, and near the owners. All three winery owners—Slade, Flynn and Will—were hometown boys, several years ahead of Shelby in school and relative strangers until recently. They'd made their fortunes by designing and selling a popular farming app. And now, they wanted to breathe new life into the town, bringing back jobs and people.

Redheaded Flynn had one hand resting on little Truman's shoulder, and the other resting on his wife

"Here they come. Our harvesting crew." By the pride in Christine's voice, one might have thought she was talking about her own children, the ones Agnes was waiting to dote on. "This is going to be perfect." Christine rubbed her hands together. "We'll divide them into teams and show them how to cut grape clusters. And if someone can't cut—"

"Or cuts off their finger..." Ryan muttered, crossing his gangly arms over his chest as he inspected their volunteer crew.

"Think positive," Shelby urged her co-worker.

"That's right." Christine gave Ryan the stink eye. "If they aren't skilled at cutting, they can transport grapes to the de-stemmer and then the crusher. Everyone works. Everyone should feel needed, even our youngest helpers." She gestured to Truman and the girls. "That's the most important takeaway from this experience tonight. They're getting paid with a T-shirt, a bottle from our first vintage, a thank-you on the web site, and our graciousness."

"Compensation enough to come back for the Cab harvest?" Ryan stroked the long, sparse whiskers on his face. His dark hair curled in disobedient waves that nearly brushed his shoulders. It was a mark of pride that male winemakers didn't shave or cut their hair from the beginning of harvest season until the last grape was picked and crushed.

Female winemakers were more civilized.

Shelby elbowed him. "No more glass half-empty. Wasn't this your idea to begin with?"

"It was." Christine smiled at Ryan, but it wasn't a pleasant smile. "Was it just a few months ago that I hired a sweet, shy assistant?" Christine shook a finger at Ryan. "Whatever happened to him?"

"He blossomed under your tutelage." Ryan grinned.

"More likely in my grandmother's kitchen eating her homemade strudel. She's spoiled you." Christine turned away again, and rubbed her hands together as she took in the group on the porch. "Let's welcome our workers." She led Shelby and Ryan down the steps and into the growing crowd.

The young volunteers embraced their elders, called out greetings to their other hometown friends, hugged each other and shook hands, looking as if they were coming to a family reunion instead of a race to pick grapes before they over-ripened.

Shelby mingled with friends from her past—Emily Johnson, Carl Quedoba, Tanya Romero, Umberto Escobar. She met the recently hired town sheriff for the first time, as well as a woman who was thinking about opening a bed-and-breakfast in her grandmother's ancient Victorian.

A lone vehicle turned down the driveway, its headlights high between the palms. A truck. A white truck. A white truck with a dented front fender.

It can't be. Shelby held her breath.

The driver parked and got out, flashing a dazzling smile beneath a faded red Harmony Valley Hedgehogs ball cap.

A brisk wind rustled the grapevines, chilling her.

Dead Gage.

Awareness of Shelby kicked through Gage's system like an electrical current wearing combat boots.

If Gage had been a lab rat hooked up to sensors, every time he saw Shelby scientists would record an intense release of dopamine, serotonin, and norepinephrine.

He wasn't a lab experiment, but the trifecta of his body's chemicals heightened his perception at the sight of her. Those chemicals focused his attention on the things he found physically attractive about Shelby—her slender curves, her warm smile, her big blue eyes. And the things he admired about Shelby—her intelligence, her gentle humor, her nurturing tendencies. It was all imprinted in his memory. And it all came rushing back at just a glimpse of her golden hair.

Luckily, no one kept track of his internal responses except Gage. And to this day, since he'd been careful, no one knew he loved Shelby.

Gage was a doctor, a scientist. He could catalog his physiological response to Shelby, rationalize his feelings and control his behavior. And if that control was threatened, a joke to break the tension was always the answer.

And so, upon seeing Shelby, he didn't smile like an idiot when he admired her in body-hugging jeans. He didn't let his gaze linger more than a second on her delicate features. And he didn't reenact his fantasy of staring into Shelby's sky-blue eyes as he reeled her slowly into his arms, brushed aside her soft blond curls, and kissed her.

Not when their small town friends flanked her.

Not when, presumably, her new boss stood nearby.

Not when he hadn't talked to her since Nick's funeral.

Gage took off his old high school baseball cap and wiped his brow. The hat was useless anyway, as it did little to hide his semi-nervous expression from Shelby.

Two years ago, he'd overslept and missed meeting Nick for a day of kayaking on the swollen Merced River rapids. That was the day his life changed forever.

If Gage had woken up on time, he might have talked Nick out of getting on the raging water that day. He might still spend Saturday mornings snowboarding black diamond slopes in winter. He might still spend Saturday afternoons in summer free-climbing cliffs in Yosemite. And Nick might still be alive.

Born a month apart, and raised a block from each other, Nick and Gage had been more like brothers than friends. Gage would do almost anything for Nick, even ignore the feelings he had for Shelby.

Take the day he'd met Shelby. She'd stumbled into his high school science class during his senior year. He'd felt as if he'd been sucker punched. Unbelievably, he, who'd always relied on proof and facts, had fallen in love at first sight. How else could he describe how discombobulated he felt just seeing Shelby? But while he'd overanalyzed those strange, new feelings, Nick, who'd never hesitated in his too-short life, acted right after Gage introduced them.

Once Gage discovered his feelings for Shelby were substantial and real, it was too late. He'd fallen for his lab partner, and she'd fallen for his best friend. And despite that, Gage's feelings hadn't waned. Not at their high school and college graduations. Not at Nick and Shelby's engagement party. Not at Nick and Shelby's wedding. Not at Nick's funeral.

He'd never acted on his impulses. And tonight would be no different.

"Gage?" Shelby's voice. So unsure.

He closed the distance between them slowly. The slower he approached the longer he had to take note of how she looked. That no-nonsense, short blond hair beneath a yellow knit cap. That slender figure bundled against the evening chill. That tentative look in her blue eyes.

He was the reason for that look, while she was the reason his pulse kicked up a notch.

He stopped and brought out the heavy artillery—his smile. "Did somebody call for a grape picker?"

Without missing a beat, she put her hands on her hips. "You didn't answer any of my messages."

He shook his head. The crowd of volunteers watched silently, as if this was enthralling cinema.

"You didn't reply to any of my texts or emails either," she said.

His smile dimmed.

"You un-friended me on Facebook and unfollowed me on Instagram," she accused.

The crowd gasped. A few chuckled.

"I shut down my social media pages," he told her, and the crowd. There, at least that was a defendable excuse.

"And your phone?" she demanded, not giving up.

Don't do this to me, Shel.

He'd never admitted to anyone that he was supposed to have been with Nick the day he died. The secret ate away at him. It probably always would. And that was why he'd gone incommunicado. Cold turkey.

Gage pressed his lips together, trying to make an emotional wall, afraid he was failing.

Because Shelby seemed to notice. Her hands left her hips and her eyes turned watery, melting that wall he'd been trying to create. "Gage?"

"I couldn't." The words were wrenched out of him.

Shelby made a sound that was half disapproving huff, half sob, and ran toward him, practically tripping over her own two feet. He couldn't say later if he'd met her halfway, couldn't remember much beyond her arms coming around him, pressing against the hoofprint contusion Sugar Lips had made near his spine. But the hug...the hug was worth every pang in his bruised and sore back. She held Gage as if he was a precious gift she never wanted to lose.

For a moment, Gage drew Shelby close, inhaling the intoxicating scent of her hair, imagining what life would be like if she were his: *No over-analyzing. No careful responses. No distance.*

Like there was a chance of her ever being his.

But he'd made the right choice coming tonight. He'd needed to see Shelby again, if only to say goodbye to her once and for all.

"This makes up for nothing," Shelby whispered, before pushing Gage away to introduce him to those he didn't know—her boss and coworker, the winery owners.

Christine divided the volunteers into different groups—bin runners, crush pad operators, but mostly grape harvesters. Gage ended up with Shelby's group of harvesters, along with several of their friends from school.

They were outfitted with plastic tubs, work gloves, and curved, serrated knives. Shelby led them between two rows of grapevines, halting beneath a boom with lights that illuminated three rows across, positioning them six feet apart on either side. "We'll go through each corridor tonight. You'll locate a cluster of grapes and then cut the stem as close to the cluster as you can."

Gage's breath caught as Shelby held up a very sharp-looking knife. Back in high school, after she'd sliced open her finger while dissecting a pig—*twice*—Mrs. Bernhardt had forbidden Shelby to wield sharp instruments in her biology class.

"Plant your feet. Grab hold of the vine. And…" Shelby smoothly slid her knife beneath a leaf, made a cut, freed a grape cluster bigger than her hand and set it in the bin next to her. Then she demonstrated her technique again, slower this time, surprising Gage with how capable and confident her movements were. "Hold the cluster in one hand, make a diagonal cut with your knife and then show the grapes some love as you put them gently in the bin."

"Nicely done," he said.

She ignored him and cut another grape cluster free. "Remove any leaves or excess stems. When your tub is full, empty your load into the large, wheeled bin and move ahead to another section. And if the knife makes you uncomfortable—" she made eye contact with everyone but Gage "—let me know. We'll find something else for you to do. Nobody's getting hurt on my watch."

He realized in the past two years he'd missed out on something: *Shelby had changed.*

She wasn't the cute, naively optimistic, bumbling young woman he'd fallen in love with, the one his best friend had married.

She was something more.

Something that made it hard for him to remember he should only have come to say goodbye.

Each winery's harvest was different. The weather, the slope of the property, the crew.

Some crews spoke very little English. Some sang rowdy songs.

This crew was like being at a high school reunion without the alcohol or cocktail dresses. They fell into an easy camaraderie—joking, reminiscing, telling stories about college, jobs, spouses, and kids. Everyone, that is, except Shelby and Gage.

"Three kids already?" With a waggle of eyebrows, curvy Tanya ribbed Emily. "You've been busy, girl."

"I love my kids." Emily had that look about her that many young moms seemed to have—equal parts joy and weariness. "But every mom needs a break. That's why my husband is home with them tonight."

They all laughed.

Carl hadn't changed a bit. "I couldn't wait to get out of here after graduation. Santa Rosa has everything I need—sexy cars, fancy women, and the food..." He'd always been focused on the trappings of success and quite the talker. Only now, his brown hairline was receding, and he'd gained a paunch, presumably from all that good food. "I sell solar panels for swimming pools. I drive a company truck, and as a perk they put solar panels on my roof for free. If anyone needs to heat up their pool, let me know."

"Dude, I can't afford a pool much less solar panels." Umberto's teasing grin was as wide as ever. "Do you still play baseball? Or are you too busy being a big shot?"

Shelby laughed along with the others, but she didn't join into the conversation.

Seeing Gage triggered too many memories. Bright ones—laughing with their heads bent over a science book, racing Nick and Gage on bikes to school, dancing with Gage on her wedding day. And darker memories—her calling to ask Gage if he'd heard from Nick, him showing up at their apartment in the middle of the night to drive her to identify Nick's broken body, Gage fading into the crowd of mourners at the funeral.

A part of Shelby ached anew, trying to imagine the reason he'd disappeared. He must have been hurting as much as she'd been. A part of her rose up in indignant anguish. He'd left when she'd needed him most.

Wounded pride stiffened her backbone. She refused to need anyone anymore. Needing, attachment, loving. It all led to heartache.

For two years, she'd coped with the loss of Gage's friendship by creating the metaphor of Dead Gage. If she was dead to him and not worthy of a phone call, he'd be dead to her. Tit for tat. Quid pro quo. Right back at you.

Then why did I claim him for my crew?

Her knife slid too far, opening the skin of a few grapes. She tossed it into the bin and moved a few feet farther down the row.

Why did I claim him?

Because... Because they'd been close once. Because there'd been a shadowed look in his eyes that echoed hers on difficult days. And because his happy-go-lucky smile when he'd arrived was the one he used to hide his true emotions.

Before she could ask Gage how he was doing, Tanya started up again. "Do you remember that time Mrs. Horvath took us on a field trip to the coast?"

As the night wore on, fog blanketed the vineyard. Cold seeped through Shelby's work gloves, the same as it had seeped through her heart at the sight of Gage.

"Do you ever hear from Maria?" Tanya cut a thick cluster free.

"I heard she's living in Vegas." Emily straightened, pressing her thumbs into the small of her back. "I'm using muscles I haven't used in years."

Umberto dumped a tray of grapes into the big bin on wheels. "My grandmother said she went to prison."

"My grandfather said she's dead." For once, Carl sounded somber. "Sorry. That was rude given Nick isn't here."

The group fell silent, casting covert glances toward Shelby and Gage.

"Let's break," Christine called out shortly after midnight.

Agnes, Mayra, and Mayor Larry had arrived with hot tamales, sandwiches, chocolate cake and fresh coffee. They set everything out on the wrought iron patio tables beneath portable heaters.

Agnes fawned over Ryan, serving him a sandwich and bringing him a large piece of cake. Mayra, who owned the Mexican restaurant in town, did the same with Umberto, her grandson. But she plied him with tamales and orange soda. Mayor Larry was making the rounds, shaking everyone's hand.

Bypassing the food, Shelby headed toward the river. She didn't have to ask Gage to follow. She knew he would.

At the riverbank, she sat on a log, and turned to face him when he emerged from a row of grapevines. The moon did a poor job of illuminating his features, which were hard planes and shadows. His dark hair blended into the night.

"How've you been?" Gage surprised her by breaking the silence between them as he came to sit. He'd always been a reticent conversationalist, more likely satisfied by simply being part of the group than actively participating.

"I've been fine." It was what his parents had said when she'd asked about Gage. "Busy, I mean."

A frog sang a baritoned lament across the river.

"I miss him, too," Gage said quietly.

"Don't." Shelby's shoulders deflated as if pressed down, threatening to bend her over. She kept herself upright by pushing her palms onto her knees. "You weren't around when I needed to talk about Nick, when I needed to share the things that made him special with someone who knew him as well as I did." Her voice made her sound hurt and disappointed. She resented that he'd drawn grief and resentment out of her. "I'm sorry. I can't talk to you as if I just saw you yesterday."

But she wanted to. That once young, innocent part of her she'd assumed was long dead and buried—that stumbling, lonely misfit—wanted things to be unchanged between them.

Shelby covered her lips with her fingers, but that didn't stop the lonely misfit from talking. "My marriage to Nick...your friendship...they meant everything to me and for one precious year after college graduation, I had both. I felt I had what everyone else took for granted." Dropping her hand to her thighs, Shelby drew a shaky breath. "But now... I'm not the same person anymore. And seeing you..."

"I'm sorry."

Shelby let Gage's words drift by with the river.

"I'm sorry," he said again in a voice roughened with emotion. "I can't tell you how often I started to get in touch. But what would I say?" He clasped her hand.

It was a very un-Gage-like moment. He wasn't a touchy-feely sort of person.

She'd taken her gloves off. The warmth of his skin heated her palm. But his touch sent more than physical warmth. It offered more than belated comfort. The feel of his hand around hers—an intimacy she hadn't experienced since Nick—sent a prickle of awareness along her spine, of Gage, as a man.

Awareness? Of Dead Gage?

"There's nothing more to say." She snatched her hand back from his and hopped to her feet. Breaking their connection, she almost tripped over a tree root as she backed away. "Friendships are like seasons. There's a cycle. A beginning, an end. Ours ran its course." Friendships cooled. People moved on, except for those who stayed here in Harmony Valley. "Time to get back. We've got a long night ahead."

She turned away, one hand cold. The other, the one Gage had held, still tingled with warmth.

Awareness of Gage? It was a fluke. A product of her loneliness.

By the time she returned to the others, she almost believed it.

Chapter Three

Gage had been coldcocked twice in one week. First by Sugar Lips. Then by Shelby.

It'd been a long, physically demanding night, made longer by the residual reminders of Sugar Lips's blow, and Shelby's proclamation that their friendship had run its course. It was exactly what he needed to hear to be able to take the job in Kentucky and get on with his life.

There would be no *what-if* hypotheses about a future with Shelby. There would be no arguments about his being disloyal since Shelby was now free. There would be no middle-of-the-night, sleep-depriving worries about where Shelby was, if she was dating, if she felt as alone as he did.

Gage parked his truck in his old driveway on Adams Street. Blue sky peeked through a layer of cool fog.

When he'd informed his parents he was volunteering for the harvest, they'd told him not to go by their former house. But how could he not?

"Helping two kids through college," his dad had said. His parents lived in Santa Rosa now, both working at a livestock auction instead of their ranch. "We could only afford the taxes on the place. And now it's not as if anyone's going to buy it."

The once cheerful blue and white house seemed to have given up hope of the Jameros returning. The roof on the ranch home sagged beneath wisps of fog. Someone had been by to cut the weeds where the lawn used to be. Boards from the tree fort that Gage and Nick had built dangled dejectedly from the oak tree in front. The basketball hoop over the garage was rusted, the netting frayed.

The curtains were drawn. Not only did the house not want to see the desolation outside, it didn't want anyone to see the similar emptiness on the inside. Down the road, where Nick used to live, was much the same.

There was nothing left to keep Gage in Harmony Valley. All he needed for closure was to tell Dr. Wentworth, *"Thanks, but no thanks."*

Gage walked next door, taking the shortcut through the side yard.

Doc had the kitchen door open and waved him closer. "Heard you drive up. You're just in time for breakfast."

Mushu waddled over to meet Gage, her black curly fur was peppered with gray and in bad need of a grooming. He knelt down to give her some love, stroking her while doing a brief health inspection. No tumors, no scaly skin, no sensitive spots. Just matted fur.

The cocker spaniel didn't follow him inside, despite the tantalizing scent of bacon. "You've either been overfeeding Mushu, or she's got a hyperthyroid issue."

"She's overweight." Dr. Wentworth looked at Gage over the top of his thick glasses. "I'm busy, so I set out a dog feeder. She's like a hobbit. She eats more meals than she needs to."

"It's not healthy for her." Gage caught sight of the stacks of books and magazines blanketing Doc's living room. "What's all this?"

"My research. I'd like to discuss it with you." The old vet dished a plate of scrambled eggs mixed with bite-size chunks of potato, red pepper, cheese, and bacon, and handed it to Gage.

After the cold night he'd had working in the vineyard next to Shelby, the hearty meal was a welcome sight. Gage took a seat at the table. Whereas his abandoned home looked like a candidate for demolition, Doc's was bright and lived-in. It was on the tip of Gage's tongue to ask if Shelby knew about the clutter, when she came through the front door, looking haggard.

"Shoot. I forgot this was here and I'm too tired to go around." Shelby wended her way carefully through the tall stacks. Her blue eyes were dark-rimmed, betraying her exhaustion. They stayed firmly trained on the path in front of her. "But I'm relieved Grandpa didn't knock anything over."

"Hey!" Doc protested.

Gage held his breath, prepared to leap up if she mis-stepped and knocked over anything.

She didn't. Instead, her gaze stumbled into his as she entered the kitchen. "You didn't come in this way, did you?"

Gage shook his head, grateful that he wasn't being given the silent treatment, grateful that her effect on him wasn't as strong as when he'd first seen her last night. "I came in the back."

"Which is the door I told you to use, Shelby," Dr. Wentworth scolded, filling another plate for his granddaughter. "What's your schedule today, hot shot?"

"This hot shot is taking a nap, first thing." Looking just as tired as Gage felt, she sank into a kitchen chair opposite him, accepting the food and glass of milk her grandfather put in front of her with heartfelt thanks. "I'm meeting Christine downtown after lunch. We're going to choose a site for the temporary wine cellar."

"Aren't wine cellars underground?" Gage had the strongest urge to put an arm around her shoulders and tuck her close. Instead, he made a mental list of the salt-and-pepper shakers on the table—a pair of Mallard ducks, a pair of kissing geese, brown spotted cocker spaniels, bumble bees and Siamese cats. "I didn't think anything downtown had a big enough basement."

"There isn't. But we have to make do." Shelby's response was crisp, all business. "The wine cellar was left out of the original winery plans, made before they hired Christine. The grapes we picked will ferment at the winery's main facility in steel tanks. Then they'll be put into oak casks, which require climate controlled storage while they age enough for bottling. The sooner we get a wine cellar cobbled together, the better off we are in terms of wine quality."

"You plan to use one of the vacant stores downtown?" Gage had overheard some volunteers discussing it while taking a coffee break during the night.

She nodded.

Doc turned off the burner and moved the pan to the rear of the stove. "You can shower if you want to, Gage, before we check out the clinic." He joined them at the table with a loaded plate for himself. "I could wash your clothes while you nap in the guest room."

"That's very domestic of you," Gage said with a straight face. No offense, but he didn't want Doc anywhere near his skivvies.

"Grandpa, you're embarrassing him." Shelby grazed Gage with a glance. "And me."

"I'm being hospitable." Doc's rumble filled every corner of the kitchen. It might have even sent his stringy white hair fluttering. "Gage is here to talk details on reopening my practice."

Gage swallowed quickly, nearly choking on his eggs. "About that—"

"You're not seriously considering moving back?" Shelby blurted, her gaze intense. "I thought you didn't want to live here."

"Well, I—"

"The boy needs a job." Dr. Wentworth shook his fork in Shelby's direction.

Shelby shook hers right back. "I'm sure the boy has dreams that don't involve treating overweight cocker spaniels and aging dachshunds with back problems."

The familiar way they bickered had Gage hiding a smile.

"Are you implying the challenges in practicing here aren't good enough for him?" Doc squinted at Shelby over the top of his eye-glasses.

"Yes." She popped a bite of potato in her mouth.

Dr. Wentworth pounded a fist on the table, rattling shakers. "Why don't we wait to hear what the boy has to say?"

They both turned to him expectantly.

Gage chose a bumblebee from the collection of shakers at the center of the table, and peppered his food, wisely keeping his mouth shut.

"You see," Shelby said at the same time her grandfather said, "I told you so."

They each stabbed a bite of food.

Gage couldn't prolong disappointing Doc any longer. "I have a job. Starting in January, I'm going to be the veterinarian for a group of racing stables in Lexington, Kentucky."

They both stared at him with equal parts dismay and pride.

"So far away," Shelby murmured, while her grandfather muttered, "Dogs, all mighty. I should have called you sooner."

Had Nick been alive, the ensuing silence would have been filled with a supportive comment. To live up to Nick's standards, Gage found himself stepping in. "Shelby's right. I wouldn't be happy here. It's my dream to work with racehorses."

More silence.

Gaipan appeared at the back door, announcing her presence with the distinctive complaint only a Siamese could give.

"Two months." Dr. Wentworth stared at Gage through thick, smudged lenses. "I'll take you for two months. In that time, we can have the practice up and running again. It'll look attractive for some other vet to come in. Or maybe you'll decide to stay."

In his mind's eye, Gage could see himself shaking his head, his neck twisting to and fro. But his eyes had stuck on Shelby, on her fringe of mussed up hair beneath her knit cap and the weary set to her shoulders. She wasn't just tired. She was unhappy.

I could make her happy.

As a friend. Only as a friend.

He should have ended Doc's hopes. Instead, Gage kept them alive with a nod and a curt, "We'll see."

Chapter Four

"**M**ae, how about you? When can you work the gift shop? Saturday afternoon is still open." Agnes had a way of looking at a person and smiling that almost made you forget she was putting you on the spot. Almost.

"I won't be working at the shop." Mae Gardner sat in her chair at El Rosal, her full lunch plate lying untouched in front of her.

The first Saturday of the month used to be the widows meeting. They talked about gossip and meal planning and men.

Agnes had increased the frequency of the meetings and changed the focus of their gatherings to opening a gift shop downtown. "How many pot holders can I put you down for, Mae?"

Mae squished a piece of cold enchilada with her fork. "None."

The rest of the room gave a collective gasp. Mae always made quilted pot holders for town fundraisers, and had been for more than five decades. Her refusal was like saying there would be no Christmas this year.

Mae's breath hitched. She turned to Rose Cascia. "Did Emma's wedding dress come in yet?"

Rose shushed her, glancing guiltily at Agnes.

"Okay, how about Lila?" Agnes shifted her attention elsewhere, trying to fluff the short gray bangs of her pixie haircut. "Can we rely on you for a baby quilt or two?"

Mae swung her gaze around the room. Nineteen other elderly women were in attendance, eating and head-nodding whenever Agnes reached a head-nod moment. Were they all really interested in opening a boutique?

A glass clinked in the corner. Rhonda Matson was on her third mimosa. That usually meant her son had cancelled plans to bring her grandkids to visit on Sunday.

Janine Lee kept tugging down the ends of her blond wig. Was her hair finally growing back after chemo? Olly Bingmire's attention kept drifting toward the front of the restaurant. She gave a mouse-like squeak and stared at Agnes as Thomas Higby came through the door, nearly five-and-a-half feet of single senior man and a hard worker.

Mae would like to have a word with Thomas. Life was too short to live alone. She'd like to have a word with Janine, maybe congratulate her on beating the Big C. She'd like to tell the waiter to stop bringing Rhonda mimosas. But there was Agnes and this boutique business. And that, plus her sour mood, had Mae silent.

"The next item on the agenda is a name for our venture." Agnes tapped her pencil against her palm. "Ladies, we need something unique and creative."

"Pretty Things," Clementine Quedoba piped up. "I enjoy pretty things." She had, but the poor dear had hocked many of her pretty things over at Snarky Sam's pawn shop.

Such a shame.

"Harmony Valley Boutique?" Linda Sue suggested in her kitten-soft voice. She always came across like a fragile flower. You'd think she would have gotten over her husband's passing five years ago. Instead, Linda Sue had cats. She could be dating a well-preserved retired fireman who rescued cats, but no. She and the cats lived alone.

"A Stitch in Time," Meg Galinsky blurted as if the thought had just come to mind. She still had both her God-given hips and mobility. Why wasn't she dating someone in the town's bowling league?

Mae mashed up her enchilada some more, waiting for the meeting to be over. Maybe then she'd be able to get to the really important things—the emotional status of her friends.

But Agnes clearly had other plans. She bee-lined to Mae as soon as she adjourned their meeting. "Are you okay? You look like you've lost weight again."

"I'm fine." *Liar, liar, polyester pants on fire.*

"Oh, Mae," Agnes said softly.

Shoot. Linda Sue was heading out with Meg and Olly. Janine and Rhonda were gathering their purses.

Agnes worked that smile of hers. She was the sweetest member of the town council. "You know we'd love to have some pot holders to sell in the store."

Janine and Rhonda drifted outside with the crowd. Mae wasn't moving fast enough to catch them. She had so little joy left. Why was this being taken from her, too?

"Agnes, do you really want to spend the last few years of your life selling pot holders in a store?" Mae didn't wait for her friend's answer. She left.

Chapter Five

What happened to believing Gage was dead to her?

Dead Gage shouldn't make Shelby want to smile just by seeing him sitting at her grandfather's kitchen table.

Dead Gage shouldn't tug at her heartstrings when he talked about leaving town.

Dead Gage shouldn't open up long-shelved feelings, ones that made her feel bad for thinking of him as Dead Gage.

"Grandpa, I'm going to my meeting." Shelby kissed the crown of her grandfather's head. She'd had a nap, coffee, a shower and almost felt human.

Her grandfather was working at the computer desk in his bedroom. He acknowledged her announcement with a soft grunt.

It was just under a mile to the town square, so Shelby decided to walk. Someone on a motorcycle passed by her and waved. Shelby waved back, trying to reach her parents on her cell phone. There was no answer. The message she recorded was brief: *Call me. I'm back home.*

She passed by a house that was boarded up. There were too many boarded up houses in town. People were returning to Harmony Valley, but slowly.

A block from the town square, Flynn and Slade were building a ramp over the front steps of Mr. Hammacker's house. Truman, his dog, and the twins ran around the yard playing keep-the-ball-away-from-the-dog. Their laughter was infectious.

Shelby stopped on the sidewalk and waved at one of the girls before catching Flynn and Slade's attention. "I would've thought you guys would be catching up on your sleep."

"Kind of hard to sleep when your to-do list is as long as your arm and you've been drinking coffee all night." Flynn stood and shook out his shoulders, seemingly grateful for a break.

Drill in hand, Slade shaded his eyes as he turned toward Shelby. "Off to that wine cellar meeting?"

"Yep."

He gave her a half grin. "Make sure Christine doesn't offer anyone any money before she talks to me."

She laughed politely, but instantly sobered. Like she was going to get between the owner and her boss. The safest course of action was to smile and move on.

Gage would be moving on, most likely sooner rather than later.

Funny how Gage's announcement about Kentucky affected her. She'd had to fight the urge to ask him why he couldn't find a job closer to town. But she hadn't because she understood how things worked. People leave. And yet, it was his leaving that jostled her emotions this morning.

She felt restless, as if something needed to be done. Today. Something more than a search for a temporary wine cellar location.

Shelby crossed the town square.

Agnes opened the door to El Rosal and waved her over. The primary restaurant in town served breakfast, lunch and dinner, as well as sold grocery staples in what used to be the lobby. The bright primary colors of the restaurant's interior—red tables, blue chairs, green walls—were almost too much for Shelby's sleep-deprived eyes.

Agnes was having coffee with two other elderly women while the waitstaff cleaned up the tables around them. "I know you're probably in a hurry, but neither Rose nor Mildred have had a chance to say hello since you returned."

"Unfortunately, I only have a few minutes." Shelby sat with her grandmother's friends, just as she'd sat in their kitchens back in the day and mixed cookie dough or tried to learn how to make a decent casserole. Hands down she'd been the worst of their culinary students.

"I seem to remember you performing in a version of West Side Story I directed for the high school." Rose Cascia smoothed her already smooth, white chignon as she studied Shelby. She had a regal, tightly-wound posture. In her youth, she'd performed in ballets and on Broadway. "But I can't recall what role you had."

"I was in the chorus." Where Shelby had tried very hard not to trip her way into the orchestra pit.

Rose tsked. "That will have to do. On Sunday nights—"

"She's going to be too busy to sing theatricals with you on Sundays." Agnes patted Shelby's hand. "I know because my granddaughter works 24/7. That's a term, isn't it?" She arched a silver brow as she looked at Shelby. "24/7? Or is it 7/24?"

"24/7." Shelby tried hard not to smile. "It was lovely to see you all again, but I really need to be going, I'm meeting—"

"Tell me." Mildred's round white curls complemented her plump pink cheeks, but her gaze was unfocused, giving away she had deteriorated vision, even with thick glasses. "What kind of car do you drive?"

"A white SUV. Why?"

Mildred shook her head. "Young people nowadays. No imagination. No spunk." In Mildred's youth, she'd blazed many trails, including being one of the first female professional race car drivers. "I expected more from you, Shelby. Weren't you named after Carroll Shelby, the famous race car designer?"

"I don't think so." Shelby made a mental note to ask her parents when they returned her call.

"Leave Shelby's vehicle choice alone. She's practical," Agnes pointed out kindly.

"But boring." Rose patted Shelby's other hand. "No offense, dear."

"None taken." Shelby pulled her cell phone out of her pocket and checked the time.

"She needs to take some risks," Mildred interjected. "Fast curves, fast dancing, fast men. Before she's old."

"O-kay." Shelby stood. "It's been lovely, but I'm going to be late if I don't leave now."

She hightailed it out the door.

A brisk breeze ruffled Shelby's bangs as she turned down Main Street. Summer was waning. Harmony Valley was far enough north and close enough to the ocean that fall often tried to elbow summer aside before late September.

The stuccoed buildings, brick sidewalks, and classic gas streetlights were postcard perfect. There were still plenty of vacant, cobweb-draped windows to be worrisome—the ice cream parlor where kids hung out after school, the fabric store where she'd worked part-time, the beauty salon where her grandmother received her monthly pin-curl perm.

But there were signs of life, too. A couple of coming soon signs posted in windows. The small pizza place was still open, if only for lunch and take-out for dinner, and some of the elderly ladies were planning a gift boutique with handmade quilts, crocheted baby things and the like.

Christine stood in the sunshine outside the barbershop with three local residents, who were or had been business owners. They weren't exactly the traditional butcher, baker, and candlestick maker.

The youngest of the three, Mayor Larry, was rumored to own most of the commercially zoned property in town. He wore a purple and green tie-dyed T-shirt beneath a worn jean jacket. He smoothed his long gray ponytail as Shelby approached, looking more rested than she felt.

Phil Lambridge, the town's barber, was a scarecrow's collection of gangly limbs and ill-fitting clothing. Two years ago, Shelby'd accompanied her grandfather to have his haircut and nearly had a heart attack. Phil's hands undulated like a hula dancer's hips. She'd feared Grandpa would lose an ear. But miracles did happen. He'd come out unscathed.

The final member of the trio was Mae Gardner, who leaned heavily on a cane. The former bridal shop owner had sold Shelby her prom and wedding dresses. You wouldn't know it from looking at her brash red hair, layers of wrinkle-sunken makeup, and the flowery polyester blouse that hung loosely from shoulder pads on her too-thin shoulders, but the woman was a savant when it came to matching a girl with the right dress.

Christine greeted Shelby, then turned to the three locals. "Thanks for meeting us today. As you know, the winery needs to build a wine cellar. We'd like a property downtown and we're willing to pay cash."

"Actually—" Phil gestured with a shaky hand toward his shop "—my property isn't available. I have a good business. Real popular."

Hoping that wasn't true, Shelby tugged her knit cap more firmly over her ears.

Mayor Larry patted the barber on the back. "If you're taking yourself out of the running, Phil, you can play for me in the weekly bridge tournament at Yolande's. They start in ten minutes and then there'll be dessert."

Phil grinned. "An unclaimed slice of Yolande's key lime pie? How can I turn that down?" Waving, the old man walked off with deliberately measured steps.

"Let's get down to business." The mayor may not have been as old as Mae, but his smile creased his face in wrinkles as webbed as his tie-dyed designs. "You need a good bit of square footage, Christine. The largest space is where the grocery store used to be." Owned by none other than Larry.

Mae tsked, then said in her sultry smoker's voice, "If we're trying to rebuild the town, shouldn't we save that space for a new grocery store?"

"Now, Mae." Mayor Larry's smile wavered almost imperceptibly. "It might be better for a grocery to build a new facility out by the highway."

"You own that land, too, I suppose." Mae pounded her cane against the sidewalk and arched a penciled brow. "You always were an opportunist."

"Actually," Christine said diplomatically, "I'd like to avoid any space on Main. We hope the winery's success will eventually draw the tourist trade. Best reserve locations on Main for that. What about something on King or Polk?" The streets flanking Main.

"My store is on King," Mae said smugly. "You remember Dream Day Bridal, don't you, Shelby? You bought your wedding gown there. Nick was so sweet when I told him no grooms allowed."

Shelby's breath hitched. The brisk breeze danced around her ankles. She'd forgotten Nick had wanted to vote for the dress. He'd laughed when Mae shooed him out the door, promising he'd get his vote in somehow. That was Nick, always breaking the rules.

"I had the most marvelous shop," Mae continued, moving in careful, mincing steps toward the corner. Larry offered her his arm, which she graciously accepted. "Four dressing rooms. A lighted dais surrounded by mirrors. Prom creations. Quinceañera dresses. Wedding gowns." She sighed. "I do so miss it."

Despite escorting his rival, the mayor wasn't giving up that easily. "There's the Brown Jug Bar around the corner."

"That vacant dump," Mae scoffed. "It's only as big as my storage room. Christine said they wanted a large space."

Christine glanced in amused amazement at Shelby, who wished she could share in the unexpected sparring match, but the closer they came to Dream Day Bridal, the more apprehensive she became about another first to soldier through. Suddenly, she didn't care where Christine put the wine cellar, as long as it wasn't in Mae's building.

Mayor Larry cleared his throat. "The butcher shop has—"

"A stench that permeates the walls to this day." Mae had the upper hand and wasn't giving in.

"And then there's the real estate office." The mayor quickly rebounded.

"That might work." Mae's kohl-lined eyes narrowed. "If you don't mind low ceilings. That's the only one story building on the block. Flat asphalt roof. Didn't you have a problem with leaks every year?"

The mayor frowned.

"We'll start with the real estate office and then look at the bridal shop." Christine continued being the diplomat.

Shelby continued to feel off-kilter. If only she could have a moment alone.

The real estate office had low ceilings, which were a deal breaker. By Shelby's calculations, they'd need to move at least four large, upright casks from the winery to this location. Eight-foot ceilings were far too low. Besides, Christine wanted to age smaller amounts of wine in barrels and bottles for years. The square footage seemed short.

"Last resort only," Shelby said when Christine asked her opinion, trying to keep from sounding disappointed. If it'd been perfect, there'd be no reason to visit the bridal shop. "We'd have to raise the roof and find a place somewhere else to age bottles."

"Onward," Mae said, moving slowly off.

Dream Day Bridal was only a few doors down. But between Mae and Shelby's slow steps, it took a long time to get there.

From the sidewalk, Shelby could see Mae had left a few mannequins inside—fully gowned—along with the dais where brides evaluated their appearance, and the chairs where mothers and bridesmaids sat.

They went inside.

And just like that, Shelby was sucked into the past.

Nick had held open the glass door for Shelby, her mother and his. He'd sat in a chair against the wall with a broad smile on his face. And then Mae gave him the boot. Not ten minutes later, he'd sent Gage in as his representative. The women had laughed but welcomed him into their midst.

Gage smiled every time Shelby came out in a gown cinched and clipped in the back. But none of his smiles was a wow. Not until she appeared in an ivory satin A-line that draped elegantly over her curves did his smile beam so bright it hit her midsection. It was official. That was the dress.

"Wow." His smile faded and he looked at her with wonder in his eyes and said, "Shelby—"

"Shelby." Christine brought her back to the present. "I like it. The ceilings are high. The size will suit us until we can build a proper cellar. And then it can serve as our overflow storage. We can convert a dressing room into an office for you."

The mayor groaned in defeat.

Shelby's gaze drifted to a chair near the wall. She could almost hear Nick's laughter, almost see the amused glint in his eyes. He'd found so much joy in the little things in life. She clenched her hands behind her back, turning away from the dais, away from her memories, away from her lost dreams.

"The mannequin with the arms in the main window is Conchita." Mae lowered herself carefully into one of the chairs. "She and that dress—Spanish designer—have been with me from the start."

Shelby smiled politely. The Spanish dress had been stunning at one time—sweetheart neckline, long tight-fitting lace sleeves, lace overlaying a white satin train. "Do the other mannequins have names?" The ones without heads or arms.

Mae flashed a smile, displaying her missing bridgework. "You don't name headless mannequins. That's bad for business." She took stock of Shelby and Christine. "If I was choosing dresses for you girls to try on today, I'd pick a black satin evening gown for Christine because of her elegant carriage."

Christine chuckled and said cryptically, "I hope it comes with feathers."

The old woman turned faded gray eyes toward Shelby, seeming to see past Shelby's worn blue jeans and stained work jacket. "And a soft yellow calico sundress for you because you used to lay in the grass in the town square, stare at the blue sky, and watch the clouds drift past. From the shade of your complexion, you could definitely use some fun in the sun, girlie."

"I get outside." Occasionally. When she wasn't busy in someone's dark wine cellar. Shelby did a quick shoulder roll, trying to shake the effect of her being back in the bridal shop for the first time.

Christine looked thoughtful. "I bet you'd look great in that sundress, Shelby."

"I bet men would fall over each other at the sight." Mae sighed dreamily. She was still a hopeless romantic.

"Let's not get carried away," Shelby said, hearing Gage's voice and his wow, as if he was in the room with them.

Mayor Larry leaned against the wall. "Is there any hope for one of my buildings?"

"Nope." Mae hadn't lost any of her chutzpah or her selling skills. "The bonus to my property is it also has an apartment upstairs." She knew what to say to demoralize the competition and increase a customer's value perception. It was like choosing a dress, and then being sold a tiara and matching earrings at a bundled price. "Very efficient to live and work here if you aren't going to enjoy the sunshine."

Christine nodded, then looked at Shelby. "Free rent, Shelby. What do you think?"

Shelby wanted a moment of quiet reflection to make peace with the shop. This was a place of dreams and happily-ever-afters. Shelby's dreams had crashed into a dead end.

The front door swung open. Gage filled the doorway—tall, broad shouldered, the black hair over his forehead spiked up as if he'd run his hand through it in frustration. Once she would have smoothed the silky strands of his cowlick in place, making a joke of it. Now, she didn't dare touch him for fear of that tingle of awareness.

Gage greeted each of them in turn. Then he gave Shelby a look that questioned: *Are you all right?*

He'd always been able to read her mood. Despite their friend hiatus, his presence was comforting. Her angst over the past and the aura of happy brides faded. In its place came a sense of guilt over her private nickname for him. Turns out, Dead Gage wasn't quite so dead anymore.

On a sigh, she caught his glance, and brushed at her bangs with her fingers, telling him without telling him that his hair needed attention.

Gage impatiently and ineffectively swiped at his hair. "We were just walking by on our way to Doc's office. I didn't realize it would tire him out. Wow."

"Quit saying wow," Grandpa called out.

Peering through the front window, Shelby spotted her grandfather. Sure enough, he was sitting on a sidewalk bench, looking winded. He gave her a dismissive, don't-treat-me-like-an-invalid wave.

Shelby responded by crossing her arms and sending Grandpa a stern look. "He doesn't want to admit he needs help getting around. A cane or a walker or one of those motorized chairs would be ideal."

"Stubborn coot." Mae laughed huskily. "Just like the rest of us old fools."

"Leave him his pride, ladies, while he takes a breather." Gage stepped forward, glancing from one end of the room to the other. "I remember this place."

Eventually, his warm gaze landed on Shelby, making the whole thing seem faintly reminiscent of when they'd been here the first time to choose her bridal gown. "Is this where your new wine cellar is going?"

"Apparently," Mayor Larry muttered. "I suppose I'm done here."

"I'm afraid so, Larry." Ever the one to smooth ruffled feathers, Christine kissed his cheek. "I'll see you for yoga in the morning. We can talk about that acreage you own at the base of Parish Hill."

Mayor Larry brightened and left, pausing to chat with Grandpa outside.

"Let's check out the apartment," Mae said, even though she didn't look fit enough to climb stairs. Without waiting for an answer, she shuffled toward the back. Her cane echoed throughout the store.

Christine, Shelby, and Gage took the stairs at Mae's pace. Poor Mae paused every other step to catch her breath.

It was stifling in the stairwell. But with four bodies and a tight space, of course, the air would grow hotter. Surely it had nothing to do with Gage, who was a mere step behind Shelby.

She willed herself to be reasonable, but the intimacy of being this close to Gage persisted and she searched for a cause. Maybe she'd developed claustrophobia. Maybe the angst from downstairs was building again. Maybe the building had retained the heat of summer along with bridal dreams.

All they'd ever been to each other was friends. All she'd ever felt for him was warm affection and the pain of desertion. Until he'd touched her hand last night.

"A lot of stores downtown have apartments upstairs, but most are studios," Mae rasped. "This is a one bedroom." She took the last step, opened the door, and moved into the living space, wheezing as she practically collapsed onto a lone dining room chair. "I lived here in between a couple of my marriages."

Christine went to stand in the middle of the room, turning to survey the apartment's assets.

Unsure if she'd appreciate any assets, Shelby hesitated by the stairs.

Other than Mae's chair, the place was vacant. The opposite of the optimism downstairs. The hardwood floors were stained and covered in a layer of grime. Purple striped, velvet wallpaper had started to peel. Dust-moted sunlight filtered through grungy windows. A musty smell threatened to clog Shelby's lungs.

But the most difficult obstacle to breathing seemed to be Gage, looming behind her.

His footfalls behind her on the steps had been steady, measured, and reliable. Everything she'd longed for in a friend. If only he hadn't bailed, she'd believe in the dependable facade he presented. If only she believed in the long-term.

"It's bigger than my apartment in Davis." Gage put both hands on Shelby's shoulders and inched past her. As his hands dropped away, he seemed to take her tension with him, allowing her to breathe again.

"It's...nice," Shelby allowed, finally coming forward. She moved to the kitchen nook, opened the ancient refrigerator and immediately closed it, backing away. "There's something growing inside there."

Gage checked it out, grimacing. "I think it was a carton of milk once." He shut the fridge just as quickly as she had. "It's like something Mrs. Bernhardt had us experiment with in science class. Your mold was always the worst smelling, remember?"

She did. It had smelled awful.

They exchanged smiles. His was full-wattage charming, plus something that hadn't been in his expression in the past. Something almost...flirtatious.

I'm imagining that.

Whatever was in that smile, it unnerved her. He stopped smiling so hard, as if sensing it affected her.

Shelby blinked, and suddenly the *something* signal she thought he'd been sending was gone. And the awkwardness she'd been feeling dissipated. But she continued studying him.

Why had she never noticed how perfect his lips were before?

He smiled, but it was the smile he used to disguise what he was really thinking. She didn't know enough about what was going on in his life to pinpoint whatever he was concealing. Was he still grieving? Was he overwhelmed, as she was, by Harmony Valley memories? Was he regretting abandoning her two years ago?

Don't open the door to caring.

He was Dead Gage. And he was leaving soon.

"We'll outfit the space with all new appliances," Christine was saying. "This is the Taj Mahal compared to the condition of the sheriff's apartment when he moved in above the station."

"On a clear day, if you stand on your tip-toes, you can see the bend in the river." Mae spoke in a faraway tone, more to herself than anyone else.

Gage entered the bedroom.

As if magnetized, Shelby followed, pausing in the doorway and hearing Christine come up behind her.

"They used to hold dances in the town square on summer nights." Mae continued to speak as if drifting between memories. "It used to be a privilege to live downtown, didn't it, Oliver?"

"Who?" Christine whispered.

"Uh, she means Gage, I think." At least, Shelby hoped so. "Gage, did it used to be cool to live downtown?"

"How would he know?" Mae coughed deeply, reaching in her pocket for a crumpled tissue and spitting in it. "This place has always brought me luck in love. If Shelby lived here, she'd be engaged again in no time, perhaps to that young man right there. You two would make beautiful babies. His midnight hair. Her sky-blue eyes."

The man under question was scanning the perimeter of the room, hopefully unaware of the heat collecting in Shelby's cheeks. He pointed to the baseboards. "Mice droppings. You'll need a good mouser."

"Ew." Shelby backed out of the doorway, bumping into Christine, making a mental note to ask her grandfather about Mae's mental health.

"Give me a month." Christine took in the bedroom with an assessing glance. "An exterminator, new appliances, new countertops, a new shine to the floors and windows, and you won't recognize the place." She turned to Shelby expectantly. When Shelby didn't immediately jump at the offer, her boss added, "Hurry, before I change my mind and offer it to Ryan."

"Whether it has Mae's love karma or not, you should take it." Gage gave Shelby a small smile, moving next to her and bringing a mix of comfort and excitement. "As your friend, I'm advising you to at least consider living here."

Her friend? Shelby refrained from pointing out friends came when you called. She refrained from commenting at all.

Her silence grew until it bordered on rudeness. She didn't want to offend Christine. It was a generous offer. But the building and its faded optimism...

Living here would make her feel like a hypocrite. She didn't believe in love and happy-ever-afters anymore. Years ago, anything had seemed possible—an interesting career, happiness, everlasting friendship and love. Shelby knew better now. She had to keep her head down, her gaze firmly on the path beneath her feet, and protect what little joy she had left.

Not that she could say that to anyone without being considered as out of touch with reality as Mae.

But everyone continued to stare at Shelby, waiting for her to answer. Mae with her unflinching expression. Christine with curiosity. Gage with understanding.

She wanted to tell Gage he understood nothing. How could he know where she was emotionally after two years of ignoring her?

They continued to wait for her response.

The weight of their scrutiny finally broke her. "Sure. Of course. I'll consider it," Shelby blurted, feeling as fake as a two-dollar wine paired with a filet mignon.

She'd consider it the same way Gage was considering her grandfather's proposition to stay in Harmony Valley.

Not at all.

Chapter Six

"Don't be discouraged by the dust and age of the basic equipment." Dr. Wentworth unlocked the door to his office. "It's the insight of a vet that makes a practice thrive, not the age of your exam table."

It was pointless to allow Doc to show him the practice. Gage didn't plan on staying in Harmony Valley for two more days, much less two more months.

An image of Shelby a few minutes earlier rankled him—her arms were crossed, expression barnacled at the sight of the apartment above the bridal shop. She'd looked so determined to be unhappy. He'd wanted to shake her, to embrace her, to kiss her unhappiness away.

Dangerous thought, that.

Her lack of friendship and easy forgiveness was harder to take than he'd anticipated. So much for being the unflappable horse-whispering vet.

Dr. Wentworth flipped the wall switch off and on, squinting expectantly at the non-working light fixture in the lobby ceiling. "We'll need to get the electricity turned on. And the phones."

Gage gave the rotary phone at the reception desk a disparaging glance, imagining he looked much as Shelby had in the bridal shop apartment.

"All my old equipment is here, which should be good enough to get us up and running." Dr. Wentworth's haystack white hair seemed to quiver with excitement.

They walked past reception, through one of two exam rooms, into a back room that branched into surgery and X-ray, and past a wall of empty cages. The equipment was protected by plastic covers with a thick layer of dust. The dust wasn't the worst of it. There were cobwebs across doorways, and an unclean smell that made Gage want to bolt.

"I've still got a small paddock and the kennels in back." Dr. Wentworth led Gage out the rear door. Weeds as tall as Shelby grew in the large corral. Dandelions thrust through cracks in the pavement. Dr. Wentworth studied it all in silence for a moment. "It needs a bit of work, doesn't it?"

A bit? Compared to the state-of-the-art equipment at the university and the Thomason Equine Hospital, even with a good scrubbing and weeding, a vet operating out of this office would be in the dark ages.

Gage approached the metal fence that surrounded the paddock. Harmony Valley was a small town even when he'd grown up here. There'd been about thirty kids in each class at high school. So when Shelby moved into her grandparents' place the weekend before school started, everyone knew she was coming. But Gage had an in with her, as he lived next door, had been working for Dr. Wentworth for several years and had been assigned as her lab partner on the first day of school.

Dressed in a pair of jeans and a T-shirt, wearing minimal makeup—not even shiny lip gloss—she didn't emulate rock stars or fashion models. He'd taken one look at Shelby and that sunshiny hair, and felt the beginnings of something wonderfully awful in his stomach.

The girls in school had latched on to her that first week, giving Gage time to explore the strange, tongue-tied feeling he got just by looking at her. For days, he'd studied Shelby as completely as he'd studied his lab notes, afraid to act on his new feelings even as they deepened.

At Doc's office after school that first Friday, she'd helped him clean the paddock, shoveling manure without so much as a wrinkle in her nose. They'd been talking about careers in science when Nick showed up. Gage trusted that Shelby wasn't Nick's type, only to watch in amazement as Nick asked Shelby out, easy as one, two, three. Meanwhile, Gage's heart sank as Shelby blushed and accepted.

She'd chosen Nick.

Nick who'd been a shooting star—good-looking, quick with a comeback, captain of every sport and club he joined, always assuming Gage would be his second.

Gage had watched the couple mature and fall in love. He'd told himself he was too late, gave his feelings a cease-and-desist order, tried to contain his affection for Shelby in the boundary of friendship. He explained away his feelings with logic, just as he would have explained the outcome of a science experiment.

Through high school and college, he'd put on a good front, keeping up a friendship with the two. He'd dated—although never seriously—and tried to get on with his life.

Staying in Harmony Valley now, even for two months, would be a serious mistake. If anything, Shelby's effect on him was more powerful than before. Staying meant acknowledging that little spark that refused to give up hope. Staying meant more sleepless nights, more days spent wondering how things would have been different if he would've asked her out first.

In other words, it'd be the same old torture.

This was where Gage thanked Doc for the offer. This was where Gage told his mentor he couldn't stay. This was where—

Doc. He had to find Doc and tell him. Harmony Valley? He couldn't stay. He'd have to be firm with the old man and—Gage's phone buzzed, alerting him to a text message. It was from Shelby: *When are you leaving? Don't go without saying goodbye.*

She expected him to disappear again. It was like a knife to his gut, but in his case, it felt as if he'd been dying for years.

If he turned down Dr. Wentworth, he'd have no excuse to stay. No excuse to reconnect with Shelby. He didn't answer Shelby. He couldn't.

Leaving would be torture to his heart. Staying would be torture to his head.

And so he listened to Dr. Wentworth as he rattled on about supplies and insurance, feeling undecided, and knowing only torture loomed nearby.

Dead Gage. Dead Gage. Dead Gage.

Shelby felt her private moniker for her former best friend needed repeating.

She couldn't fathom the sad look in his eyes. She couldn't decipher the reasoning behind that look he'd given her in the bridal shop apartment. She couldn't understand how it seemed as if no time at all had passed. That if only she could get past the Dead Gage moniker that she'd be able to tell him anything, the way she had before.

But things had changed. He'd left her. Years went by.

And still, thoughts of Gage filled up her lonely, empty spaces like a gentle incoming tide.

Dead Gage. Dead Gage. Dead Gage.

Repeating her inner mantra became a way to fortify the defenses she'd erected against the inevitable anguish when friends moved on. Because he hadn't answered her text message.

"No, I'm not going to let you walk home," Christine was saying to Mae. She opened her truck's passenger door and gestured to the older woman to get inside. "What would my grandmother say if I did that?"

"Agnes would say I'm stubborn." Mae paused to cough deeply. She produced a clean tissue from the pocket of her purple polyester pants. "I like to walk. Everyone knows it. Who needs gyms? I used to walk all over this town. In heels."

Christine was smiling, but hers wasn't the smile Gage wielded. And hers was chipping around the edges. They'd been arguing with Mae about a ride since Gage and Shelby's grandfather left to visit the clinic.

Shelby had been dealing with Grandpa long enough to know the pressure points of the elderly. "There's a chill wind out today, Mae."

And the older woman didn't have so much as a sweater on. "I like the fresh air." Mae crumpled her tissue and tossed it into the trash can next to the bench.

A bracing breeze blew past them, feeling like it had just come off the ocean, billowing Mae's blouse. Mae's shoulders hunched. Shelby shoved her hands deeper into her jacket pockets and moved to the curb in front of the older woman.

"I bet you watch the evening news, Mae." Shelby met Christine's gaze reassuringly. Trying to tell her that she had this. "My grandfather does. He watches the news while he takes his pre-dinner pills." Shelby faced Mae, trying to smile as easily as Christine despite another gust of wind sweeping past them. "When do you take your pills?"

Mae worked her jaw, studied Shelby's face, and then began a slow walk toward the truck, cane striking the pavement angrily. "Don't think you've got my number. I've got your number, young lady. I see your clothes. Don't think I don't."

Shelby glanced down at her black sweater and blue jeans. Whatever number Mae thought she had, Shelby was certain it was her mind wandering again.

"Pale and covered up. No wonder your ring finger is bare." Mae stopped in front of the truck door. "Well, don't just stand there. Help me up."

Christine and Shelby hurried to do just that. Shelby hopped in the back seat.

"My daughters are both happily married," Mae said as Christine pulled away from the curb. "I like to see people happy."

"I'm happy," Christine and Shelby chimed in.

"One of you is happy." Mae patted Christine's shoulder. "The other needs a man. You had a perfectly good one upstairs. Why waste time?"

Shelby knew Mae meant well, but she still didn't want to have this conversation. Feeling compelled to tell her something she said, "Gage was my...is my..." Might be my... "*Friend*."

"Friends make the best husbands," Mae countered.

Christine laughed.

Mae crossed her arms over her chest and harumphed. She was silent for the rest of the drive.

"What was that all about?" Christine asked after Shelby escorted the older woman to her front door, which was painted a vibrant red, a red flag set in a bright purple house.

Shelby shrugged, buckling in. "I struck a nerve, but I have no idea what nerve that was."

They returned to the winery where Christine called Slade to discuss an offer for Mae's building. Shelby joined Ryan to perform quality checks on the crush and final cleanup of the night's harvest.

Shelby was grateful for the physical work. It kept her mind off Gage and Mae.

The Chardonnay grapes they'd harvested had been transferred directly from the picking bins to the crusher and de-stemmer. While initial fermentation occurred during the next week, they'd be taking samples from each tank several times a day. When the juice reached a certain level of distillation, they'd transfer the wine to barrels. And when the wine cellar was built, they'd transfer the barrels there for temperature controlled aging.

"The weather's helped us out lately. We had such a warm July, and then it was mild all the way up to this weekend." Ryan examined the circulation equipment on the tanks to make sure it was functioning properly.

Shelby swept out the last of the debris from the night before with a push broom. "All we need is an Indian Summer to ripen the Cabernet grapes." A cool breeze slipped through the winery's open double doors, as if to blow away any idea of a warming trend.

"And pray harvest falls on another weekend so we'll get all those volunteers back." Christine sounded stressed. She was bench testing crushed juice samples from every tank. "Ryan, can you take the Cab sugar readings?"

"I live for my lab kit." Ryan shrugged into a lightweight jacket, grabbed his test kit, and headed for the Cabernet Sauvignon grapes still ripening on the vine.

"I wish I had his energy." Christine slid off her stool and stretched her back. She headed toward the massive barn doors, staring out at Ryan walking away.

Shelby racked her broom. "Give Ryan another three years and give yourself another three cups of coffee. It'll all equal out."

"He won't be here three years from now." Christine leaned against the door frame, still looking out on the vineyards and, presumably, Ryan. "He's young and there's nothing here for him."

"By nothing here, you mean women his age?"

She nodded, glancing over her shoulder to survey Shelby. "You won't stay either."

"Don't start on Mae's lucky-in-love apartment." Shelby shook her head. "I was married before. I don't aspire to it again. Besides, lightning only strikes once."

Christine chuckled. "This is wine country. I know several people who've been struck by lightning three or more times. Mae Gardner, for one." She sobered. "Are you sure there's no lightning between you and Gage?"

"We were friends once and..." Shelby paused, blaming her lack of sleep and the increased stress of a new job for her off-kilter sensory meter. Gage was handsome, wicked smart and caring... Or he had been. On paper, he was any girl's dream. Too bad she was no longer any girl.

"If you two are only friends..." Christine smiled. "Sheriff Nate's single."

Shelby held up a hand.

"I'm sorry. That was out of line, especially after all the things Mae said today." Christine smiled graciously. "Slade and the other owners promised the town council they'd bring business here, along with people. But it's a slow process. Not only is the dating pool here nearly non-existent, there aren't many people our age to hang out with apart from our gang." Christine fiddled with her engagement ring. The diamond was impressively large and glinted in the sunlight. She didn't often wear it to the vineyard. Something else flashed across the yard. Something large. Larger than Christine's ring.

Shelby ran to Christine's side and pointed. "What was that?"

"I didn't see it. Was it a skunk?" Christine turned to look out on the vineyard again. "We've had problems with skunks."

"It was too large to be a skunk." Shelby peeked past her. The grapevines swayed in the cool breeze, leaves rustling.

"Coyote?"

"It was bigger than a coyote." Much bigger. The kind of bigger that got the adrenaline pumping. She'd thought it was a dog. Roaming dogs weren't always the friendliest of creatures and Ryan was out there unaware of the potential danger. "Do any of the neighbors have dogs?"

"The closest is Abby. Truman's dog. Big, she's not." Christine stepped outside and called for Ryan.

Instead of Ryan, a fur-matted Saint Bernard skidded to a halt at the end of a row of grapevines twenty feet away from them. He chuffed, as if he'd been running a long time. His tongue hung out the side of his mouth. And he was thin. So thin.

Without thinking, Shelby walked toward him. "Come here, fella. Come on, boy. We won't hurt you."

"Are you nuts?" Christine whispered. "That dog is huge."

"It's also hungry and—" She gasped. "There's blood on his back hip." Shelby tugged her cell phone out of her pocket and dialed Gage.

The Saint Bernard perked his ears, taking a few steps closer, limping.

"Shel, I'm with your grandfather." Gage sounded distracted. "I'll text you when I leave town."

Shelby kept her voice calm and stayed on task, when she'd have preferred to give him a dig about the first time he'd answered her call in more than two years. "We've got a stray over at the winery. St. Bernard. Blood on his haunches."

"Is he erratic?" Gage's voice sharpened. "Drooling? Crazy eyes?"

"No, his eyes have more of a lost, sorrowful look to them."

"Are you somewhere safe?"

"We're standing in the winery doorway. Ryan's out in the vineyard somewhere."

"Call Ryan and tell him to stay away until I get there. Better to be cautious."

"But—" She stared at her phone. "He hung up on me."

"Hopefully that means he's running to our rescue. That dog weighs more than either one of us."

"He doesn't look rabid." Shelby didn't know how she knew, but she did. "He looks afraid. And hungry."

Shelby called Ryan on his cell and relayed Gage's message. Then she whistled and snapped her fingers, but the dog stayed put, shying deeper into the row when Gage ran up, barely winded.

"Over there." Shelby pointed to where she'd last seen the dog.

A large, faded green Buick drove up next. Agnes was behind the wheel and her grandfather was in the passenger side.

When her grandfather got out, Shelby called him over, "Grandpa, come over here with us. Agnes, stay in the car."

Her command ruffled the old dear, stiffening his already erratic gait. "I'm a vet. I'm not going to hide with the women-folk."

"You should get over with Shelby, Doc." Gage projected authority with every syllable and every step, at odds with the tuft of black hair out of place above his forehead.

Unused to him in the lead, Shelby was briefly taken aback. Nick had always directed. She and Gage had always followed. Watching Gage stride forward, she was struck with the beauty of him, the power, the rightness.

For so long, she'd thought of him as a sweet boy. She knew she'd never think of him like that again.

"You're not as nimble on your feet as you once were, Doc," Gage said evenly, commandingly. "Best stay back."

Being dismissed poked at her grandfather's pride. "Have I lost all usefulness? Why don't you just put me out to pasture and shoot me?"

"Grandpa—"

Gage held up a hand for quiet as he neared the row where the dog had last been seen. He produced a piece of beef jerky from his pocket and whistled.

Her grandfather stood in the drive and bent his knobby knees to see beneath the bushy tops of the grapevines.

The chuffing noise of the dog became louder, as did the uneven padding of big paws on dirt. There was no hesitation this time. The huge dog ran right up to Gage and inhaled the piece of beef jerky.

Gage slid his fingers under the dog's collar. With his free hand, he scratched behind the dog's ears. "I need a rope," he said softly, so softly Shelby didn't realize at first that he was talking to them and not the dog.

She and Christine rushed to find some. When they came back, Gage was feeding the dog more beef jerky and Shelby's grandfather was looking at the dog's bloody hip from a few feet away with a critical eye.

"It's either a puncture wound, or he's been shot," Grandpa surmised. "Any tags on the collar?"

"No." Gage fed the dog another piece of jerky. "Dogs without tags usually mean dogs without inoculations. Ladies, please stay back. This big guy could have rabies."

"He doesn't have rabies," Shelby scoffed, handing Gage the coil of rope. "He was probably more afraid of us than we were of him. Weren't you, big guy?"

The dog was huge. He panted through a friendly, toothy smile. He was mostly white with a blanket of mahogany across his back, black freckles on his nose and beautiful brown eyes that spoke of disappointment.

"Come on, boy." Gage led him toward the driveway. Or tried to.

The dog cringed and backed away, lowering his body until he was almost lying down.

Gage pulled on the rope, but the Saint Bernard was having none of it.

"Hey, boy." Shelby pitched her voice sweet as sugar as she came at the dog from behind. "Be a lamb and walk to the clinic with Gage."

"Don't come any closer, Shel. I mean it." Gage so seldom gave her a command that Shelby froze. "I've got to get him to the clinic. We can put him in a kennel. I'll see what kind of treatment he needs and run into Cloverdale for meds."

"I found him. I'll go with you to the clinic," Shelby said stubbornly.

"Shelby, I told you it's dangerous." Again with the commanding tone.

"And I told you I don't care." Something about the dog called to her. That sad, hopeless look. It told her he was no threat. She'd seen that expression staring back at her from the mirror for months after Nick died. She'd seen it the other night in Gage's eyes.

"Barnacles," Gage muttered.

Suppressing a smile, Shelby spoke to Christine. "I'll be back later."

"Call it a day. We all deserve a break," Christine said. "Let's meet tomorrow at nine to establish our priorities for the week. I'll phone Ryan and give him the all clear."

Shelby faced Gage and his cowlick bristle of hair. She reached up to smooth it, her fingers combing through his thick, ebony locks. The contradictions faded away—Dead Gage, Leader Gage, Lost Gage. Her friend. Her lab partner. Her safety net. He was all those things and none of those things.

He was just Gage.

Gage held himself so still, she thought he'd forgotten how to breathe. And then that smile of his—the one he used to bamboozle people—slid into place. That smile said more than Gage ever could. It said distance. It said detachment. It said denial.

Her hand drifted to her side.

She stepped back, facing Dead Gage once more.

Chapter Seven

G age was mad. At Shelby.

It was a first for him.

She questioned his decisions. She touched his hair. She wreaked havoc with his control. And it hadn't stopped. Not at the winery and not on the walk to the clinic.

"Don't walk so close to us." Gage crooned, the same as he would to a mare in the throes of labor. Tone was everything with animals. He'd never tried it on a woman before. "I don't know this dog and even underweight, he's one hundred pounds of unpredictability."

"If he was going to hurt me, he would have done it by now." Shelby walked shoulder-to-shoulder with Gage through town. She was focused on the asphalt ahead of her. Each footfall landed with crisp precision.

The Saint Bernard ambled along a few feet ahead, limping on his injured leg, his large ears perking up to hear what was being said.

"At least walk behind me, so I can protect you." Gage took Shelby's hand and pulled her back. The bruised muscles at the base of his spine shuddered in protest.

"Gage." Shelby's gaze landed on him reproachfully as she stumbled to return to his side. Her thin, army-green jacket flapped open, revealing a shapeless black sweater that hid her curves. "He won't hurt me. He needs someone to love him."

Gage hesitated at the emotion in Shelby's voice, her words echoed in his head: *he needs someone to love him.*

Dopamine, serotonin and norepinephrine sped through his veins. He glanced away from the spark of stubborness in her eyes, pretending to focus on the dog, all the while aware of every nuanced move Shelby made.

"It's okay, big guy." Gage caught up to the animal, patting him on his massive head. He spoke softly to Shelby. "Please work with me." He noted her tightly sealed lips. Graceful brows a severe slash over intent blue eyes. She wielded that barnacle expression like other women wielded a pout. How he'd missed it. "Please, Shel."

Those brows rose. "When did you become so bossy?"

"Don't mistake my caution for browbeating."

"Gage," she said with equal boundary-laying tension as they crossed Main Street. "Don't mistake my acquiescence for capitulation." She blew out a breath. "Is this your bedside manner? If so, it needs work."

What needed work was his reaction to her. "Maybe you're right about the dog being tame and disease free. But look what happened when I tried to walk him. He's unpredictable and I couldn't live with myself if something happened to you because I wasn't being careful."

"Oh." Her voice. So small. "Thank you."

They continued in silence through the quiet streets of Harmony Valley, reaching the vet office without incident.

Doc had been driven there by Agnes and her green Buick. They arrived ahead of them. Doc waited, a slip of an old man, holding the main kennel door open. He should be permanently retired, ensconced in a recliner with his remote, great-grandchildren playing at his feet.

And he might have if I hadn't overslept that one day.

Eyeing the fresh bowl of water, the stray dog ambled in, easy as you please, and started drinking. Gage untied him and backed out. Doc latched the door.

The dog lifted his head. Water dribbled from both sides of his mouth. His gaze questioning. He made a small noise, reminiscent of a child just realizing he may have lost his mother and was unsure if he should panic or not.

"It's okay, boy." Shelby waggled her fingers through the cage.

Mollified, the dog settled himself on the concrete with a heavy sigh, as if he knew all his problems would soon be taken care of.

"Granted, he seems to like you, but I've seen ponies smaller than that dog." Gage carefully guided Shelby away from the kennel. "And I've seen ponies bite."

"He's not a pony. He's harmless," she insisted.

Gage and Doc conferred on which supplies they'd need to treat the animal. Gage recorded the list on his phone.

"Wouldn't it be quicker and easier to take him to a clinic in Cloverdale?" Shelby asked.

Gage clasped a hand dramatically over his chest. "You might just as well question my manhood."

"Ditto," her grandfather growled.

Shelby gestured in the general direction of the highway. "Then shouldn't you manly men be racing down the hill for supplies? The dog is clearly—"

"Uncomfortable," Gage interrupted. "He's uncomfortable, not in agony." He laid his hands on her shoulders, much as he'd done in the bridal shop apartment. And as had happened there, he had trouble releasing her, even as he turned her toward the exit. "I'm going to make the supply run. Your grandfather is going to stay here. And you? You're going home to get some rest." She looked spent.

"I can stay with him." Shelby backtracked, edging toward the kennel.

"No." His hand shot out to stop her. Gage had visions of Shelby sneaking into the kennel to cradle the big dog's head in her lap. All kinds of bad images ensued.

"But—"

"No," he repeated. "It's my practice. My rules."

Dr. Wentworth's grin spread across his narrow face. "Well done."

Gage's announcement sidetracked Shelby. "You're staying? Here?"

"Until my job in Kentucky starts, I'm staying." Secretariat, help him.

"You'll stay with us," Doc insisted. "Your family's house isn't fit for sleeping. I thought I saw a possum coming out of the kitchen window the other day."

Shelby frowned. "He can't stay with us for two months." She didn't say why. Was it because their friendship had run its course as she'd claimed? Or...

Gage couldn't come up with an alternative hypothesis, which bothered him. It bothered him far too much.

"You'll be expecting me to cook, I suppose." Shelby blew her bangs from her forehead.

"You're a horrible cook," the old vet said.

The two began bickering about privacy and responsibilities, what Grandma Ruby would have wanted and what skills Shelby did or didn't have in the kitchen. Gage could listen to them forever.

Every day could be like this, his traitorous heart whispered. *If you stayed. Permanently.*

He couldn't stay. He couldn't live near Shelby and be her invisible man.

"You're upsetting the dog." Gage pointed to the Saint Bernard, who'd moved to the far corner of the kennel and turned his back on them.

The Wentworth family suitably chastised, Gage left the pair and drove to Cloverdale.

He was staying. At least, for now.

This could only end with a long drive to Kentucky and plenty of time to think about what should have been.

And his heart. Broken, as always.

Shelby enjoyed food as long as someone else cooked it.

She'd had a great college roommate who loved to cook. She'd married Nick and he'd been the king of the grill. As a widow, she had no reason to do more than heat something in the microwave.

And so, when dinner was lobbed in her court, she went with an old stand-by—spaghetti. Add a bag of salad and slices of bread slathered with butter, and *voila*! Dinner was served.

Gage would know she was shortcutting it. In the old days, he would have called her on it, claiming she only knew how to make three things in the kitchen. She didn't think he'd say anything today. There was too much tension between them as they danced around each other trying to figure out how to interact. It wouldn't be like this for the full two months, would it?

"How's your patient?" Shelby asked when Gage came in through the kitchen door, followed by her grandfather, who looked worn out by the day's excitement.

"The dog didn't get shot. It was a puncture wound." Grandpa sank into his chair at the head of the kitchen table and rubbed his shoulder. He needed to slow down. "He probably fell along an embankment and landed on a Manzanita bush." Manzanita shrubs had dense branches that didn't bend.

"That dog's a trooper." Gage washed his hands in the sink. He glanced at the stove, at her, then away, a hint of a smile on his lips. "I should have known we'd either be having spaghetti, pancakes or chocolate chip cookies." The three things he claimed she excelled at making.

Busted.

"Don't push it or I'll serve you frozen pizza." Who was she kidding? She'd do that anyway, sometime soon. Shelby dished up the spaghetti and passed them each a full plate. "I looked online to see if anyone posted anything about a lost dog. Nothing."

"I asked at the clinic in Cloverdale and called animal control. Nobody reported a missing Saint Bernard there either." Gage dug in.

"It's likely someone couldn't afford to keep him. He's a very big dog." Grandpa accepted a glass of water from Shelby and drank deeply. "He probably eats his weight in kibble every month. A lot of people used to drive out to the country and dump animals, back before gas prices were so high."

Shelby's heart panged at the idea of anyone dumping the dog and leaving him behind. The look on his face—so lost and alone—returned to her. "I'm going to keep him."

Gage put down his fork, despite it being wrapped with spaghetti. "Don't rush into anything. You don't know this dog. When he feels better, he'll show you his true colors."

Shelby drew a breath, preparing to argue, but Gage beat her to it.

"Don't barnacle me, Shel. I'm serious. Normally, I'd jump for joy at someone adopting a stray. But when this dog is healthy, he's going to put on another thirty to fifty pounds." Gage shifted in his chair to face her. "Flynn Harris's nephew Truman stopped by the clinic after you left. He has a little dog. Maybe you've seen Abby around."

Shelby nodded.

"What if this Saint Bernard doesn't like kids or other animals, Shel?"

"He will. I have a good feeling about him." He'd been lost. She'd been lost. They had a connection. "You'll make him better and you'll see. He's going to be perfect for me."

Gage shook his head. "Dogs are like kids. They need your time. You have a demanding job."

"Friendships take time, too, in case you'd forgotten," Shelby countered. "I'd rather have a dog."

"You've given up on relationships? That explains a lot." Looking grim, Gage finally took a bite of spaghetti.

"I don't... I haven't... You know nothing." Shelby tore off a piece of bread and popped it into her mouth, muttering darkly, "*Dead Gage.*"

"What did you call me?" Gage's volume nearly reached Grandpa's decibel level.

Shelby felt a twinge of remorse. But it was just a twinge.

"Dogs, all mighty." Grandpa leaped into the fray, louder than Gage. "You two used to be as inseparable as peanut butter and jelly. I haven't heard one nice word exchanged between the two of you since Gage came back. Friends know when to give a person space and when to mend fences."

Gage ignored Grandpa. His black brows drew low. "You called me Dead Gage?"

Shelby swallowed the bread and lifted her chin unapologetically. "You left without a word and never looked back. You might just as well have been dead and buried in the cemetery, too."

"That's harsh."

Shelby gave no ground. "So is the way you dumped me."

"That's it!" Grandpa's white, haystack hair quivered angrily as he stood. "I'm going to eat outside with Mushu. At least she can forgive me for ignoring her sometimes."

The screen door banged. The kitchen became oppressively silent.

Shelby pushed spaghetti around her plate. Ignoring? Gage had gone beyond ignoring her. He'd ended contact completely.

The nausea of loss rose in her throat.

Breathe, girl. Breathe.

Her grandfather was right. Friends knew when their friends were going through a tough time. They made allowances. They forgave. They mended fences.

Much as she didn't want to mend things with Gage for fear he'd just desert her again, she still cared for the man. She set down her fork, smoothed her black sweater over her hips and cast about for some way to begin the conversation.

Grandma Ruby used to say it was hardest to extend an olive branch when you were in the wrong.

Shelby sighed. She hated being wrong. "The Dead Gage label might have gone a bit far."

"You think?" Gage's brown eyes had never seemed so unforgivingly black.

She swallowed back two years of hurt and gripped the arms of her chair with both hands. "You know how I struggled to keep friends while I was growing up."

"I was in a dark place, Shel."

She waited for him to say more. The Gage she'd known had been reticent, but not purposely uncommunicative. When he didn't answer, she asked, "Do you remember that time I dropped my science homework in your bull's pen?"

He nodded, his face a study of sharp edges. He used to be strong and brave, not hard and unyielding.

"You jumped in, Gage, grabbed my homework and jumped back out before that old bull ever saw you." Before Shelby had a chance to be scared for him. Tentatively, she reached across the table and touched his shoulder. "That day, I realized you'd do anything for me. To me, that's what friendship is all about." Her throat threatened to close at the memory, as if admitting its significance exposed her to too much hurt.

Gage leaned in, covering her hand with his. "Your friendship was important to me."

Past tense. She had to swallow twice to speak. "Can't you tell me why you left?"

He withdrew—shuttered his eyes and removed his hand, expelling a breath that seemed to cool the very air between them. "Shelby, I..."

Gage wasn't ready to tell her the truth. In fact, he might never be ready. To reforge their friendship, Shelby would have to rely on blind trust. But a relationship built without truth had a weak foundation. She wasn't sure she had enough trust left inside her for that.

"After I check on the dog in the morning, I'll drive to Davis to get my things." His black gaze collided with hers, sending her a confusing rush of signals too overwhelming to separate and decipher. "I'll move in tomorrow night."

He's staying.

Hope inside her chest expanded at his words, like a tulip stem breaking through a layer of snow, determined to blossom despite the harsh conditions.

And yet... Despite his promise, he might not come back tomorrow.

It was a warning. A warning her heart wanted to ignore.

The truce they'd come to was fragile and hung heavily in the air.

After Shelby did the dinner dishes, she rounded a corner in the hallway and bumped into Gage coming out of the bathroom in only a towel.

Apologies were quickly exchanged, and they gave each other a wide berth.

With a hand on her bedroom doorknob, Shelby glanced over her shoulder at a retreating Gage, and gasped. "What happened to you?"

The lower half of his back was like an impressionistic painting in purple, red, and black.

Shelby rushed toward him. "Why didn't you tell me you'd been injured? You shouldn't have been harvesting last night."

Gage put his discolored back to the wall. Clutching the towel with one hand, he held her off with the other. "It's nothing. I got a little love tap from a mare."

"Let me see." She reached out.

He drew back. "Don't worry, Shelby. It happened days ago. It's just a hazard of the job."

A hazard of the job... Why hadn't she realized a large animal vet put himself at risk every day?

"This isn't like a mosquito biting a gardener." Shelby's voice was near hysteria. And yet, she felt as if the world was spinning downward. "A kick like that could paralyze you."

Fear gripped her throat, making further speech impossible.

What if she lost Gage, too?

Her vision blurred around the edges, tunneling to Gage's bare, muscular chest.,

"Shelby?" Gage's voice sounded far away.

And in that faraway place, Shelby dreamed of Gage's lips pressed to her forehead, of him tenderly whispering her name.

Chapter Eight

"Here she comes." Dr. Wentworth sat in a chair at the end of Shelby's bed amidst suitcases and wardrobe boxes. "You see it in their eyes first."

Shelby's eyes were indeed fluttering.

Gage forced himself to loosen his grip on her hand. As she'd dropped to the worn avocado carpet, so had his heart and his towel. He'd been cradling her, nearly naked, when Doc emerged from his bedroom. Back spasming in protest, Gage had carried Shelby to bed before hastily pulling on his clothes. "Breathe deep, Shel."

Shelby did as Gage asked, her chest rising and falling regularly. Her face was pale against her pink flowered sheets. Her eyes inched open, a deep blue, deeper than usual given her pupils were dilated.

"Atta girl," Dr. Wentworth said gruffly. "You shouldn't scare me like that."

Shelby smiled weakly. Her gaze drifted toward Gage. She reached a hand toward his chest, grabbing a fistful of T-shirt. "You put a shirt on."

"Well, yeah. It upset you to see me half-naked." Gage tried to joke, more worried about her than Sugar Lips' love tap. He squeezed Shelby's hand. "It upset me to see you pass out."

She blinked. Sat bolt upright. Almost fell over. Her steadying grip on his shirt was so tight the cotton stretched. "You were nearly killed."

Gage slipped an arm around her shoulders, lengthening sore muscles in his back that didn't want to be disturbed.

"Today?" Her grandfather's bushy white eyebrows pinched together.

Shelby shook her head, which caused her to teeter again.

"Easy," Gage whispered, pulling her closer. She smelled like sweet nectar and sunshine. "I'm fine, Shel."

"Don't ever tell me you're fine again," she snapped, scowling as she looked at her grandfather. "Did you see his back?" And then she raised her head up to look at Gage. "Is that an everyday thing?"

Gage tried to make light of his injury by bringing out *The Smile*. "Horses kick sometimes."

"Horses kick you!" She poked his chest repeatedly. "What if that was your head?" She crossed her arms and looked at him menacingly. "Your smile won't work on me."

The need to kiss away both their fears was nearly overwhelming. But there was Doc and there was the past. Gage drew a deep breath, inching away from her. "My head's not good for much anyway."

"How can you joke about this?" Shelby cried.

Because he didn't want her to worry. He should have known it was the wrong approach. "Doc, can you get Shelby some water?"

"You should listen to him, honey." The old man stood, bobbing like a row-boat on rough seas until he found his balance. "A horse kick? It's as common as a dog bite to me."

"I'm surrounded by adrenaline junkies." Shelby closed her eyes.

Gage waited until the old man left the room. He eased Shelby back on the pillows, brushing a short lock of blond hair off her forehead, committing the silky feel to memory. "As your friend, I appreciate your concern. But this type of incident doesn't happen often. How often do you pass out?"

"Incident? You think that's what this was?" Her pupils were returning to near normal size. "No, Dr. Jamero. I'm not in the habit of passing out."

He nodded, unable to resist stroking the back of his hand across her cheek. When he spoke, he kept his voice soft and steady, as if he was talking to Sugar Lips, a high-strung mare who felt things had gotten out of control. "I'm good at what I do, Shel. Yes, sometimes the mare gets the best of me, but it's a chance I have to take when a foal's life is in danger."

"Promise me—" her voice took on that small fragile quality that had the strength to tug his heart "—you won't put yourself at risk like that again."

The urge to please her was strong. "I can't. No more than I can promise you a long and happy life. We both know that things can go bad in seconds. I take precautions, but that's all I can do."

"In a blink," Shelby murmured, tugging his shirt once more. "It's not fair."

He tightened his arm around her shoulder, intending to kiss her forehead. Instead, Doc's return had Gage sitting back in his chair.

But in his mind, he imagined pressing his lips to Shelby's in a gentle kiss that lingered, and healed, and made the unfair world a little more bearable.

Sunday morning, Shelby turned into the winery's gravel driveway lined with palm trees.

Ryan's vehicle was just ahead of her. The sun crept above Parish Hill and peeked through the palm fronds.

After a hot California June and July, they'd been blessed with a milder August and what seemed to be a milder September. The lack of heat meant the danger of early frost or rain, either of which would be disastrous to the Cabernet grapes. With the mornings were growing colder, the grapes wouldn't need much more time on the vine.

Disasters. The threat of which kept Shelby awake at night.

Although to be fair, she'd woken to an image of Gage kissing her at three a.m. That had kept her awake for far too long.

But in her dream, his lips had been as gentle as his voice had been last night when she'd come to. Hard as Shelby tried, she couldn't shake how secure it felt to have Gage's arms around her when she collapsed. Her overactive imagination insisted he'd whispered her name as if she was the most important person in the world to him.

Shelby knew better. So she rejected the idea that she was starting to fall for Gage. Didn't help her sleep though.

Shelby parked her small white SUV in front of the two story tasting room, beside Ryan's old gray truck. The running horse weather vane on top of the main building turned lazily as she and Ryan got out of their vehicles.

"Over here," Christine called from the farmhouse porch. She waited until they joined her, then led them to the back of the property, blond braided hair swinging between her shoulder blades with each step. "I've got an idea about a permanent wine cellar. I'm interested in your opinions."

Shelby walked faster, thoughts of Gage drifting away. She'd be managing two wine cellars soon. Not one. Two!

"We're sacrificing grapevines for a wine cellar?" Ryan questioned Christine with his usual forthright manner. "How much will that decrease our tonnage?"

"It depends on how large a wine cellar we build." Christine looked to Shelby. "I have enough bottling permits to expand production from five thousand cases to eighty. Slade, Will and Flynn are willing to invest in further expansion if it creates more jobs. In order to do so, we can't compromise on quality, and we have to raise capital with the unused permits." The government regulated how much wine could be produced in each region by issuing permits with production limits.

"I'm assuming you'll raise funds by leasing the excess permits?" Shelby's brain circled the eighty thousand case figure with excitement. For tax purposes, each case contained a dozen regular-sized bottles of wine. That was a lot of wine to manage. At some point, she'd need help.

Christine paced in front of them. "Yes, we'll lease, but we'll slowly increase our production each year, always within our quality standards. I'd like to have the capacity to produce eighty thousand cases a year someday, but not only do we have to make it, we have to sell it."

"Eighty thousand cases sounds like a grotesquely large number," Ryan said. "Especially if we're starting at five."

"It's still not large," Shelby told him. "Most wines available in grocery stores sold millions of cases."

"And we won't increase production without quality assurance. But back to the wine cellar." Christine pointed toward the gravel entry. "Months ago, we were considering building a wine cellar across the road with an underground piping system from the barn to barrel or bottle juice. Mayor Larry owns that land. But the slope between here and there is uphill and works against us."

Shelby shook her head. Poor Mayor Larry. That's twice he'd lost out on a sale.

"The property has a natural drainage toward the river back here." Shelby walked into a sloping row, trying to envision the size needed for such a large storage facility. Grapevine creepers bent toward her in the breeze, their leaves browner than even two days ago. "Anything we build behind the main facility will capitalize on gravity."

"Anything we build here will mean sacrificing grapes," Ryan pointed out.

Shelby nodded absently, engrossed in the square footage calculations.

"Don't worry, Ryan," Christine said. "Not only does my new growth plan include buying an additional fifty acres at the foot of Parish Hill, but it includes hiring a vineyard manager." She beamed like a kid in a pet shop about to adopt a cute little puppy. "Anytime I suggest hiring someone, my fiancé gets behind the idea."

"More vineyards." Ryan brightened. "Gotta love a winery backed by the fortunes made in the tech world. It's the gift that keeps on giving."

"Consensus. Love it." Braid swinging, Christine led them toward the tasting room. "That's one thing off my list. I'll call a couple of architectural firms tomorrow to get some quotes. Between planning and city approvals, it's going to take at least a year."

They climbed the narrow stairs to the office. It was a decent space with dormer windows and swag curtains. Shelby had been given a small table in one corner. Christine sat at her desk, indicating Shelby and Ryan should sit across from her.

"If we're pursuing new construction, we'll need to be more visible about town. Get folks on our side. Explain all the positives of expanding the operation here. It took months to get the town council to approve this little winery to start with." Christine tapped a pad of paper covered in scribbles with a stubby pencil.

"I need both of you to network. Make friends. Be helpful. Put a strong face to the winery so that people will support us building a wine cellar.

"First order of business is Mae," Christine continued. "Shelby, I want you to keep Mae happy. We can't afford the sale of her building to fall through. We'll need that space in both the short and long term." Christine printed Shelby's name next to Mae's on her to-do list.

"But-but-but..." Shelby sounded like a sputtering motorboat. "How would I do that? Besides, I'm just not...uh, the hearts and rainbow girl who appreciates Mae's romanticism." She'd been hoping to put off the idea of her moving into the apartment above Mae's shop. This would put her smack dab in the face of Mae's meddling.

Ryan sniggered.

Shelby scowled at him.

"And Ryan." Christine raised her voice sweetly, ignoring Shelby's protest. "I'm assigning you to the ladies on the town council."

"I'll take care of Mae," Ryan blurted, jerking back in his seat. "Or Mayor Larry."

"No, you won't." Christine shook her head. "I'll work with the mayor. He and I do yoga every morning and given all the property he owns, economic growth is in his best interest."

Ryan turned to Shelby, "Wanna trade?"

"Ryan!" Christine's frown had no effect on Ryan.

"Why don't you want to work with the town council?" Shelby asked, suspicious of her coworker's reason for a trade.

Ryan stared out a dormer window, a blush creeping up his cheeks. "They think I'm cute."

Christine snickered.

"It's not funny." Ryan ran a hand through his shaggy locks.

Christine laughed harder. "It's your own fault."

"That's the worst part." He slumped. "It is. I should never have let them feed me." Ryan's honesty was part of his boyish charm.

Shelby couldn't help but smile.

"Those meals you mooched weren't the problem." Christine pointed her finger at him. "It was the mending. And the laundry. And those truck repairs."

Ryan cast Shelby a hangdog glance. "Word of advice. Always check with Mildred before you take your car in for service. Because she used to be a race car driver, she can diagnose a problem just by listening to your engine."

Shelby was skeptical, recalling Mildred's unfocused vision in El Rosal. "Isn't Mildred legally blind?"

"She doesn't need to see anything." Ryan nodded morosely. "She's a savant. If she was sixty years younger, I'd marry her."

"All right," Christine said briskly. "All kidding aside, you'll do it. Those three old ladies adore you."

"I'm a grown man. They treat me like I was six now." With the fight back in him, Ryan turned to Shelby. "When Agnes brought sandwiches the other night, she tried to put a napkin inside my shirt. Like a bib."

Shelby hid a smile behind her hand.

Ryan winced. "I'm doomed."

"You let them baby you." Christine printed Ryan's name next to town council on her notepad. "Someday, when you're running your own winery, you'll thank me for this experience."

"Highly improbable." He rubbed a hand over his forehead. "Your grandmother is on the town council. You could at least handle her yourself."

"Rose, Mildred, and my grandmother are practically inseparable. You'll need to charm them all at the same time." Christine tapped her pencil on the list. "I've been talking to my grandmother about this, but you need those three to stand as one."

Ryan sighed in defeat, slumping farther in his chair. "I guess I know where I'm going for lunch."

He may have known, but Shelby needed clarification. "What are you asking me to do with Mae? Didn't she agree to the sale?"

"Yes, but Dream Day Bridal is her life's work." Christine's volume dropped into serious territory, the space occupied by doctors, lawyers, and morticians. Shelby's skin prickled. "Mae lost her husband this spring. She'll need someone who understands..." Christine paused, and Shelby's skin prickle spread. "She'll need someone compassionate as she clears out her things from the building."

Shelby knew Christine had been about to say, *"Someone who understands losing a spouse."* There was a skill set Shelby didn't want on her resume: *widow hand-holder.*

Before Shelby could challenge the assignment again, Christine, the queen of efficiency, pushed forward. "You can use the winery truck to move her things out of the shop as soon as the contract is signed. I'll schedule a dumpster for delivery midweek. Mae gave me a set of keys." Christine handed Shelby a key ring with a purple high-heeled shoe charm. "Her children live in another state. She's alone. If you could just be a sympathetic ear to her and watch for any more of those out-of-touch episodes, I'd sleep easier at night."

"I asked my grandfather if he'd noticed anything unusual about her behavior." The metal key ring felt cold in Shelby's hand. "But Grandpa hadn't seen or heard of Mae doing anything like what we witnessed." The drifting conversations. The dialogue with a dead husband.

"Do you want to reconsider trading?" Ryan whispered.

Shelby shook her head. She supposed widows should stick together. She'd just be clear with Mae over and over again, if necessary. There'd be no talk of Shelby getting married or pairing up with Gage.

"Moving on..." Ignoring their irascible assistant winemaker, Christine reviewed her list. "I called in a favor with Utley Construction. They can assess the basic work needed at the bridal shop to prep for our casks and tanks. We used them for all the original work here, and they have experience remodeling and installing wine cellar equipment. Can you meet them at the shop by seven Tuesday morning, Shelby?"

"Yes." Shelby tried to recapture some of her excitement at learning she'd have not one, but two wine cellars to manage.

All she had to do was keep an older widow happy and even-keeled. How hard could that be?

Gage rested against the stall door, watching Sugar Lips and her colt.

The maternity barn at the equine hospital was unusually quiet. The hushed sound of hooves on hay, nickers and snorts were a soothing backdrop to his confusion about Shelby.

They'd achieved some sort of common ground where she actually looked at him when they spoke. But what did it mean? More important, what did he want it to mean?

What he wanted it to mean was a pipe dream.

His mind wrestled with the potential outcomes, reaching for science.

Hypothesis Number One: in two months, he'd leave Harmony Valley, completely over his infatuation with Shelby. Since Nick's death, she'd changed. He'd changed. It wasn't outside the realm of possibilities that his attraction to her would fade.

And pigs fly.

Hypothesis Number Two: in two months, she'd fall in love with him, and they'd leave Harmony Valley together, bound for Kentucky.

And pigs regularly fly.

Hypothesis Number Three: in two months, he'd give up on Kentucky regardless of how Shelby felt for him and stay in Harmony Valley.

And flying pigs always came to roost where they weren't wanted.

Gage knew himself well enough to be truly concerned about the third outcome. That worry slid beneath his shoulder blades, unbalancing and unwelcome.

Sugar Lips twitched her ears in his direction, but otherwise ignored Gage.

Her chestnut foal blinked wide eyes at him from around his mother's tail. With bold steps, the colt approached Gage, tilting his head as if trying to figure him out.

"You wouldn't compromise your dreams for a girl, would you, buddy?"

The future Triple Crown winner came nearer, stretching his graceful neck toward Gage. His velvety chin touched Gage's forearm as he tried to nibble his first human.

Gage moved his arm out of the way. "I'll take that as a no."

Footsteps at the entrance to the barn sent the colt bolting to the other side of his mama, who stomped impatiently.

"You're not fooling anyone, Sugar Lips," Gage told her. "When it comes to your son, you're a total softy." As was Gage when it came to Shelby.

"Dr. Jamero?"

Gage bent backward to see who'd entered the barn, only mildly twinging in his spine. "Dr. Faraji." The last person Gage wanted to see was Leo. He knew how to capitalize when Gage stumbled.

"What's this I hear about potential scheduling conflicts? Are you leaving early for Kentucky?" Leo carried a clipboard, wore a lab coat, and a satisfied smile. "Dr. Thomason warned Far Turn Farms that you might not be present for the next maiden delivery."

The satisfaction in Leo's tone stomped on Gage's nerves like an angry, rearing stallion. "I told Dr. Thomason I'd come if he gave me enough warning."

"No need to bother." Leo's smooth accent should have soothed, but Gage had heard those notes a few times too many for him to take Leo's words at face value. "I'll be here for the next Far Turn delivery. You will be surprised how quickly they will learn to ask for me instead of you."

Gage rejected several uncharitable retorts.

"What is it that's taking you away?" Leo barely glanced into Sugar Lips's stall. For a vet, the man had practically no personal interest in animals.

"I'm helping out back home." Gage struggled to keep his voice even. It nearly killed him to admit, "Small town. Small animals."

Leo raised a brow and chuckled. "Sounds like destiny, my friend." In the elite equine world, treating everyday pets was perceived to be low on the importance scale.

It may have only been perception, but Leo's laughter stung Gage's pride nonetheless. "It's only until my job in Kentucky opens up." Only until the current vet retired. Gage tried to sound confident. He was afraid he came across as angry and defensive.

"You're not as coldhearted as you'd have the interns believe," Leo said cagily. "Can I have your picture of Secretariat?"

"No." Gage stared his rival down. That picture had been a gift from a grateful horse breeder.

Leo crossed his arms over the clipboard. "Small animals don't admire greatness like his. Why not leave it here?"

The colt stuck his nose over the top of the door, sniffing and angling his head for a peek at them. Leo continued to ignore the little guy, being more interested in the glory of being a veterinarian at a prestigious facility than in the animals that were his patients.

How can I give this up?

"Leave the picture where it belongs, Dr. Jamero," Leo pressed.

How can I give this up to him?

"It belongs with me." The steel in Gage's voice stiffened his backbone. "In Kentucky."

Leo moved toward the next stall. "You're a small animal doctor now, Dr. Jamero. Best to accept it and move on." He laughed, each note a jab at Gage's wounded pride. "And while you're at it, submit your regrets to Kentucky. I knew all along I was the better fit for the job."

There was no way Gage was letting his infatuation with Shelby grow, no way he was staying in Harmony Valley permanently.

That's what he told himself anyway, mile after mile on the drive back to town.

Chapter Nine

"You came back." Shelby sat at the kitchen table with her laptop open, dark circles beneath her eyes.

Gage grimaced as he approached her. "You thought I wouldn't?"

Shelby hesitated a little too long before answering. "Grandpa's excited about reopening the clinic." She straightened papers into a neat stack, and then shoved them into a folder. "He went to bed early."

"While you stayed up because I left two years ago, and you thought I'd do it again." Gage felt as if he'd come home before curfew and been accused of wrongdoing when he'd been studying at the library.

He set the picture of Secretariat against a floor-level kitchen cabinet.

"What a pretty horse."

Secretariat wasn't just a pretty horse. He was *the* horse, at least to Gage, and his blood ran in Sugar Lips' veins.

Despite that, Gage ignored Shelby's attempt to change the subject. "I gave you my word I'd be here for two months. If I say I'm going to drive to Cloverdale to get you coffee, will you doubt me returning then, too?"

She surprised him by smiling, albeit sadly. "I might."

Her not trusting him was perfect. Oh, make no mistake, it hurt. Like a horse's hoof aimed right at his heart. But it blew all his hypotheses to pieces. There was no need to wait two months for rejection. Shelby was giving it to him straight, right now. Kentucky was all but assured. Gage could lock it into his GPS. Put a security deposit on an apartment in Lexington. Wrap the Secretariat picture in packing material.

"I don't put my trust in people or situations anymore," Shelby whispered. "It's like you said last night. Life can be lost." She snapped her fingers. "Like that."

Gage opened his mouth to rebuke her. Closed it. Then said, "I wish there was a way I could restore your trust."

The personal pep talk he'd given himself while driving back to Harmony Valley? The advice about Shelby and keeping his distance? A wasted exercise.

He wanted to thunk his head against the wall. More than once.

Maybe that would knock his thinking on track. But there was her barnacle expression and her comments about living her life alone. Without any kind of relationship.

Before he could stop himself, he said, "You're going to love again, Shelby."

She pressed her lips together.

Barnacles.

"What kind of life is it without love?" Gage refused to back off. Her blue eyes stared blankly at the kitchen wall as he answered his own question.

She'd be alone. She'd be less than the person she could be. And what a further tragedy that would be...

She'd laugh less, smile less, try less. Suddenly, Gage saw the results of her locking away her heart. She'd never have a baby, never know how love created one of its greatest gifts.

That's not right.

The words in his head sounded as if Nick had spoken them.

Gage's insides twisted with a sense of frustrated obligation. In the two years they'd been apart, she'd become more confident in some ways. In others, she'd withdrawn, her sense of humor conspicuously absent.

"Hearts don't stop loving just because they're broken once or twice." How he wished they did.

She slid her folder into her black laptop bag, careful not to look at him. "Did you check on my Saint Bernard on your way in?"

She cared too much about that dog, but maybe... "You think it's safer to love a dog than a person?"

He could see her answer. It was a yes. A slight blush tinged her cheeks.

"Animals can leave you as abruptly as people, Shel. Don't put your love—don't put your trust—in that dog. He's too well behaved to be left behind. His family will show up one day. Soon."

She shrugged. "Is he better?"

"Why do you always have to make things so hard?" Gage rubbed the back of his neck, wishing she'd participate in this conversation instead of stalling it. "Yes, he's improving." Gage had stopped by the clinic before heading over here. "He'll need exercise in another day or so."

"I'll walk him." Her eyes sparked with enthusiasm. For a dog. Worse still, for someone else's dog. "Or I could take him to work with me. In fact, he doesn't need to stay at the clinic at all. Mushu would enjoy some company at night."

"You're getting carried away. Don't get attached." Not to a dog.

And not to me. I'm Kentucky bound.

"He needs me." Shelby closed her laptop. "You want to know how to restore my faith in you?"

"Yes." Heaven help him, he did.

She rested her elbows on the table and stared up at him with the enthusiasm he'd seen in her eyes when she'd talked about harvesting grapes. "Let's put your dog adoption conditions on the calendar. If no one returns for him, when will you consider him officially adoptable?"

She was on cruise control, ignoring the warning signs that said Slow Down and Curves Ahead. But what could he do? "Shelters have varying policies. A week. Ten days."

"What do you consider the right amount of time?"

Whatever he said, she was going to hold him to it.

Gage considered carefully. He weighed the fact that the dog looked as if he'd been loose and without food for several days against Shelby's capacity for patience. "A week. Give it a week."

"Deal." Shelby came around the table, presumably to shake on it.

Suddenly inspired, Gage stepped back. "What do I get out of this deal?"

Shelby hesitated. "My trust?" She phrased it like a question. Trust was something she clearly had no intention of giving him again.

All those mountains he and Nick climbed with rope, crampons and axes had never seemed as treacherous as the climb to regain her trust. There was a cavernous hole inside him, he'd lost everything that mattered to him once and had only been fooling himself up until now. "We both know it'll take more than this for you to trust me again."

Shelby crossed her arms, knotting them tight. "You could tell me why you left after the funeral."

The tilt to her chin would have sent him tumbling in defeat if it hadn't hit him then. An idea. One that would put her on the path to love again. "Here's what I want. When a week has passed and you take the dog home, you'll go out on a date."

"Yeah, right." She rolled her eyes. "With who? Mayor Larry?"

"I'll find someone." Worst case? He'd set her up with Leo. "Deal?"

She paused.

"If the dog's still here in a week, he could be yours." Gage smiled and held out his hand.

She hesitated before grasping it firmly.

And then her grip shifted. She took both his hands in hers, holding out his arms in a sort of informal exam. "You were with that mean horse today. Show me you didn't get kicked or bit or whatever it is peevish mares do."

He froze. What was she asking? To examine his body for fresh wounds?

She squeezed his hands. "Show me."

"No." He took a step back.

Her hands fell away, but she moved closer to him. "Don't be embarrassed. I've seen you without your shirt on. I put antibiotic on your back after the brambles got you, remember?"

He did. He'd been pretending to sleep in the raft, watching her instead of where they were going. He'd lunged forward to protect her from being scraped by blackberry brambles. "I didn't get in a stall with any mares today. I don't need medical attention." Talk about mistrust. Shelby didn't take him at his word.

He took another step away from her.

She matched his stride. "I'm not offering to give it. I just want to make sure you aren't keeping something from me."

He was keeping a huge secret from her, but it had nothing to do with medical attention and horses. "This is not how you build trust. You can't just back me into a corner." But she had. He glanced over his shoulder. He had another three feet until the kitchen door.

"It's not about trust, Gage." He had to strain to hear her voice. "It's about reassuring me you're safe."

She reached for him, resting her hand on the hem of his T-shirt.

He wanted to tell her she was out of line and playing with fire, but her hand...her warmth. It tested him as he'd never been tested before.

He silently hoped for the appearance of Doc, a sudden rumble of thunder, a phone call, anything to distract her.

"Please." Her blue-eyed gaze softened. "I won't be able to sleep tonight wondering if you were in danger today."

"I packed my things and tied up loose ends. No more," he said gruffly. Her fingers tugged at the gray cotton at his waist. "If you took me at my word, you'd know I was safe. Trust is about not needing proof."

"I trusted Nick when he said he'd be careful. I trusted you when you told me at the funeral we'd talk soon." Her voice hardened and pressed upon him, edging him closer to obeying her wishes. And then he had to strain to hear her add, "I need to see for myself."

The pain and vulnerability in her voice nearly undid him.

It was a small thing, really. Her gaze showed no embarrassment. No heat either. There was merely concern.

Okay, then. She wants a clinical exam.

Showing her his bare torso would be like doing a good deed—helping a granny cross the road or returning a stray dog to its owners. He'd strip and she'd sleep better tonight. The exhaustion would ease around her eyes tomorrow.

He removed her hand from his hip and peeled off the gray cotton. "There's nothing new here to see."

She blinked once at his chest, then walked behind him.

"No new bruises." Her whisper danced across his shoulders. He felt the barest of touches near Sugar Lips' strike zone. "And this one is turning green."

He stared at the picture of Secretariat, patron saint of horse enthusiasts and foolish veterinarians.

"Another two days and it'll be yellow."

"Don't say things that imply you have a wealth of experience with gigantic bruises."

He couldn't look at Shelby as he turned and stepped away. "You know, friends worry about each other. But they trust each other, too."

"I'm trying. Don't push me." She touched a scar over his biceps. "A bite?"

He nodded. "Last spring."

"Ever broken a rib? Punctured a lung?" She moved back to the table, sliding her computer into her laptop bag.

She'd left him standing like unwanted beefcake in the middle of the kitchen. Gage drew a shaky breath. "I've been spared that, thankfully. Can I put my shirt back on now?"

She disappeared down the hall, laughter in her voice as she said, "You never had to take it off."

Chapter Ten

The next morning, Shelby was still wondering what had come over her with Gage.

She hadn't been brave enough to look back into the kitchen to see if he was smiling when she'd pointed out he never had to remove his shirt.

Yes, she'd wanted reassurance he was unscathed. Yes, he needed something to erase that lost look in his dark eyes. But it was bold and brazen, not like her at all. She'd practically run to her room, closed the door and sat on the bed. Heart pounding. Hands shaking. Watching to see if Gage came in to...do what?

Shake his finger at her in reprimand?

Share a laugh about her besting him?

Or...or...

The word *kiss* floated about in her head.

What had happened to her? How long had it been since she'd joked or flirted with a man? It seemed like forever. Shelby didn't used to think about Gage this way.

Well, duh. He was a man, all right. It was just that he'd been her friend long before she'd ever thought of him in romantic terms and now...

When she looked at him and saw the pain in his eyes, she wanted to hug him. Which would have been fine, if she hadn't recently noticed the perfect bow to his lips, the breadth of his solid chest or his take-charge attitude.

When she thought about embracing him, instead of a quick, friendly hug, she imagined his strong arms around her.

But Gage hadn't knocked on her door or barged into her room. It was all anticlimactic.

She gave up on sleeping in the gray light before dawn. She dug in one of her suitcases and found her running shoes. She hadn't been running in two years but running had always cleared her head.

Her running shorts were wrinkled. So was her red polyester exercise tank. She didn't bother popping them in the dryer for a heated shake-out. She grabbed a thin, neon-yellow hoodie.

Her grandfather was sitting at the kitchen table, head resting on his hands. He started at her exclamation and jerked his head up. "What? Who? Shelby, I…" He straightened his glasses. He glanced around the kitchen as if checking to see where he was.

Shelby hadn't seen Grandpa so unsure since her grandmother died. She wrapped her arms around herself. "I went to bed late. What time did you get up?"

"Three. Maybe four. I had a theory… I can't remember it right now, but…" He rubbed at the white whiskers on his chin.

"Is this something I should be worrying about? You not sleeping. You forgetting things." She gestured toward the living room. "You turning into a hoarder?"

"Dogs, all mighty!" He pushed to his feet. He wore faded red flannel pajamas and a scowl. "I haven't lost my marbles. You should be happy my brain is so active it keeps me up at night."

Shelby opened her mouth to argue but realized something. "You're right. You're fine. Who am I to cast stones?" She drew up her hood.

"Where are you going?"

"For a run." Shelby stepped out into the bracing air.

After a few minutes of a slow pace, her muscles warmed and the nip in the air didn't seem so bad. Fog hung low over the town, thickening the closer she came to the river. Streetlights did little to cut through the haze. She ran from one halo of light to the next.

Rounding the corner onto King, she stopped at Dream Day Bridal. Winded, she wiped away the moisture on her forehead, and stretched her hamstrings using the bench out front. Taking in the shop out of the corner of her eye, she tried to persuade herself it was just a building with a fond memory or two. Like the Chinese place where she and Nick used to order takeout in Davis. The Chinese restaurant had gone under after Nick died, replaced by a cupcake business. She'd gone in once before she'd moved to the mountains, just to see how it felt. She'd ordered a red velvet cupcake and waited for the melancholy. There'd been none. As soon as the bridal shop was transformed into a wine cellar, there'd be no residual sadness there either.

She heard the footsteps of another runner, but with the fog so thick, she couldn't tell which direction the person was coming from. A scuff of sneakers on pavement had her turning toward the town square. Gage emerged from the fog wearing a pair of black basketball shorts and a navy sweatshirt. He hesitated when he saw her, slowing to a halt.

She couldn't remember him being reluctant to approach her. Ever.

"So this is what we've come to." She leaned against the back of the wooden bench and crossed her arms over her chest. "Out-of-sync and awkward moments."

"And mistrust," he added. She expected him to walk toward her, but he stayed where he was—twenty feet away in front of the sheriff's office. "Don't forget mistrust."

"Nick would be disappointed." Her gaze fell to her toes. She'd often crumpled in the weeks after his death. This morning, her legs were sturdy, only her morale was weak. "He'd expect us to lean on each other."

"He might," Gage allowed gruffly.

Shelby pulled her gaze from the ground to study him. Pursed lips, tense jaw, distant eyes. He clammed up like that every time she brought up his two-year absence from her life. "There's something you're not telling me." Something that had made him leave.

He didn't leap forward to share.

Maybe if she repaired their friendship, he'd tell her. Maybe then awareness of Gage as a man would recede and things could go back to normal.

She blew out a breath. "I should probably apologize for last night. You just seemed so defeated and I—"

"Let's not get maudlin. You got me." He shoved his hands in his hoodie pocket and walked toward her. He stopped near the shop window, that winning smile of his returning to his lips. "I'm wondering why you haven't figured out how to use an iron."

She glanced down at her wrinkled sweatshirt. "Who irons at five in the morning?"

He glanced down at his unwrinkled clothing. "And while we're on the subject of domestic goddesses, I suppose you'll be cooking again tonight."

"Lucky you." How easy it was to fall into the rhythm of their familiar banter in the semi-darkness. "Thrill seeker that you are, you should appreciate sitting down at the table not knowing what you'll get."

His smile vanished. "I'm not an adrenaline junkie. I haven't been snowboarding or kayaking or mountain climbing ever since..."

"But your job—"

"Listen, if I made a living climbing electrical poles, would you still label me a thrill seeker?" Everything about him hardened. His posture. His expression. His words. This was a Gage she didn't know anymore.

"No, but—"

"Or if I worked as an engineer on an offshore oil rig?"

"No."

He propped his foot on the brick sill below the shop's framed window and stretched his hamstring. It seemed pointless of him to stretch since it seemed the tension hadn't left his body. "Point made?"

Point made? It was a phrase he'd often used when he was presenting his side of an argument.

"Point made?" she repeated. "If your point is that your job doesn't make you a thrill seeker, then yes. But if you want me to believe you've chosen a safe specialty, then no."

His frown said more than his words did. It spoke of endings and loneliness. That frown tugged at her insides.

Because that frown said their friendship was irreparable.

She swung her arms, preparing to jog away with what little dignity she had left when Gage said, "Did you poke a hole in that back wall?"

"No." She moved closer to the window, peeking inside. There was a hole the size of a bicycle tire where yesterday there'd been none.

Gage tried the door. It opened. He entered.

Shelby's pulse hitched up to worry-level. She propped open the door with her hip. "Shouldn't we call the police or something?"

As if reading her mind, the sheriff pulled up in an older model blue truck with a gold star on the door. He rolled down the passenger window and nodded to her. "Starting early on that remodel?"

"Nate, I'm so glad you're here." She glanced at Gage studying the hole that gave her a clear view of the downstairs toilet. "Did you hear anything weird last night from Mae's shop?"

The sheriff's body seemed to coil as his cop sensors perked up. In no time, he was standing next to her on the sidewalk, hand on a gun holster at his belt. "I spent last night in the Bay Area at a law enforcement workshop. Just got back. What's wrong?"

"I think someone broke in." Shelby gestured to Gage, who helpfully pointed to the large hole in the wall.

"Looks like they took all the copper pipe used in the plumbing," Gage said.

"Copper sells at a premium at recycle centers." Nate examined the lock on the front door before moving inside, each step made as if he was on patrol in enemy territory, ready to turn and shoot at the slightest sound.

It was unnerving. Gage must have been put off by it, as well. He came to stand by Shelby's side and took her hand. She linked her fingers with his as if they'd been holding hands for years.

Nate finished his inspection with a single pronouncement, "Clear."

Shelby released a breath she hadn't realized she'd been holding. "There are so many empty buildings and houses around. I'm surprised they haven't broken in here before."

Nate's brows drew together. "They wouldn't come all this way just to rob one store." He strode to the vacant business next door.

Shelby and Gage followed. From one store to the next. Each location had been broken into.

On the corner, the Brown Jug's door was slightly ajar. The vacant pub had a long, narrow bar. Perfect for copper thieves to hide behind.

"Stay outside." Nate drew his gun and entered.

Shelby was happy to oblige.

Somewhere nearby, a vehicle started up.

Shelby and Gage exchanged glances.

Gage spoke first. "I can't say for sure which street it's coming from, but most of the shops are on—"

"Main Street," Shelby finished with him. "It's very unusual that anyone would be out and about at this hour."

The engine accelerated. Gage and Shelby both started running toward the sound.

With his long legs, Gage quickly passed her. Looking up rather than down, Shelby's toe caught on an uneven slab of sidewalk, and she belly flopped on the pavement. Before she had a chance to register the sting of skinned flesh, Gage helped her up.

A late model, gray sedan squealed around the corner onto Jefferson and disappeared into the fog.

"Did you see the license plate?" Shelby asked.

"No. Are you okay?" Gage held out her arms, much as she'd done to him last night. He inspected her scraped hands, then knelt to look at her reddening knees. "You're shaking."

She was surprised to find it was true. "My clumsiness strikes again. Don't worry about me. Let's find Nate."

The sheriff came sprinting up to them at full speed, carrying his handgun, pointed end down. "They took the pipe from the bar, too. I heard a car. Did you see them leave?"

"Gray. Four door," Gage said matter-of-factly. "On the small side. California plates. Couldn't make out the number."

Nate turned to Shelby, who agreed.

"I'll contact the Cloverdale police. Maybe they can catch the thief before he gets on the main highway." Nate holstered his gun and hurried toward the jail.

"Well, that was exciting." Shelby was still shaking, and her palms and knees were beginning to throb. "Probably doesn't compare to frantic mares in the throws of labor, but—"

"It was stupid. What if the thief had a gun and decided to shoot at us? Over copper." Gage put his arm around Shelby's shoulders and started walking. "My knees are shaking, too."

She smiled because he'd known she needed physical contact. It wasn't every day a girl ran into criminals making a getaway, rarer still in Harmony Valley. They crossed Main, but Gage stopped her from heading toward the town square and home. Instead, he drew her south.

"Are we going to the clinic?"

He nodded. "I bought some antiseptic yesterday. Plus I want to make sure they didn't break in there, too."

"My dog." She quickened her pace, ignoring her throbbing scrapes.

Gage mumbled something about dogs and lost causes.

It only took a few minutes to reach the clinic. The doors were all locked, but Gage had a key. The Saint Bernard was in his kennel in the back. He gave them a tail-wagging welcome.

"He looks happy," Shelby noted. The lost look had disappeared in his eyes but was back in Gage's.

"Dogs have simple needs." Gage tested the lock on the rear gate. "Food, water, a roof over their heads when it rains."

"Sounds good to me." The sun was starting to come up, trying to break through the thick fog as it rose over Parish Hill, and with it she started to feel the pressure of the day's to-do list. She was supposed to keep Mae happy. How would Mae take the news that her shop had been vandalized?

Gage led Shelby inside the clinic proper. "People need more than the basics, Shel. Companionship. Friendship. Love."

"People need safety," Shelby argued, albeit weakly.

He paused at the doorway to an exam room. "More than love?"

"It's hard to love someone when you're dead." The words dropped between them like an unexpected explosion, destroying their easy camaraderie. "Skydiving, BASE jumping, big wave surfing. I could go on. You and Nick would try anything. I used to worry you'd be okay, but I was naive. I never worried either one of you would die and leave me."

Gage opened his mouth, closed it, tugged at his ear, then muttered, "Dead Gage."

He was going to hold that against her for the rest of her life. "Can we talk about something else?"

"Sit there." Gage pointed to a chair in the exam room. He produced gauze pads and antiseptic from a cupboard. "This might sting a little."

There were other things that stung—his abandonment, her callousness. They'd never move beyond his leaving and Dead Gage if they didn't talk about it. "What happened to you when Nick died? Why did you leave?"

Why did you leave me?

He soaked a square of gauze in antiseptic. "I needed time to heal."

"We could have helped each other heal."

He knelt at her feet, inspected her knees, then daubed at her scrapes.

Her indrawn breath echoed through the empty clinic.

"Sorry. It won't get any easier." He moved on to her palm.

Her hand looked small in his, smaller when she flinched. "If people need all those things you mentioned—companionship, friendship, love—why did you give up on our friendship?"

The old building groaned, as if resenting her interrogation.

"I stopped...because I felt guilty," Gage said slowly.

"About what?"

"A lot of things." He doused a clean piece of gauze with antiseptic and applied it to her knuckles.

She tensed at the stinging. "Help me out here, Gage. Give me a hint. Was it something I said? Something someone else said?"

"Can't we drop this?" He shoved at the hair on his forehead with the back of his hand, straining his cowlick until it thrust into the air.

"No." With her free hand, she smoothed his hair, softening her voice. "There was a time you'd tell me anything."

"There was never a time—"

"You're saying our friendship wasn't real?" Shelby tugged her hand away. "You're saying you didn't tell me your private dreams when I told you mine? What was that year we spent here? A joke? That's it, wasn't it? I was a joke to you. You only put up with me because of Nick."

"For the love of Pete." Gage tossed the gauze into the trash. "You push and push and…" He hung his head, turning his face away as if he couldn't stand to look her in the eye. "I felt guilty about Nick dying, okay? He asked me to go kayaking and I said yes. Then I was invited to watch a mare deliver a foal at the university in Fresno. I stayed up most of the night, drove back, and slept through my alarm." He lifted his head, meeting her gaze.

Had she thought Gage didn't care? His black eyes sparked angrily, but it was anger at himself.

Shelby felt burned to ash, as if the weakest breeze could scatter her away.

"I woke up thinking he'd be okay." Gage's voice flooded the tiny room and bounced off the walls. "I woke up and he wasn't. He went out on the river alone. On raging rapids. Without me." Gage twisted the cap back on the bottle of antibiotic. "He's dead. I overslept and he died alone. Is that what you wanted to know?"

His question echoed through the empty clinic.

Shelby didn't answer. She couldn't speak. She couldn't seem to do anything. Except run.

"Don't go!" Gage stopped following Shelby when he reached the front door.

Despite the sun's rays angling through the patchy fog to the pavement, there was no warmth. Harmony Valley was cold and gray and heartbreaking. "Shelby, please."

"I can't talk to you right now." Shelby marched into the parking lot, hugging herself.

"You wanted to know." Gage's entire body felt weary, as if he'd been playing football and been pounded all game.

His pride, buoyed by logic, encouraged him to let her go. He had Kentucky.

His heart, shackled with unrequited love for too long, encouraged him to follow her. He needed her.

"You asked me why I left, and I told you, Shel." This was it. The moment where he'd know if he'd lost her forever, or if they'd go on as they always had—on the pretense of friendship. She could never love the man who'd let her husband die. "You have every right to hate me. For a long time, I hated me."

She stopped walking.

He willed her to face him so that he could see the damage he'd wrought.

"I don't... I could never hate you." She half turned, but he couldn't read her expression. "I just... Since... I don't let anyone see me cry."

He took the steps out of the clinic two at a time and swept her into his arms. "I'm sorry." It had been the last thing he'd said as he stood over Nick's grave, long after the other mourners had departed. "I'm so sorry."

Shelby clung to him, her face buried against his chest. Her body shook with silent sobs.

"I've got you." He held her tight. He'd abide by whatever she decided, or whatever her gut reaction was to his confession. Because he loved her. Because he'd always loved her. He'd love her until his dying day.

Her shudders subsided.

Gage had to know. He had to ask. "Shel, can you ever forgive—"

With a wounded cry, she pushed out of his arms and fled, this time not stopping and not looking back.

Chapter Eleven

"**M**ae?" Shelby knocked on the bridal shop owner's front door shortly after eight that same morning.

Gage's revelation had knocked her sideways. Pain, sharp and persistent, filled her chest.

It had taken a long time to come to terms with the randomness of Nick's accident. If anything, she'd blamed Nick for his death. He'd been reckless tackling the river on his own.

To learn that Gage was supposed to have been there brought all the anger back, this time directed at Gage.

He was right to leave me.

Two years ago, she'd wanted a reason for Nick's death. Someone to blame. Now she had one. Sort of.

She couldn't blame Gage completely. He stood Nick up, yes, but Nick could have turned around. Why hadn't Nick turned around? Why hadn't he wondered where Gage was?

Because he'd loved testing himself.

Nick had probably thought he'd get to the bottom of the rapids and find Gage waiting to pick him up. And if Gage hadn't been there? Nick would've bummed a ride off another kayaker and tracked Gage down. But he'd have done it after his run on the river. Not before.

No. Gage wasn't at fault for Nick's death. But his confession dredged up the pain of Nick's passing, this time with more resentment.

A therapist would say that she was harboring toxic feelings. But Shelby had learned she needed to embrace the hurt before she could let it go. She blew out a frustrated breath. She had no idea what she'd say to Gage the next time she saw him.

If she spoke to him at all.

Mae still hadn't answered.

Shelby knocked again, her hand as pale against the scarlet door as her spirits.

Red was an odd choice for the color of a front door considering the rest of the house was painted deep purple. That might have worked on one of the town's many painted ladies, but on a 1950s ranch house? Not so much.

"Whoever's knocking doesn't understand the need for beauty sleep." Mae opened the door a crack, and then the crack widened, and Shelby stumbled back due to purple overload.

Mae's living room walls were a cheerful purple, as were her carpet, couch, and a recliner. She wore a short purple cotton robe, displaying a set of mottled, knobby knees leading down to purple fluffy mules. Her neon-red hair was in purple and pink rollers that looked torturous to sleep in. Her face was devoid of makeup, revealing skin with a blue, mottled cast. Or maybe it looked that way against all the brash red and deep purple.

"It's the lonely young widow," Mae rasped as if she'd just finished a cigarette. "Dressed in black again, I see."

"Black hides stains," Shelby retorted. Every science major knew that.

Mae arched a brow. Or she would have if they'd been penciled on. "Black reflects your mood. Who wants to date a woman who wears black every day?"

"I don't wear black every day," Shelby said defensively, belatedly reminding herself she was here to make Mae happy.

"You've worn black every time I've seen you." Mae wagged a finger at her. "You make widows a cliché. Be quick about your business. I don't accept visitors until after nine."

Shelby took a deep breath, preparing to start over. "Did the sheriff call?" Shelby had a sinking suspicion he hadn't or else they wouldn't be having a discussion about black. They'd be talking about the hole in the wall at Dream Day Bridal.

Mae shook her head and the curlers followed. "He knows I don't answer the phone or accept visitors until I'm fully awake. After nine."

Shelby explained about the break-ins and the stolen copper, trying to put a positive spin on things. "As a winery representative, I'm sorry this happened, but it doesn't change our interest in the place or our offer." Christine had reassured Shelby of that earlier on the phone.

"They didn't take anything else?" Mae sagged against the doorjamb. "My dresses?"

"I don't think so," Shelby said.

"I want to see. Come and get me at nine."

"But—"

"Come back and get me," Mae commanded, slamming the red door shut.

Gage spent the morning cleaning the clinic.

It was better than thinking about the look on Shelby's face when he'd told her he was the reason she was a widow.

He started at the top of the clinic, brushing cobwebs from the ceiling and walls with a broom, wishing he would've kept his mouth shut when she'd pressed him for answers. He sanitized counters and storage drawers, wiping them down until they looked like new. If only he could clean things with Shelby. He swept and mopped the linoleum floor until he could see his shadowed expression in it.

Dr. Wentworth manned the phones, placing orders for supplies in between talking to people about the copper thefts and their intent to reopen the clinic. The thefts were big news.

Gage was wiping down the plastic chairs in the lobby, wondering if any of Shelby's scrapes were bothering her, when one of the old man's conversations caught his attention.

"Now, Felix, you can't go making accusations like that." Doc paused to listen to Felix's reply. "If it makes you feel better, tell the sheriff." He slammed the receiver into the cradle. "You won't believe what people are saying about this copper thief."

"Try me." Gage took a seat.

"Some of the Nervous Nellies think it's a drug gang moving into town."

"Very few people have moved into town lately. What did you tell me? Four? Six? All of them former residents, except the sheriff."

"Exactly why that theory doesn't fly."

"And you have one of your own." Of course. Gage rocked back in his chair, waiting.

Doc cleared his throat. "People get funny when they feel threatened. My theory is more sensible."

"Which is?"

"That someone who came to help with the harvest did it." Doc's eyebrows waggled. "Think about it. Only the businesses that aren't open were hit. The thief cared."

"But if the thief cared, he wouldn't have broken into all those places to begin with." *The thief knew.*

The phone rang again.

"Mark my words," Doc said gravely. "It's someone who was here this weekend."

"What?" Christine's voice carried from the upstairs office down to the kitchen where Ryan was making a cup of tea and Shelby was doctoring her coffee. "Of course I'll cooperate."

Ryan and Shelby hurried upstairs with their mugs.

"That was Nate." Christine finger combed strands of blond hair back from her face. "We need to give him a list of our volunteers from the harvest. He suspects one of them is the copper thief. So far they've found six businesses that were vandalized."

"Do we have a list?" Ryan frowned.

Shelby hurried to her desk. "I have the call list."

They reviewed the list together. No name shouted guilty.

"We saw a small gray sedan drive away this morning," Shelby said. "Do you remember anyone driving something like that?"

"A gray four-door sedan?" Ryan stroked his long, sparse whiskers. "Isn't that the most popular car model and color in America? We might as well mark down who didn't drive one."

Shelby checked the time. "I'm late getting to Mae's house. I'll drop the list off with the sheriff."

"We'll enter the wine readings you took this morning into the database for you." Christine looked worried. "I hope it wasn't someone who came to help. That casts a shadow on the winery."

"Not unless it was one of us," Ryan said matter-of-factly. "And none of us drives a car like that."

"Any bad press is bad press." Christine sighed. "Since when are you the upbeat one?"

"I like to keep you guessing about me, boss."

"You are nothing like the boy I hired," Christine quipped.

"But you love me anyway," Ryan predicted.

Chuckling, Shelby made a photocopy of the list of names and numbers, and left, stopping by the sheriff's office. Which turned out to be a good thing, since Mae was sitting there when she arrived.

"You're late." Mae sounded like she'd smoked a pack of menthols since Shelby had seen her last. "I called the sheriff to pick me up. He showed me the horror. I needed a moment to collect myself."

"I'm sorry, Mae. I got busy." Shelby approached the tall counter separating the lobby from the sheriff's desk. "Here's the list of attendees from our harvest, Nate."

"So it's true." Mae's tone turned serious. "If it wasn't for your winery bringing people back, my store wouldn't have been violated. I knew that winery was a bad idea."

So much for Christine's plan to butter up the residents to approve the expansion of the winery.

"Let me do the detective work." Nate picked up Shelby's list and began scanning the names from the other side of the counter. "Look on the bright side, Mae." Shelby infused her voice with cheer. "You don't have to make an insurance claim. The winery wants to buy your property as is."

"Maybe I shouldn't sell." Mae pounded her cane on the floor. "Maybe selling will bring more crime here."

"Maybe you should take a breath and think about the future." Nate looked up from Shelby's list. "What good is that place doing you?"

Mae sniffed. "It's where my memories are stored."

"Last I checked, memories are stored up here." Nate tapped his temple.

"Fat lot of good my memories will do anyone after I'm gone if I keep them to myself." Mae's grip on the cane tightened. "Do you see the thief on that list? I'd like to kick him in the shins before you arrest him. I've got big feet for my size."

"Justice takes time, Mae," he deadpanned. "Not boot size."

"I don't have a lot of time, sheriff."

"Now, Mae," Nate soothed, finally giving her his full attention. "Shelby's going to take you home, where you can relive all your glory days in the comfort of your recliner."

"Oliver, you were always a pain in my patoot."

"Who's Oliver?" The sheriff's gaze intensified. "I'm Nate. And this is Shelby. Do you recognize us?"

"Of course I recognize you. The nosey sheriff and the lonely widow. You'd make a cute couple, but I think that veterinarian with the cowlick has a soft spot for Shelby."

"I'm sorry," Shelby said softly to Nate. "She seems fixated on matchmaking."

Mae blinked and gazed around the jail. "What were we talking about?"

Nate didn't miss a beat. "You calling your doctor."

"What for?" Mae harrumphed. "My doctor was born in the nineties. I have spandex leggings older than he is."

"Call him." The sheriff caught Shelby's gaze, then nodded toward the door.

Shelby took the hint. "Time to go, Mae." Before the stress of the break-in had her drifting deeper into confusion.

"Don't take me home," Mae ordered, unflinching. "People are gathering at El Rosal. After I visit, then you can take me home."

Like Shelby had a choice.

El Rosal was crowded with perhaps forty residents, although no one seemed to be below age fifty.

The residents' faded clothing, white hair and pale complexions were nearly lost in the bright room. Mae and her red hair being the exception. She'd always stand out in a crowd.

While Shelby got Mae settled in a chair, Gage and her grandfather pulled up out front. She'd been hoping she wouldn't have to face Gage until tonight at dinner. She still had no idea what she'd say to him.

"You see," remarked Rose, pointing with the graceful precision of a ballerina at Gage's truck. "Wrong vehicle. He couldn't be the devil who stole all that pipe. He's driving a truck."

"You think it was Gage?" Shelby blurted.

"Some of these old fools are personally vetting everyone physically able to work a blowtorch or wrench." Agnes shook her head. "Don't worry. You were the first one crossed off our list."

Shelby bit her lip to keep from boasting that she'd picked up a few mechanical skills since she'd left town. She could change a tire and release the pressure seal on a vat of wine.

"And Gage isn't driving just any truck. Remember how that boy got that dent?" Rose turned to Shelby with a smile, while others chuckled. That dent had a reputation far and wide in Harmony Valley. "Do you remember, Shelby?"

Of course Shelby remembered. She ignored the comment and fussed over Mae.

Mae seemed the only one who had no recall of the event. "Did you hit Gage's truck with a baseball bat, girl?"

"No." Why hadn't Gage fixed his fender or traded in the truck?

"Did you give it a karate kick?" Mae released a raspy chuckle that morphed into a cough.

"No." Shelby's cheeks heated as she rubbed Mae's back.

Gage and her grandfather entered the dining room. Everyone quieted. Grandpa crossed the room with his rolling gait to sit next to Mae. Gage claimed a chair close to Shelby.

What to say? What to say?

"Mae, let me refresh your memory about that truck." Rose stood and made a dramatic flourish with her hand. "Gage was teaching Shelby how to drive a stick shift and she missed the turn in front of Bea's house. That dent is where they slid into Bea's goat pasture and hit a post."

Shelby had pumped the clutch instead of the brake. If Gage hadn't grabbed the wheel, they would have hit some goats. As it was, they narrowly missed plowing through the next fence and into the muddy pigpen.

"I could have taught you how to drive a stick shift." Mildred stared in Shelby's general direction, eyes half-hidden behind thick circles of glass. "I still could."

Several people groaned.

"I could," the former race car driver said louder.

"I remember now." Mae's gaze turned speculatively to Gage. "Gage had to have stitches on his right temple."

Shelby slouched in her chair, suddenly not so fond of small towns where there were no secrets.

Gage touched his scarred temple, then leaned toward Shelby, his scent of woodsy aftershave setting off her awareness meter. "Why are they talking about our accident?"

Without looking at him, she whispered, "Because they have very long memories, and you can apparently wield a wrench." Whew. Check done. Their first conversation since his admission. Impersonal, but okay.

"Wait a minute." Olly squinted in her grandfather's direction. "Doesn't Doc own a silver sedan?"

"It was my wife's," Grandpa admitted. "She loved that car."

"They could have driven Ruby's sedan," Olly pointed out. "Silver. Gray. In the fog who can tell the difference?"

"Anyone who isn't legally blind," Grandpa muttered, adding an apology when Mildred protested being lumped with the accuser.

Despite his protests, the amateur sleuths took to Olly's hypothesis hungrily.

"I'm embarrassed to call myself a Harmony Valley resident," Mae said. "Have you people listened to yourselves?"

"That car has undisturbed cobwebs in the wheel wells." Shelby couldn't keep sarcasm from her voice. "Not to mention the Lincoln is longer than the car we saw."

"We only have their word about the car." Felix's burgundy polo shirt was sprinkled with what looked like cat hair. The retired fireman rescued cats and kittens from all over the county. "For all we know, they could have been driving a truck."

Grandpa was done with muttering. This time he bellowed. "Or Santa's sleigh."

The crowd quieted.

"We're the ones who reported the break-in at Dream Day Bridal," Gage patiently pointed out, further dampening the group's enthusiasm toward them as suspects. "We were there with the sheriff when the culprit drove away."

"See?" Rose gloated. "Airtight alibi. Cross Gage off the list."

Gage leaned in once more, whispering to Shelby, "I was getting worried."

His warm breath on the shell of her ear created a yearning that she shouldn't have if she was going to hold tight to her upset over his confession.

Mae yanked on Gage's arm. "If you're serious about this girl, you'll need to get her a ring. Not too big, not too small."

Shelby put her hand on her forehead, wishing she was elsewhere.

"Don't start matchmaking, Mae." Grandpa removed his glasses and cleaned them with a tissue.

"Hypocrite." Mae sniffed. "Have you forgotten I set you and Ruby up on a blind date? I am a soldier of love."

Shelby covered her mouth with her hand because her grandfather was speechless and blushing. That never happened.

Gage chuckled. And Shelby wanted to laugh along with him, but she couldn't.

It should have been Nick chuckling next to her. It should have been Nick. And she should have felt anger at Gage. Why didn't she feel anger?

Because...because...

Everything over the past few days tumbled together—her awareness of Gage as a man, her feeling happy and comforted when he was around, her fear that he'd be hurt by a horse. She was afraid of what it might mean. She had to go.

Shelby stood and dug in her purse for her keys. Between the bright colors, the gossip, Gage, and this crazy rejectable idea forming about him, she needed air. "Come on, Mae. Your taxi is leaving."

"I'm staying. I want to hear all the gossip." Mae looked around the room happily. "Don't worry. I'll defend your innocence, Shelby."

"My innocence doesn't need defending, but you do need a ride home." Shelby was all too aware of everyone's gaze upon her, most especially Gage's. "Please, Mae. Let's go."

Mae shooed her off. "Agnes can drive me home. Despite the idiocy of the crowd, it's the most exciting thing to happen in town since Will proposed to Emma at the spring festival. I can't miss this."

Agnes nodded absently, listening to Mona Kincaid present her theory of an alien invasion.

Gage stood when Shelby did. "I'll walk you out."

He wanted to talk. Shelby wasn't ready. She had to sort out her feelings. About him, about Nick.

She turned and rushed out. He was right behind her.

Shelby fiddled with her keys when she reached the sidewalk, forcing herself to look Gage in the eyes. "You were right not to tell me two years ago. I would have hated you."

He flinched. "I'll understand if you never want to see me again." He'd understand, but the pain in his eyes said how hurt he'd be.

A part of her wanted to take Gage up on the offer. A larger, stronger part of her rebelled. This was Gage. Nothing was simple where he was concerned.

His cell phone rang. It was a welcome distraction. "Excuse me. I need to take this." He answered his phone and his eyes lit up at whatever was said by the caller. "You think she'll deliver tonight? Sure, I can be there."

Worry knotted in her stomach. Shelby clenched her keys and waited for Gage to disconnect. She wanted to say, "Don't go." Instead, she told him to be careful. The distance between them was clear, as if he was Dead Gage once more.

"I'm always careful." He flashed his trademark smile. False, flawed, phony. He was infuriatingly glib when what she wanted was reassurance that he'd be alive in the morning.

She took a breath, tried holding her fears at bay. "Careful? That nasty bruise on your back tells another story."

The charmer's smile faded. "And what does the scar on my temple tell you?"

"That you care," she begrudgingly admitted. She needed to get back to work and find that emotional space she'd been in before he'd shown up again. If they hadn't reconnected, she wouldn't have discovered her feelings were still vested in someone who might get hurt going about his daily business.

As his friend, she had no right to ask him not to go.

Foolishly, she said, "Don't do this."

He affectionately stroked her cheek. "It's who I am. I can't give up what I love, Shel."

She wanted to turn into his touch, to clasp his hand in both of hers and keep him here where it was safe, but there was the way he let Nick down on that fateful day. She turned toward her SUV.

"Don't wait up," he called after her.

They both knew she would.

"Is that you, hot shot?"

Shelby paused as she entered her grandfather's house after work. Once more, she'd used the front door instead of the kitchen one. But it was a good thing she had. Grandpa had gone deep into the stacks again. "Let me help you out of there."

Something fell at his feet. He bent over.

"I'll get that," she said, moving quickly between the piles.

"Got it." Grandpa stood up in that wobbly manner of his, steadying himself with a hand on the mantle. "Don't block the aisle. I'm coming out."

"Grandpa..." She backed up. Everywhere Shelby turned lately, there was someone to fret over.

That wasn't true. It was mostly Gage she worried about. Gage who occupied her thoughts. His strength, his compassion, his fondness for her grandfather. It all resonated with her.

"I hope that worry in your voice isn't for me. I told you I'm not packing my library away. No need. I'm as solid as a rock." His rolling steps and a slight stumble contradicted his words. He picked his way carefully through the stacks. Three steps. Two. One.

She drew him into her arms, hugging that sweet old ornery bag of bones as if she'd nearly lost him.

"What's this?" His voice rumbled in her ear. "Has something happened to that giant dog of yours?"

She released him and stepped back. "Is Gage here yet?" It was nearly nine.

"No. And you shouldn't be spending time worrying about him either. He's a professional."

"I'm not worried about Gage."

Both his white brows shot upward.

She held on to the fib as long as she could. "Okay, I am worried about Gage. And you."

Grandpa patted the top of her head, just like he used to when she was a little girl and she'd caught her skirt on a fence rail or tangled a brush in her hair. "He'll be fine, hot shot."

"He'll be fine until the day he's not. That's how it was with Nick." Inevitably, she'd blink and things would change. "Have you eaten?"

"Yes, but if you're cooking, I'm more than happy to eat again." He winked.

"I love the way you lie to me."

Chuckling, her grandfather clasped her hand and allowed her to lead him to the kitchen. "It's not lying. I was married once. I know how this works. You make an effort and I am vocally appreciative."

Once he was settled in a chair, Shelby took bacon and eggs out of the refrigerator. How could she screw up breakfast for dinner? Rather than go to the stove, she sat next to Grandpa at the table.

"Whatever's bothering you," he said quietly, "you can tell me."

And so, she did.

She relayed why Gage disappeared two years ago. She admitted how hurt she was, and how sad she felt for Gage. "I want to forgive him, but part of me can't."

Grandpa held her hand through her entire speech. Those frail, age-spotted hands gave her comfort. "I need to tell you something, something your mother should have told you a long time ago."

Shelby summoned what strength she could and waited.

"You know your mother never lets a challenge pass her by. When she was a girl, she was the fiercest competitor in town. Checkers, softball, swimming, holding her breath underwater. She hated losing." He shook his grizzled head.

"Nowadays, she uses that determination on her career." He fell silent, as if lost in thought.

Shelby squeezed his hand.

"Your grandmother and I wanted a houseful of kids. But it wasn't meant to be. We were lucky to have your mother. When she and your father came home for a visit one winter and told us they were pregnant, we were ecstatic. Our first grandchild."

"Me."

"No, just listen." There was hurt and disapproval in his voice. "This was before you."

"But—"

"Let me finish."

Shelby waited. She waited so long, she squeezed his hand again.

That did the trick.

"Your mother was invited on a skiing trip to Aspen with some important clients."

"Mom doesn't ski." Not ever.

"Not anymore." He drummed his fingers on the table. "Her competitive streak got the better of her. When the group decided to take a Black Diamond run, she couldn't turn them down. At that elevation, the air is thin. Four months along, her body was changing and not as able to take fast turns."

Shelby didn't want to hear the rest, but she couldn't keep running away from truths either.

"Your mother?" He gnawed on his lip. "I'm sure she came down that slope like a bat escaping the devil. She told me she was ahead of everyone when she fell."

Sorrow burrowed deep in Shelby's bones.

"There's a cost for every reckless decision that's made, I suppose. Your mother spent a week in the hospital in critical condition. But that baby...that precious little life. Lost." His voice broke and he cleared his throat. "Your mother should have known better. She should have been more careful. She should have placed more importance on the value of life—hers and that child's—than in the thrill of the moment."

"What about Dad? Did he just let her go skiing when she was pregnant?"

"He couldn't do anything to stop her, just as he can't stop her now. People like your mother…" Grandpa fixed her with a hard stare. "People like Nick. They live in that moment. Their enthusiasm for life and living it their way is magnetic. I'm sure that was part of Nick's appeal to you. He was a lot like your mother, just not as fortunate."

Shelby recalled how well her mother and Nick had gotten along. There was an energy between the two that instantly drew others to them.

"Whereas people like you and Gage, you're a different breed." His wrinkles smoothed. His voice softened. "You watch your step and consider the consequences of your actions. You assume that everyone else does, too. It's what makes the mistakes of others so hard to accept. I always thought you and Gage were the better match because of your similarities."

Obviously, it wasn't the first time someone had paired Shelby and Gage. People in their university science classes. Mae. Christine. But it was her grandfather's perspective that finally joined the pieces together for Shelby.

How right it felt when she and Gage were in the same room. The interests, values and beliefs they shared. His rare, genuine smile. His wit, his humor, the way he'd named her stubborn expression barnacles.

"I loved Nick," she murmured.

"I'm not saying you didn't." Grandpa's normal burly voice sounded strained. "But I'm not saying you shouldn't look around. The heart's a fickle organ. Doesn't work as well when lonely."

"Doesn't work as well when heartbroken." Now it was her voice that sounded stretched thin against her throat.

"You've been in limbo, hot shot. And along comes Gage, one of your closest friends, telling you what you dreaded hearing, what you needed to hear. That type of honesty deserves forgiveness. Think about it." He patted her head again. It was an accepting pat. A loving pat. An everything will be all right pat. "If Gage had gone with Nick that day, most likely, both men would've drowned, perhaps while one was trying to save the other."

The truth in his words sank in and silence... Silence closed around her, filling her ears the way it did when she swam under water.

"It's late. And I've lost my appetite." Her grandfather pushed himself to his feet. "While you're cooking dinner, you think about these so-called hurdles of yours in the way of forgiveness, think about how lucky you are that one of your men survived."

Shelby had waited up for him.

Or at least, she'd tried.

Gage found Shelby slumped over her laptop at the kitchen table, the Siamese cat in her lap.

He paused inside the kitchen doorway, storing the image in his memory. The flyaway wisps of short golden hair. The thick lashes and pink cheeks. The wrinkled black T-shirt. Her hand lay across the table as if inviting him to draw closer.

It's been a long couple of days, Jamero.

"Come on, Shel. Time for bed." Gage gave her shoulder a gentle shake.

The cat hopped to the floor with a plaintive meow.

Shelby sat up, finding his hand when her eyes were barely open. "What time is it?"

"It's after two." Her hand was soft. Her grip possessive. His heart lost. "I don't think either of us will be running in the morning."

She yawned. "Did you deliver a baby?"

"Yep." He'd delivered a beaut. "No nips, no kicks, no trampling." At least, none that connected. After the mare settled down, it'd been an easy delivery.

Shelby released his hand. Blinked. "Let me see." She tugged at his shirt.

He dodged behind a chair, pulling his T-shirt free of her grip. "I'm not taking my shirt off again."

"I'm awake now, and I need to make sure you're safe." There was a clear note of urgency in her voice.

She'd admitted valuing safety over love and even friendship. It was the exact opposite of Nick's philosophy.

"I'm telling you I'm fine. Not a scratch." And then he saw the scrape down the back of his hand where Misty Bog's hoof had grazed him.

Shelby saw it, too. She blanched. "You did get kicked. What if you have internal bleeding? What if you go to sleep and you don't wake up?"

He tugged his shirt off and turned around slowly so that she could see the only place he'd been touched was the back of his hand. "We're going to have to talk about your phobia."

"I'm only scared for you." She sounded miserable, looked it, too. "Which makes no sense."

"Because I'm Dead Gage?" It hurt to say it out loud, to acknowledge that he'd been successful in cutting her out of his life. "We don't have to do this if it's too painful. I can leave, though you'll have to explain it to your grandfather."

"We're different when it comes to risk." She used the same tone that Gage used when telling a client there was no hope for an animal.

Different. His heart ached so bad that it spiraled up into his throat, making it hard to speak. "It's why I stayed away," he rasped.

"Yes."

"It's why I should go." But there was his promise to Doc. His feet didn't budge.

"No. You shouldn't leave." Her voice strengthened. She sniffed, blinking back unshed tears. "I can remember sitting at this table dozens of times and listening to Nick tease you because you didn't want to climb a dangerous cliff or snowboard down a challenging trail. What I can't remember, ever, is sitting here and listening to you convince him of the danger about something. No one ever talked Nick out of doing what he'd set his mind to." Her words cut through the guilt and the uncertainty. It reached deep into Gage's heart, offering absolution.

"You wouldn't have stopped him from going on the river that day, Gage. It didn't matter if you showed up or not."

Gage wanted to believe her.

But he'd wanted to believe many impossible things before.

And been disappointed.

Chapter Twelve

"I was hoping plumbing wouldn't be an issue." Sleep deprived, Shelby unlocked the door to Dream Day Bridal early Tuesday morning for Dane Utley. He was the contractor who'd remodeled the winery's one hundred year-old farmhouse and rebuilt the barn. "And then someone came in and stole our copper pipe."

The thieves had broken into six businesses in all. Speculation about the thieves' identities still ran high on the gossip meter. The elderly residents created a number of interesting theories about potential suspects. Since the suspects were always related to folks in town, each theory ruffled someone's feathers.

Gage ruffled Shelby's feathers. She was at a loss now as to how to act around him. She couldn't—wouldn't—try to ignore him any longer. Still, it didn't mean she could see a future for herself with him, or anyone else. There remained the fear of loss.

"People ransack old buildings and new construction all the time." Dane drew her back to the present as he glanced around the main room. "It's become an annoying part of the business. In this case, I wouldn't worry about missing pipes. You'll probably want to move the bathroom to the rear of the building to allow for your storage tanks anyway."

"Agreed." Dane's foreman, Joey Harris, a short, wiry man with a sharp gaze had followed them in. "Is it me? Or is there something a little zombie-like about the mannequins in here? The one with arms seems like she wants a dance and is reaching for me."

Dane smiled sheepishly at Shelby. "Construction humor. Every old building has a character and a story."

Ignoring looking at the bridal dais, Shelby stood up for the place. She led Joey directly to the window display. "Would it help if I introduced you? Her name is Conchita and she's been here since Dream Day Bridal opened for business."

"Get out." Joey flicked back his steel-gray ponytail. "They have names?"

"Just Conchita. She was stunning in her day. Nothing to fear." Shelby fingered her delicate dress.

"Nice to meet you, Conchita." Dane tipped an imaginary hat. "Now, let's get to work."

With one last speculative glance from Joey at Conchita, the two men set about measuring the space and poking at walls, stomping on the stair treads and knocking on the ceiling. Shelby followed them around, always keeping her back to the dais, answering questions when she could, stepping outside a few times to field calls from Christine and Mae.

"Structurally…" Dane began his summation in the storage room thirty minutes later. "This is the best building I've seen in Harmony Valley all year."

That should have reassured Shelby. "I sense this is a good-news, bad-news moment."

Dane nodded. "If you want to convert this into a wine cellar, you've got a few challenges. Those large plate glass windows in front face the west, letting in the afternoon heat. I'm afraid you won't have any natural light in the place when we're done."

"Dark is good," Shelby said. Depressing, but good for the wine.

"Dark increases the efficiency of the special cooling unit you requested, too." Dane tucked his clipboard under his arm and led them back to the main room. He gestured toward the front door. "We'll also need a wider entryway so you can get a forklift in here."

Joey eyed Conchita as if she might suddenly attack. "After we give the mannequins a proper burial, we'll widen the space."

"They won't bother you if you don't look at them," Dane teased.

"There's three of them. Three's a powerful number, with heads or without." Joey joined them by the dais. "Tell her about the rodent problem." He shivered emphatically enough to send his ponytail swaying. "I hate rats. But boy, do they love fancy dress boxes."

Shelby couldn't stop a small shiver of her own. She must have been on her phone when they made that discovery.

"You need to work on your delivery." Dane's smile heightened his strong, handsome features. Yet Shelby felt no uptick in her pulse. "The rats chewed through a wall from the abandoned building next door."

"The good news is the cats." Joey took up the tale. "Didn't see any but smelled 'em downstairs and in back. Hopefully, they've kept the rodent population down."

Sniffing, Shelby peered around nervously. She didn't see or smell anything rat-like or cat-like.

"You'll need new plumbing, of course," Dane said louder, giving his foreman a pointed look. "But we're particularly concerned with the electrical. Your circuit board is from the fifties. Add to that a rat's fondness for wires, and I'd highly recommend rewiring the entire building."

"Wouldn't it have been easier to build from scratch?" she mused.

Dane and Joey shared a laugh.

"It might be different now, but it took months to get the first winery permits past the town council," Dane explained. "The older residents don't want to see the town change in character. To them, growth means big-box stores, fast food, and crime."

The need for Christine's game plan to woo the town council made more sense. If only Shelby wasn't high on the town's copper thief suspect list.

"Can we move some of these mannequins into the back?" Joey rubbed his arms.

Dane frowned. "Why? You'll be moving them into a dumpster when we demo."

"We could move the nameless mannequins to the back," Shelby offered, almost certain that Mae wouldn't mind. "But let's move the mirrors and dais first." Okay, that was a cowardly thing to do, but the dais affected her more than the mannequins did.

"The things I do so you don't freak out, Joey." Dane set his clipboard on the floor.

"It's like being married, isn't it?" Joey winked at Shelby.

Chapter Thirteen

M ae wanted to know what was going on at the shop.

She'd heard a rumor from Rose, who'd heard it from that boy, Ryan, who worked at the winery, that a contractor was taking a look at her shop early this morning.

Despite being a firm believer in beauty sleep, Mae had risen at the indecent hour of six a.m., put on her makeup, teased out her hair and called Shelby for a ride. She'd been too late. Shelby was already at the shop with the contractor and refused to come pick Mae up until after they left.

No papers had been signed. It was still Mae's shop. Having long ago given up her driver's license, Mae grabbed her cane and headed out.

The first block was easy.

In the midst of the second block, her legs began to feel heavy.

When she reached the town square, her breath came in ragged gasps.

"Should have quit smoking a decade earlier," she grumbled to herself.

The sheriff noticed Mae sitting in a chair on the patio outside El Rosal. Hoping he wouldn't stop, she waved and looked away, as if waiting for someone.

He parked his blue truck with its gold star and got out.

Shoot and darn.

It was times like these that Mae hated living in Harmony Valley. If she'd lived in a bigger town, she could wander about as she pleased.

"Sheriff Nate."

"Mae." His gaze scanned the town square as if anticipating criminal activity about to occur. He must be good at waiting, she figured. Until the copper thefts, the only criminal activity in Harmony Valley had been Franklin Oscar's evening walks in his speedo during the summer months. Mostly, Sheriff Nate corralled wandering elderly and wayward pets. Just last week she knew there'd been a 911 call because Bea's milk goats had escaped and invaded Etta's vegetable patch.

The ability to wait was what made a good cop, or so one of Mae's husbands had said. "Wait long enough and people will admit to anything." He'd been a detective in Cloverdale. Took a bullet in 1992. Recovered. And divorced her. The jerk.

The sheriff swiveled back to study Mae. Waiting.

She bit her lip. He'd have to ask what she was doing. And even then she wouldn't tell him. Last she checked, it was a free country.

The sheriff's gaze was hypnotic. He raised one black brow.

She broke. "No need to worry about me, sheriff. I'm going to my shop. Go help some poor old sod." Mae might have succumbed to his finely honed interrogation technique, but she stopped short of admitting what was on the tip of her tongue: she had lung cancer and could go to the big bridal shop in the sky any day.

Instead, she asked, "Where are you headed?"

He ignored her question and held out a hand. "I'll drive you." He didn't look her in the eye.

Was he not looking at Mae because she was old? Or because he knew she was sick?

Men used to look at Mae appreciatively, fondly, flirtatiously. And she used to look back. The fun had gone out of looking.

She considered refusing Nate, but when you were this close to the pearly gates, you didn't have time for pride. And the walk this far had taxed her. She was tempted to go home and rest.

"May as well roll over and die if I go home," she mumbled, taking Nate's hand. It was where she preferred to depart this world. No cold, colorless hospital. No tubes in her veins. Nope. She was checking out in her Purple Palace.

Without a word, Nate helped Mae into his truck and buckled her belt.

"You'd have a good time with my granddaughter, Annie," she said, feeling cantankerous. "She talks a lot and has tattoos. All that talking wears on me because I can't get a word in edgewise. But a man like you, who doesn't say much, would appreciate a talker."

"Don't be so hard on her," he surprised her by saying. "At least she loves you enough to talk to you. Have you seen her recently?"

"No." Which only reminded her that she owed her daughters a phone call. She was still coming to terms with the doctor's diagnosis. Ava and Andrea would want to know the bad news.

Nate let the conversation drop.

Minutes later they were parked outside Dream Day Bridal. Inside the shop—her shop—men in work boots carried the mirror panels to the storage room.

Mae wanted to gnash the few teeth left in her mouth. She wanted to scream. She wanted to raise her fist and rail. Instead, she gripped her cane handle and glared at the sheriff.

He frowned. "Be nice."

She didn't want to be. She didn't have to be. Husbands had loved her, come and gone. Her girls had grown, married, and moved away. Dream Day Bridal was the one constant in Mae's life.

I don't want it to end.

Her life cut short. Her body frail, weak, lacking the curves she'd flaunted and flirted with. Her face. How it sagged and wrinkled and disappointed her. The dance between a man and a woman was what she'd enjoyed most. There'd be no more dancing. No more people watching, no more matchmaking, no more advice-giving.

"Help me out of here," she commanded, realizing that the sheriff had been waiting to see if she'd want to be driven home. "This is my shop and I'm not dead yet." She struggled to open the heavy truck door. It was stuck or had some trick to opening it.

It was still shut when Nate came around to her side. He opened the door, and lifted her down as if she weighed nothing, making her feel even more helpless. To make matters worse, he held her arm as they took the few remaining steps, as if he knew her legs were too unsteady to go it alone.

"Stop!" she cried, entering the store like a queen about to order a beheading.

A man with a graying ponytail had been about to grope one of the armless mannequins. His hands were grimy and would leave a mark on the pristine, green satin dress.

"Everyone stop. Now." Her voice cracked. "If anyone touches anything else, I will never sign. *Never*."

Shelby appeared on the stairs, holding the chair Mae had sat on the other day. "We were just clearing things out of the way."

Mae gestured for Shelby to put the chair down and she hobbled across the sales floor and sat in it. "You can stop. I knew something like this would happen. These are my things." She hated how fragile she sounded. She needed to turn the conversation in a new direction. "I made dreams come true in this shop. Women walked in and with my help transformed themselves into a vision. Men took one look at that dress on that mannequin—" she pointed to Conchita "—and realized even *they* could be Prince Charming. All they had to do was stand at the top of the aisle and say, I do."

Everyone looked at Conchita. Everyone, but the sheriff.

Sheriff Nate had positioned himself with his stiff back to Conchita and her traditional Spanish lace dress, as if he couldn't bear to look upon a bride, even a plastic one.

Mae would have smiled, if not for the vandalism and the disrespect of her merchandise, as well as the absolute exhaustion her outburst had cost her. She might have smiled, too, because she recognized that the sheriff had a secret. He had someone, after all. Someone he'd lost if that forlorn look on his face was any indication. Perhaps even someone he'd promised to meet at the altar.

Her attention was drawn to Shelby next, hiding in that ugly, thin green jacket. Who did she think she was kidding? She wore another black shirt today. This one a rumpled button-down. The young widow needed a kick in the patoot if she was ever to escape widowhood's doldrums.

Mae might not fall in love one more time, but there were secrets to unearth and people who needed her.

Even if they didn't want their secrets unearthed.

Even if they didn't know they needed her.

Chapter Fourteen

There was nothing like moving someone else's stuff around for selfish reasons and being caught at it. Shelby apologized to Mae as Dane and Joey made their escape. She wasn't doing a good job of keeping Mae happy.

"I found her wandering the streets." Sheriff Nate obviously disapproved. "She seemed distraught."

"I'm not a runaway." Mae's retort lacked snap. Shoulders bent in her purple polyester, belted, vintage eighties jumpsuit, she was clearly fatigued. "I protect what's mine. And this... This was unauthorized mayhem."

Guilty as charged. "We were just—"

"Ah!" Mae cut Shelby off with a chop of her hand. "Apologies mean nothing to me. It's actions that count."

"I'll be next door at the jail," the sheriff said to Shelby. "Come get me when she's ready to go home. And next time you want to visit your store, Mae, call me and I'll drive you over."

After the sheriff left, Mae leaned forward in her chair. "What did we learn today about dealing with me?"

"To ask before we move anything." Shelby bit her lip. When would that contract be signed? Not soon enough.

"It'll always be my shop," Mae insisted. "I'll come in and look at these walls, look out these windows and relive the excitement of all those brides and prom queens." She stared at the mannequin in the front window. "Can you keep Conchita in the corner? Wouldn't people find her charming?"

Uh-oh.

Thick cobwebs connected the shoulders of the mannequin's dress to the wall like gossamer girders. The right half of Conchita's dress, the part facing the window, was yellowed with age. Mae's eyesight was probably so poor she didn't take note of any of that.

"People aren't going to come in here," Shelby said gently. "This space is for barrel storage. Tourists and visitors will go to the tasting room on the main winery grounds."

"Oh," Mae's response brimmed with disappointment. "We need to find a place for Conchita and her dress. For all my dresses." Her voice had become as fragile as the rest of her. "There are thousands of dollars' worth of inventory in the stock room."

That was some expensive rat chow.

Shelby fidgeted.

"Not that I care about the money. Each wonderful dress deserves a wonderful woman to wear it." Mae batted her mascara-caked lashes coyly. "How about you? There's a beautiful knee-length white sheath in storage that would be perfect for your next wedding."

"No." Shelby should have traded assignments with Ryan. How troublesome could three elderly town councilwomen be?

"I won't even charge you," Mae continued her sales pitch. "It would be a gift, from one widow to another when you marry Gage."

"Whoa." Shelby hadn't even gotten to the first comes love part and Mae had accelerated to the then comes marriage part.

Mae scoffed. "You're blinded by all that black. Don't be such a cliché. You're young. Wear something bright. It's late summer. Practically fall. Orange is in and it's a passion color." She sighed dreamily. "My favorite bridesmaid dresses were orange." Mae's gaze shifted to the display window. Her tone became a soft whisper. "Your bridesmaids wore teal, high-waisted halter dresses."

Shelby was impressed. "You have a great memory."

"A great dress leaves a lasting impression." Mae shook herself. "I'd like to show you something."

Shelby glanced toward the back of the shop. "Something in the storage room?"

"No. Never mind. You're not ready." Mae pointed at Shelby's torso.

She glanced at her black shirt. "Sorry, Mae. Black's my color of choice at the moment."

A car drove by with a white poodle barking from a window, headed in the direction of the clinic and Gage. Shelby hoped he was having a better day than she was.

"There aren't enough quality, single men in this town," Mae lamented, staring at Conchita's wedding dress.

"I'm not looking to date anyone." And even if she was, the one person who interested her had a job waiting for him in Kentucky. That made her a nervous wreck. How could that be love?

"Who said anything about you?" Mae sniffed. "You're still defining yourself by your last husband. You wouldn't know love if it struck you on the noggin."

There wasn't a good volley for that lob.

"And Sheriff Nate is mourning a lost love. Closed to happiness, the both of you." Mae tsked. "Wasted youth, if you ask me. If you don't change your mind, ten years from now you'll be pining for kids, staring at your ever-widening hips, lying in bed alone at night wondering when life passed you by."

Bittersweet truth coiled around Shelby's heart and sunk in its claws.

She's not right. She can't be right.

Mae winked. She knew when she was spot on target. "When you find yourself with ten cats and the label of neighborhood eccentric instead of a second husband and two babies, you'll know I'm speaking the truth."

The soulful face of the Saint Bernard came to mind.

Still, Shelby refused to believe she was about to fall down Mae's rabbit hole. Mae was just...just...exasperating. A hopeless romantic when Shelby had lost hope.

"Tell the sheriff I'm ready to leave," Mae commanded regally, ruining the effect with a bone-rattling cough.

Shelby retrieved an unopened bottle of water from her bag and offered it to the old woman, but she waved Shelby off. "Go."

Shelby hesitated. "I'll get Nate when you've recovered."

"I'm not recovering." The fight seemed to drain out of Mae, and with it Shelby's exasperation.

There was a line outside the vet's office before Gage and Doc unlocked the front door.

News of their reopening had spread quickly. Just as swiftly, Gage began matching names to faces.

Bea Larkin and one of her milk goats. Gage directed her around to the back.

Mr. Mionetti with a small, squealing guinea pig.

Miss Shephard cradling a black-and-white Shih Tzu with rheumy eyes and matted hair.

"Will we be seeing you, Dr. Wentworth?" Mr. Mionetti asked, carefully avoiding Gage, who was standing in the hallway almost next to him.

"You will not," Doc barked out. "There's a new vet in town."

Mr. Mionetti hesitated, his thin frame wavered like a reed in the wind. Finally, he leaned forward to whisper. "But the copper—"

"Dogs, all mighty, Gino! You think I'd turn my practice over to a thief?" Doc chastised as he leaned over the front counter. "I've never turned away an animal in need, but you tempt me. Oh, how you tempt me." Eruption complete, Doc sat back down, and waved Mr. Mionetti toward a chair.

The guinea pig owner retreated to a seat, looking as enthusiastic as a child about to receive a tetanus shot.

Other cars pulled into the clinic's small lot.

Gage sighed. It was a good thing he'd been inquisitive at vet school and had started his upper division courses with dual streams—both small and large animals. It was only after Nick's death that he'd concentrated on large animals and found his niche with horses.

Doc cleared his throat. "Who knew we'd be so swamped? This is a very lucrative practice."

Gage ignored the hint. "If everyone could please sign in." He gestured to a clipboard on the counter. "We'll get to you in the order you arrive, barring any emergencies." Gage made his way to the paddock in the back, passing by the kennel and stopping to check on the Saint Bernard. "How're you doing today, boy?"

The dog rubbed his cheek against the kennel fence, begging for an ear scratch. He was a loving, well-adjusted dog. Whoever had lost him wouldn't give up the search easily. And when the person did show up, Shelby would be crushed.

Meanwhile, a weight had been lifted off Gage's shoulders last night. He still found it hard to believe that Shelby didn't blame him for Nick's death. When she'd reminded him of Nick's approach to life, she'd struck upon a truth he'd forgotten, a possibility he hadn't been brave enough to consider: *I couldn't have prevented Nick's death.*

Bea's white milk goat bleated behind him, oddly reminiscent of Leo's laughter at the equine hospital.

Gage proceeded to the enclosed paddock where Bea was waiting patiently with her goat. "What seems to be the problem?"

"Sissy has a cough." Like the Jameros, Bea's family had always worked the land. Her skin was brown, and age spotted. Her hands gnarled and calloused.

The goat's calm demeanor and clear eyes contradicted her wheezy cough, immediately providing clues to a preliminary diagnosis.

"Do you put her feed in a metal drum?" He ran his hands over Sissy, head to hoof, finding nothing out of the ordinary.

Bea nodded.

"A rack is healthier." He pulled the goat's lips back, checking her teeth warily. Goats weren't particular about what or who they nibbled. "Racks allow the dust on hay to dissipate. Sissy might have developed bronchitis. Can you leave her with me? I want to take her vitals and run some tests." The tall, wild grass in the paddock would get a nice mowing from Sissy and wouldn't hurt her.

Bea shuffled her booted feet. "She's been fed in a drum for years and this just came on."

Getting a vote of no confidence when it came to veterinary medicine was unusual for him. Gage was momentarily speechless.

"Do you have experience with goats?" Bea asked.

He suspected goats weren't the issue. "I have more experience with horses."

Bea chewed on her lip before responding. "Maybe I'm just used to old War. He's been treating my farm animals for decades. I take his word, no questions asked."

In the past year, Gage had become used to his word being law—Far Turn Farms didn't question his methods with mares, and no client asked for a second opinion.

"Soooo." She squinted at the position of the sun as if calculating the time. "I'd like to get his opinion about Sissy."

Gage opened his mouth to say, "*No.*" He was certain of his diagnosis, calling in Doc was a slam to his ego. So when he said, "Yes," he paused and ran a hand along his spine.

Yep, backbone still present and accounted for. It was his pride that lay on the floor at his feet.

"If it would make you feel better, of course, you can talk to Doc."

"Thank you." Bea leaned over to scratch Sissy behind the ears, switching her tone to baby talk. "You like War, don't you, Sis? Just don't nibble on his clothes and make him mad."

Gage sent the older vet to the paddock and called the next patient into the exam room.

Mr. Mionetti stepped forward with his guinea pig. The brown long haired little beast had an ulcerated front paw. "Been like that since Friday," the old man said. "She can hardly hobble about her cage, and she's not eating. My wife is worried sick."

Gage could tell Mr. Mionetti was, as well. Everything about the bean-pole thin man was wound tight, from his laced arms to his worry-stitched frown. Gage probed the guinea pig's swelling gingerly. The bottom of her foot was crusty. "You keep her in a metal cage?" He'd seen something similar in domesticated fowl housed in cages.

"Yes."

"She needs a change of environment. No cage. You can keep her in a plastic storage tub or a plastic cage, but no metal wires." Gage rummaged through his memory for the term to describe the rodent's ailment. He couldn't recall the scientific term. "I suspect she has bumblefoot. She'll need foot soaks, equal parts warm water and Epsom salts. If you give her foot soaks two to three times a day, you should see improvement in forty-eight to seventy-two hours."

The elderly man's chin jutted out. "No antibiotic? I was expecting antibiotic."

"Well, Mr. Mionetti, antibiotic in an animal this small can be deadly. I'd prefer to try a more natural approach first. Call me in a few days if she's not better."

Doc stuck his head in the exam room door, a thunderous expression on his face. "You don't need a second opinion, Dr. Jamero!" The door slammed shut.

And on it went. Baying dogs, a few reptiles, a demented cat. Further suspicion regarding the copper thefts. Doubt regarding Gage's diagnoses and methods of treatment. Doc annoyed with his neighbors. The longer the day dragged on, the more humbled Gage became.

He wasn't the pregnant-horse whisperer. No one cared that he'd just delivered a potential Kentucky Derby winner. There were no hushed audiences admiring his every move. He was plainly a small hometown vet, whom the residents of Harmony Valley peered at with a jaundiced eye.

It was like living in Nick's shadow all over again.

The meat loaf Shelby made that night for dinner was black around the edges.

While entering the day's wine analysis readings into her laptop, she'd over-baked and shriveled the sweet-potato fries. She'd steamed the life out of the green beans while on the phone with Christine. Garlic bread? Burned as she fed Mushu.

All the while, Mae's prediction for her clung to her spirits like cheap perfume.

The town eccentric. The crazy cat lady. Lonely days and lonely nights.

Wanting to adopt a stray dog didn't mean Mae was right. Being averse to another relationship had to do with her being scared to open up her heart and lose again so completely. New relationships fell apart after a few dates. A lot of marriages crumbled after a few years. She'd fallen in love with Nick looking at the stars and dreaming. Could she really find that again? Even with Gage?

Her gaze was now firmly on the ground. Her heart safely tucked away.

Not that Gage wanted her heart.

Not that any of her pitying thoughts would fix her botched dinner.

The kitchen door swung open, and Gage and her grandfather funneled through.

She was drawn to Gage, admiring of how he'd stuck it out here so far.

Their gazes connected briefly. It was enough to draw her in completely. She erased the image of a houseful of cats from her mind. That wasn't her future.

"What's that smell?" Grandpa covered his nose.

"Hardy-har." Shelby poured herself a glass of milk, making a mental note to call her parents in the morning. They hadn't called her back since she'd arrived.

"Somebody's in a bad mood." Grandpa gave her a curt nod and went to wash his hands.

"I just need to eat." Shelby dropped into a chair, feeling as sullen as a disgruntled teenager.

"I meant him." Grandpa gestured toward Gage with his elbow.

"I just need to eat." Gage grabbed a beer from the fridge.

"Where's Captain?" Shelby asked, glancing past them.

Both men stared at her in confusion.

"My dog. The Saint Bernard? I'm calling him Captain." So what if she'd just come up with the name? So what if she hadn't expected them to bring him home? She was feeling sorry for herself and a bit prickly, ready for a fight. "I assumed you'd bring Captain home with you today. Isn't he due to start exercising soon? Maybe as soon as tomorrow."

"Whether he's up to it or not, he's not your dog. We agreed on a week." Gage cut away a charred corner of the meat loaf.

"Nobody wants him but me." Shelby speared a bite of meat loaf. It was dry and stuck to the roof of her mouth.

"His owners will show up." Gage worked a square of burned meat loaf off his fork with his teeth.

Shelby said nothing. It was hard to talk back when she was close to choking on overcooked meat loaf.

Chapter Fifteen

After dinner, Gage sprawled in an uncomfortable plastic chair in the backyard, one hand on a cold beer, the other resting on Mushu's silky black head.

It was one of those early September nights where the air turned chilly uncomfortably quickly, before the sun had disappeared below the horizon.

His good intentions for being at the clinic temporarily had turned uncomfortable just as quickly. Two months. It seemed like purgatory, in spite of Shelby's company.

As if summoned by his thoughts, Shelby joined him, claiming the creaky porch swing. In endearingly familiar fashion, she very nearly tumbled onto the grass while trying to arrange her limbs on the cushions. "Feel better after eating?"

Gage made a non-committal noise and held back a smile. She'd never be graceful. Or a good cook.

Finally, the swing settled. She studied the purple sky that preceded sunset, a breeze ruffling her short blond hair. "Rough day? I'll vent my gripes if you vent yours."

Once upon a time, he would've told her how he was feeling without hesitation. But their relationship felt duct-taped together, with the minimum amount of duct tape.

"I know we'll never be friends like we were before." Her words were tinged with regret. "But we are friends. And maybe telling me will help." She pushed the glider in motion with a booted toe.

So much for drinking the day's frustrations away in peace. "Today was a humbling experience. Don't get me wrong. I love helping animals. But—"

"They weren't racehorses." She laughed at what must have been the dumb-founded expression on his face. "Do you think I've forgotten how you used to complain about veterinarians who thought they were gods? You've turned into the one thing you once despised, haven't you? I mean, what's higher in the vet career ladder than racehorses? Zoo animals?"

He refused to admit she was right. "It's bad enough that I don't like myself much right now." He set his beer on a white plastic side table. "You have to rub it in?"

Shelby grinned and stole his beer, sending the swing careening higher and her arms grasping for purchase. Somehow, she managed to stay on. "Hmm. Let's see. Delivering at-risk, thoroughbred horses while risking life and limb, versus treating a cat with fleas... I can see where your ego could get involved, despite the danger." She froze for a moment, as if struck with worry for him and his work.

An owl hooted in the distance.

"You make me sound shallow. It's not just the status that appeals to me."

"Why don't I believe you?" She picked at the corner of the beer label.

He rested his elbows on his knees, clasping his hands. He'd returned to Harmony Valley with several secrets he'd never considered sharing with Shelby—his role in Nick's death, his resentment toward being second fiddle to Nick and his love for her.

She'd come to terms with his first secret. What would happen if he told her the second? Would it be the last straw? A clean break would make leaving for Kentucky that much easier for both of them. He had no choice but to tell her.

Glancing at his beer in her hand, he cleared his throat. "You're going to take this wrong, but today at the clinic—"

"You realized my grandfather is off the deep end? I knew it." She pressed the beer bottle to her cheek. "You've seen his research library. He's not the man he once was."

"This isn't about your grandfather. Or the clinic, at least, not really." His growing frustration caused him to raise his voice. He quickly took a breath to compose himself. "This is about Nick."

"Nick?" The beer bottle lowered slowly to her lap.

"I shouldn't be saying this to you." But he couldn't stop now.

"It can't be any worse than the reason you left two years ago." She added softly, "Can it?"

Now Gage was the one who was worrying. Every secret he'd withheld from her made him look like a louse.

"Wow, this is serious. And it has nothing to do with the clinic?" Shelby's voice dropped to a whisper. "You can say it. You can tell me anything."

How he wished that was true.

"I'm the worst of friends, Shelby." In more ways than one.

"Gage."

"I was always a step behind Nick in whatever we did." He stared down at his shoes, realizing he needed new ones soon. "Nick was better than I was at sports. He had more confidence with people...with women...with you." Gage's voice echoed across the yard. "He just was...better." He snagged his beer from her and took a long pull. "Except with horses. It was the one area of expertise, of life, where I could do things he couldn't, where people looked up to me instead of him." Another heavy sigh. Another slug of beer. "And now, I'm cleaning wax from a dog's ears and cutting away mats of hair so they can see. I'm just another vet, second in preference to your grandfather—who hasn't lost his edge, by the way, just his balance."

"Oh." Shelby anchored the swing with her toe.

"Yeah, oh. I've been a horrible friend and I have questionable motives for my choice of career." Now she'd feel justified in ending their friendship, which would allow him to move on.

The owl hooted, taunting Gage.

"Life isn't a competition." Shelby spoke without recriminations, accusations, or anger.

Gage fell back in the chair. "Don't sugarcoat it. You can tell me what a bad friend I am. Or I was."

She shrugged. "I think Nick knew."

Gage made a derogatory sound.

"Oh, come on." She held out her hand for the beer. "It's not as if you and I weren't competing against each other in school for the highest grades in class and we were friends."

He passed her the bottle. "I have no idea what you're talking about."

"Seriously?" She drained what little beer was left. "Highest science grade in high school earned the Weinstein Scholarship. Best essay about your future earned a Lion's Club merit award. And don't get me started about vying for valedictorian." She rolled her eyes.

"You didn't care about any of those things. What did you need a scholarship for? Your parents paid for college." He darted inside for two more beers, opening one for her before sitting back down and rubbing his forehead with one hand.

"You don't know everything about me." Shelby held her beer bottle up to clink his. "Remember when I got a better calculus grade than you in college?"

"You said you were lucky and that you hadn't even studied."

"I lied." She reached over and smoothed the hair on his forehead. "I hired a tutor because I was tired of coming in second to you. I felt so guilty afterward that I bought you a steak dinner." She sagged into the glider cushion. "I can't believe I told you that. It's been eating away at me for years. Okay, so maybe the guilt wasn't dining on me like a buffet, but it definitely nibbled at my conscience."

While she drank and gazed into the darkening sky, Gage scratched his head. Could it be that he didn't know Shelby as well as he thought?

"You're having an epiphany." She licked her lips. "I can hear the cogs spinning in that big brain of yours."

He couldn't seem to look away from her lips. His mouth went dry. "I'm realizing that friends don't necessarily know everything about each other."

"That doesn't mean our friendship had less significance or that our relation-ship was shallow. Sometimes I feel like I know what you're thinking before you put it into words."

If that were true, she'd know he was thinking about kissing her. He forced himself to look away.

"I know what you're thinking," she blurted.

His gaze flew to hers.

Shelby's grin spread from here to Kentucky. "You're thinking your good friend deserves to visit her dog."

And if that wasn't proof Gage and Shelby weren't on the same wavelength and weren't meant to be, Gage didn't know what was.

He sighed. "Visiting hours at the clinic are over."

"It was worth a try."

Nothing about his return to Harmony Valley was turning out as he expected. "So what upset you today?"

"Ugh. I let Mae get to me." Shelby sounded so maudlin, Gage laughed. "I know. Silly, right? In the past few days, she's practically accused me of giving widows a bad rep."

"What?"

"I wear too much black." She spread her thin coat to reveal her black shirt.

"It hides the stains," Gage said. Anyone who'd spent time in a lab knew that.

"I know, right?" Shelby sipped her beer. "She says black means I'm lonely."

He hesitated before asking, "Are you?"

The owl taunted Shelby this time.

"Maybe I am, a little," she allowed in an odd tone of voice. "But I'll take lonely over heartbroken any day."

"That might explain the limp green beans, but it doesn't sound bad enough to make you burn the meat loaf." Or the fries. Or the garlic bread.

Instead of arguing the point, she shrugged.

Interesting. "She really got under your skin." Gage leaned forward. "Cough it up. What else did she say?"

Shelby's foot sent the glider swinging again. "She might have hypothesized that I'd become the town's eccentric cat lady someday."

Gage reached over and stopped the swing. "What did she really say?"

Shelby bit her lip, refusing to look at Gage.

Bribery was in order. There was no chocolate in the house, so... "If you tell me, I'll take you to see the dog."

Shelby hesitated.

"You know you want to see him."

"She said..." Shelby closed her eyes and started over. "She said in ten years I'd be lonely, probably regretting my life choices... Lonely and childless."

A close enough prediction of the truth.

Gage sent the glider swinging. "Weren't you just insisting you'd take loneliness over the chance at a family?"

Shelby grimaced. "I didn't say it like that."

"Yeah, but I do know you, even if I didn't know about the calculus tutor." What else had she hidden from him all these years? "And it sounds as if Mae knows you, too."

If Nick was looking down on them, he'd have given Gage a high five. Shelby had erected too many walls between herself and happiness. Before Gage left town, he was going to make sure some of those walls came down.

Shelby was losing her mind.

Or maybe her common sense.

For a second in the backyard, she'd thought Gage was going to kiss her. He'd leaned forward and looked at her mouth.

And...well...she didn't want to think about how her pulse kicked up a notch at the idea.

She'd talked to a grief counselor after Nick died. Their discussions had helped her sort through her thoughts and feelings. She'd been taking Nick's bed pillow everywhere. It smelled of him. The counselor had spouted terms like stages of healing, complicated grief, and emotional transference. Meaning Shelby held on to that pillow as if it was Nick. And that hold kept her from moving on with her life. The pillow was still with her. On her bed in Grandpa's house.

What if these strange feelings Gage seemed to be inspiring in her were along the same lines? Her bed was lonely. The nights long. Gage would be a better substitute for Nick than Nick's pillow.

That was it. Emotional transference.

Eureka!

Case closed. She breathed a sigh of relief. The chances she'd ever fall in love again were slim. She'd loved Nick too much. And on the off chance that somebody else did measure up? She'd remember the devastating pain and break things off. Cowardly, but sometimes that was safer.

She glanced at Gage as they approached the darkened clinic, seeking some transference of Nick.

But no comparison to Nick came to mind. He was just Gage, unlocking the back gate that led to the paddock and the kennels. Steady, used-to-be-reliable Gage. His shoulders seemed broad enough to carry the weight of the world. They'd certainly carried the guilt he'd been feeling toward Nick and what happened the day he died.

She reached out to rub those tense shoulders when Captain started barking.

What was she doing?

She drew her hand back before she'd touched him. "Captain's happy to see me."

"That dog is making sure whoever's coming in knows he's in charge." Gage's tone was definitive. He'd never been one to let her wrap him around her finger, unlike Nick.

She followed Gage through the open gate. "Here, Captain. Captain!"

The Saint Bernard stared from Gage to her, then back to Gage. In the dim light, his eyes seemed less soulful, less lost, less in need of her.

"I don't think he likes that name." The humor in Gage's voice flowed over Shelby.

He'll be impossible if he makes me smile.

Since Gage's confession earlier, his eyes had become less lost, as well. While she liked the idea of him coming to terms with Nick's death, the niggling idea that he might need her less put her right back at a loss—in Dead Gage mode. He'd leave. Maybe not today, but certainly in two months' time.

Shelby moved toward Captain's kennel, determined to feel the same bond she'd experienced when she'd first seen the dog. "Uh, how about Riley? Here, Riley."

The dog sat down without so much as a wag of his tail.

"Henry? Samson? Max? Spike?" She was borderline desperate. Okay, lonely and desperate. She wanted someone to love her. Someone safe who wouldn't break her heart. Like this sweet, lost beast.

Or Gage, her heart whispered.

No. Just the dog. The safe, loyal dog.

The dog in question held himself very still.

"You suck at this." Gage spun the key ring on his finger.

His sarcasm got to her in a way the frustration hadn't been able to, urging her closer. "Ammo? Gunner? Koda?"

Gage's bark of laughter made the dog's tail wag. "You might just as well try something common, like Lucky."

The dog leaped up and started barking.

"Lucky?" Shelby peered forward. "Is that your name? Lucky?"

He barked some more. Leaped around. Tired himself out. Sank onto his haunches and panted.

"Lucky," Shelby crooned sticking her fingers through the kennel wire. Lucky leaned against it so she could scratch behind his ears. "Can we let him out? He can't get away with the gate closed."

Gage's belabored sigh drifted into the crisp night air. "All right. But beware of what he's doing. Watch the perk of his ears and the lift of his tail."

Shelby nodded.

Lucky bounded out as soon as the kennel door was open, sending Gage crashing back into the fence.

"Are you all right?" Shelby laid a hand on his chest, felt his heart pound, was reminded of how she'd clung to him after she'd passed out the other night. She snatched her hand away, feeling her cheeks heat.

Lucky rubbed up against her thigh, demanding attention. She laughed and obliged. It was easier to pretend that spark of nameless something didn't exist between herself and Gage when she had something to direct affection toward. She stroked Lucky's big head, rubbing his soft ears, patting his barrel chest. She let him lead her over to a patch of dirt outside the paddock. A small white goat bleated inside. "Can I take Lucky home? I don't want to leave him here alone."

Gage's frustrated breath was a precursor to his refusal. "He's about two years old, Shel. He may or may not have given up chewing. He may take a liking to everything in the house—from your shoes to your grandfather's piles of books."

"We can't let you near Grandpa's books, can we, Lucky?" She stroked Lucky's head. "He can stay out in back with Mushu."

"And scare a life or two out of Gaipan."

"Please, Gage."

Gage closed his eyes. He was silhouetted against the inky sky, most likely preparing to refuse her. She imagined reaching up on tiptoe to plant a kiss on his lips. Her pulse applauded. But her brain... Her brain warned of danger.

There was a reason behind these feelings. Friendship or...or...emotional transference.

It couldn't be grief. Her pulse doubted her diagnosis. Her heart doubted, too. And her lips.

"Okay," Gage said unexpectedly. "Let's take him home."

Shelby launched herself into his arms, eager to shut off the careening thoughts, the debilitating doubt, and the tightrope-walking fear. "Thank you."

Lucky launched himself at his human friends, sending them crashing to the ground.

The goat bleated in the paddock, catching Lucky's attention. He bounded away.

Shelby had landed on top of Gage. "Are you okay?" she whispered, not quite meeting his eyes, not quite able to move.

He grunted.

He probably couldn't breathe. She pushed up and—

Lucky galloped back to play, planting his big front paws on her back.

And just like that, all her curves were pressed tightly against all his hard planes. Again.

"Lucky," she wheezed when the dog didn't move. He slobbered on her neck and Shelby cringed, sinking closer to Gage.

"Shel."

Gage sounded as if he was expending his last breath.

Shelby strained against the weight on her back, thrusting her chest against Gage's.

Gage lifted his head, most likely to make sure she heard his dying words.

He didn't speak.

He didn't die.

He kissed her.

Chapter Sixteen

G age had waited nearly a decade to kiss Shelby.

He'd dreamed of her soft lips on his, of her warm arms encompassing him, of their bodies drawing closer.

He hadn't imagined a mountain of a dog playing matchmaker to the point where he could barely breathe, much less resist kissing Shelby.

In that moment, as his heart pounded and his chest heaved with the excitement of a long-awaited kiss, her lips weren't soft, there was no warmth and she didn't draw closer. And he feared this was turning into a colossal mistake.

Thankfully, that moment didn't last.

Her breath mingled with his on a sigh. Her lips captured his. Her body turned languid atop him. And the kiss went on.

Maybe a little too long.

He should pull back, brush her hair from her eyes and say something romantic.

He did none of those things. The cocktail of dopamine, serotonin and norepinephrine kept his hands glued to her shoulders. He couldn't let go.

Lucky ran his slobbery tongue over them, then rolled off Shelby onto the ground next to Gage. The dog twisted onto his back and raised his massive paws into the air.

Gage and Shelby scrambled to their feet, wiping their cheeks, and expressing their revulsion to dog germs.

And then they froze, caught like a deer in each other's headlights.

I kissed Shelby.

His pulse rate reached maximum speed.

It was awesome. And wonderful. And scary.

Silence. Not even an owl hooting.

Say something tender and romantic.

"I...er," Gage said, at the same time that Shelby mumbled, "Hey, uh..."

Their gazes collided.

Lucky stood between them, panting as if he'd just run a race and beat them both.

They laughed the uncomfortable laughter of the highly embarrassed.

It's going to be all right.

Silence.

Wasn't it?

"Well, that was unexpected," Shelby said.

"Yeah." He ran a hand through his hair. They needed to talk about it, to analyze, to hypothesize. Did she like kissing him? Did she want to do it again? Did she think they could have a future together? One that invalidated Mae's prediction of Shelby as a lonely cat lady?

"Blame it on the dog." Shelby chuckled again, as if the kiss meant nothing to her.

The sound chilled him.

"Speaking of which, he probably needs another quiet night at the clinic." Shelby spoke as calmly as if they'd never pressed their lips together.

As if he hadn't just put his heart at her feet and she hadn't just hopscotched over it.

He put Lucky in his kennel and turned.

Shelby was gone.

"What's wrong with you?" Doc demanded of Gage the next morning. "You're dragging your feet. We should have been at the clinic ten minutes ago."

"I wanted to say good morning to Shelby." Gage wiped down the kitchen counter for the third time. Frankly, the longer he waited for her, the less likely the first words out of his mouth would be "Good morning."

Early on, he'd been thinking the best way to greet her would be, "Hey, we need to talk." After waiting an hour, he was leaning more toward a silent, smoldering glare that let her know they would talk, whether she wanted to or not.

"Dogs, all mighty. Shelby left this morning when it was still dark outside." The old man walked like he was a cowboy and had been riding hard for days. He paused at the back door, his age-spotted hand on the knob. "Wait a minute. Are you interested in my granddaughter?" He turned to face Gage, nearly losing his balance in the process.

"Don't go playing Cupid," Gage grumbled, sliding his cell phone into his back pocket.

"You two were always close, but..."

"Put your arrows away." The kiss had been an aberration, an outlier, an unexplainable quirk that Shelby clearly wanted to ignore.

Gage didn't usually leap into things. He studied situations and opportunities, but over the course of a few days, he'd leaped into the job at the clinic and kissed Shelby. Next thing you know, he'd be moving here permanently, giving up on racehorses and Kentucky.

It was time to man up and get a grip. Shelby was his friend. He'd do the town right by serving this two month sentence and then move on.

The old man held the door open for him. "It's like that, is it?"

Gage chose not to answer.

"I could talk to her," Doc said. "

Gage knelt to pat Mushu, who'd been patiently waiting for some attention on the back porch. "I'm only talking to Dr. Wentworth, not Cupid."

"Do you think I'd disapprove?"

"No." Gage brushed aside the way the old man's approval warmed him. "I think you'd meddle."

"I don't meddle." Doc raised his voice the way he did any time anyone tried to disagree with him. He was all bluster.

Gage unlatched the gate and held it open for the meddler. "I wouldn't be here if you didn't meddle. You told me Shelby was moving here and that she needed volunteers."

"Ha! A lot you know." Doc walked past. "I called you to make you a fine business offer."

"Meddler," Gage said succinctly heading for his truck.

"Okay. One time." Didn't matter if Doc walked slow or fast. He still pitched and rolled as he strode down the driveway. "But one time doesn't count for beans."

Gage made a disparaging noise. He'd been doing that a lot lately.

"I don't have to take this." Doc's indignation rumbled through the empty street. "I'm walking to work."

"You're not walking. You get out of breath after fifty feet." It would be just Gage's luck if Doc did walk and his ticker gave out.

"You love her," Doc accused.

Gage's fingers gripped his truck handle.

A cricket chirped.

Doc cleared his throat. "Now, son, you just need to—"

Gage turned back to the house, steering clear of his mentor, or rather, tor-mentor.

"Where are you going?" Doc demanded.

"To pack."

"Wait a doggone minute." The old man's orthopedic boots beat a slow pace as he followed. "You promised me—"

Gage whirled around. "I'll stay if you keep all interaction between us focused on the clinic."

Doc's mop of hair fluttered in the breeze. "But—"

"There'll be no speculation, no advice, no gossip in the lobby." That was what went on while Gage treated animals. Dr. Wentworth lorded over the waiting room, gleaning all the news, spreading his own. "And no matchmaking or I'm leaving."

Doc chewed the inside of his lip. "You strike a hard bargain."

Chapter Seventeen

M ae opened the front door when she saw a truck with the winery logo pull up in front of her house. It was Shelby, coming to help Mae clear out the shop.

So soon?

They were signing the papers tonight. Mae wanted more time.

I've become a foolish old woman.

More so because she hadn't wanted to acknowledge the end loomed near. She hadn't called Ava or Andrea. She kept putting it off until tomorrow. What if tomorrow never came?

Shelby hopped out of the truck. Her short, bright blond hair glinting with natural highlights, contrasted against her black T-shirt. She looked like life should have been her oyster, and yet something didn't seem quite right.

A huge dog leaped out of the truck's window and onto the sidewalk. He loped toward the front porch.

Mae gasped and slammed the door.

Big dogs were a threat. They bumped into things. Tables, lamps, people. There was nothing as scary to a person past their prime as the threat of a fall. Everyone knew the adage: A broken hip and you'd best make out your will. You'd be dead in six months.

Or less.

Mae struggled to fill her lungs. She didn't expect to celebrate Christmas. Still. Why race to heaven?

"It's after nine, Mae." Shelby knocked. "Moving day."

Mae opened the door a crack, squinting at Shelby, who stood alone on her porch. "Where's the monster dog?"

"Lucky's sitting in the backseat of the truck eating a dog treat. It's the only way I can get him inside. No need to be afraid." Shelby glanced over her shoulder. "I figured he was going stir-crazy at the clinic, so I broke him out. Nobody keeps Lucky in a cage." Her smile was halfhearted.

The Saint Bernard hung his head out the back window. A footlong drool dangled from his mouth.

"A cage." Mae harrumphed. "You might apply some of that Tao to your own life. You're living in a cage of your own making."

Shelby cast a curious glance over Mae's shoulder. "Is it purple in every room inside?"

"Of course." Mae's house was purple everywhere. She loved the color. It was powerful and passionate. "I'm a single woman. I can do as I please."

"And how is purple different from black?" There was a spark to Shelby's eyes that had been missing before.

Mae chuckled. "I can loan you a purple blouse."

"I can loan you a can of white paint and a brush."

"Got you thinking, did I?"

Shelby didn't answer. Her gaze landed above the hearth. "Who are all those men?"

Mae opened the door wider. Six framed photographs graced her mantle. "My husbands."

"All of them?" Shelby's eyebrows rose when Mae nodded. The girl might yet learn that love always returned, repairing hearts and filling voids.

"I didn't use to display all their photos. But after I buried my last husband, I became sentimental." Truthfully, it'd been the doctor telling her the cancer was back and had metastasized in her organs. "I try to think a good thought about each one of them every day."

"That's sweet."

"It's a penance of sorts." Mae leaned on the doorknob. She was getting worn out standing. "Would you like to know my secret?"

Shelby's expression grew cautious. "Secret to what?"

"Not my potato salad recipe, girlie." Mae laughed. She only got out two ha's before she began coughing. When she recovered, she said, "My secret to mending a broken heart."

Shelby's face closed down. She took a step back.

"You'll ask me someday." Unless Mae died first.

Unconvinced, the younger woman jingled her keys. "Are you ready to go?"

"In theory." The reality scared Mae. She was clearing out another section of her life. How much was one supposed to prepare for before death? She grabbed her purple sweater, and followed Shelby slowly to the truck, allowing the younger woman to help her inside.

The dog snuffled on Mae's updo. She swatted him away, missing completely. Except for the drool. That pooled in her palm. She dug a tissue from her purse.

"Do you have a plan for clearing out your things?" Shelby put the truck in gear.

"A plan?" Mae stared down her nose at Shelby.

"You know. Do you want to donate the dresses? Trash the mannequins? Except for Conchita, of course." Shelby spared Mae a glance. "We need a plan before we start."

Mae was horrified that her eyes were suddenly teary. "Can't an old woman sit and think on it?"

Shelby frowned. "You're signing papers tonight. The construction crew wants to start tomorrow."

"Why does everything have to happen so fast?" The oak in the town square looked the same as the day Victor proposed to her beneath it. Why did her bridal shop have to change? She shouldn't have agreed to the sale. But her grandchildren could use a college fund. And at least this way she'd know the shop was in good hands—Shelby's. "I suppose I'll need to go through the dresses to decide which to donate."

Shelby cleared her throat. "I should probably tell you that we found rats the other day."

"Rats don't scare me." Death did.

"I think they might have eaten some of the dresses in the storage room."

Anger coursed through Mae's frail limbs. "How dare they? What if I wanted to get married again? There are some beautiful wedding dresses in those boxes."

Shelby completed the circuit around the town square and turned down King. "Is there someone special in your life, Mae?"

"Honey, I've buried three husbands and divorced three more. There's always someone special on the horizon." That was a lie. She had no more time for a special someone.

Shelby slowed as they neared the shop. "How could you love so many men? I understand picking yourself up after a divorce. But the ones who died..."

Mae felt an urgency when it came to Shelby, a purpose in getting across what had been the guiding force in her life. "It's love. It's not a cliché. It heals. It brings back joy. It makes the risk of loss seem small in comparison."

Shelby parked in Mae's old parking space. The monster in the backseat panted with more fervor. A few spaces down, someone had parked a huge dumpster. Mae couldn't look at it.

"I know that people have made fun of the number of times I've been married," Mae said carefully. "I'm old, but I'm not stupid. The same people who laughed at my many husbands bought dresses from my shop, so I guess I'm the one who had the last laugh. I've been rich and happy."

The dog thrust his face between them and whined, ready to go.

Shelby wiped his drool with a tissue, as if he was a small child. "Which husband was Oliver?"

Mae couldn't remember if she'd talked about Oliver to Shelby before. "My last. He was from England. I buried him next to two other husbands." There was only one plot left. Hers. Someday soon she'd have to call the funeral home. Horrible as it was to plan her own funeral, it had to be done. She wanted lilies, not daisies or roses. And she wanted a casket with purple lining.

"Doesn't it hurt?" The younger woman fiddled with the key ring. "You buried three men you loved."

Had Mae ever been such a soft widow?

No. Not even the first time. "The dead ones would want me to be happy." Of that she was certain.

"And the divorced ones?" The corner of Shelby's mouth tilted up.

"They'd like to see me rot." The idea no longer turned her insides. Cancer had done that. "I'd like to spend their money first. You know, before I go." Mae admired the browns and golds of dying marigolds in the flower bed in front of her shop. "Do you see all those wilting?"

"Yes."

"They're proof that nothing lasts forever, but that life goes on."

The big beast lost all patience with them. He bounded through the open window to the sidewalk, sending the truck rocking. He lifted his leg on the back of the tree.

"Men are like that, marking their territory. But we women, we know nothing lasts forever. It takes courage to move on." Mae gazed up at her storefront. "It won't look any different, will it?"

Shelby either didn't hear or pretended not to.

Mae was no spring chicken. She'd witnessed businesses changing hands before. They'd gut the place, perhaps change the front, as well.

She couldn't seem to catch her breath.

This was worse than the time Franklin told her he wanted a divorce. Mae just wasn't up for anything that wasn't a happy ending. The shop should be thriving, filled with happy voices, and beautiful brides. Instead, it was an empty, sad place, soon to be turned into a glorified storage unit they called a wine cave.

She followed Shelby and the dog inside, leaning heavily on her cane. The beast immediately picked up interesting scents, galloping back and forth throughout the store. "I hope he eats some rats."

"I hope he doesn't." Shelby carried a chair from the storage room.

Mae stopped in the display room, looking around, seeing things as they'd been in their heyday—colorful gowns, sparkling tiaras, dazzling shoes. And smiling women.

"Why don't you sit here and tell me what we're taking to your house and what goes to the dumpster." Shelby produced a pair of canvas gloves from her back pocket and put them on.

"You're going to throw away my things." Mae knew this. But the reality—the ugly brown dumpster outside—was almost too much to bear.

Shelby returned from the storage room and stood next to Conchita. "What about her? Keep or...?"

"There's at least a thousand dollars of lace on that dress." Someone should have worn it, but Mae had overpriced the gown knowing no one in town could afford a ten thousand dollar dress. It spoke to her, that dress.

Shelby pulled the train forward delicately. "The rats have been at it."

Mae closed her eyes. It was horrid. Her shop. Her life.

"I'm taking the dress," she said determinedly. "I'll have it professionally cleaned. And I'll be buried in it."

Chapter Eighteen

T he waiting room at the clinic was full.

Overweight, nearly blind dogs barked at each other. Cats crouched in their carriers and yowled. Every person studied Gage skeptically, presumably either because they suspected him of being a copper thief or because they doubted his veterinary skills. And Doc? He was uncharacteristically mute.

But the worst part of the day wasn't the discovery that Shelby had avoided him this morning. It was that she'd snuck into the clinic and taken Lucky, the Saint Bernard. His heart was already bruised because she didn't have the courage to talk to him about their kiss. She'd taken a swipe at his ego by disobeying his restrictions and their deal regarding the dog. What was the use of being the veterinarian in charge if no one paid attention to what you said?

His cell phone rang. It was Dr. Thomason. "North Country Stables brought in a mare yesterday that's due to foal this week. Dr. Faraji just checked her and believes she'll deliver soon, possibly as soon as today. I know you're keeping office hours up there, but I was wondering how soon you could get here. Dr. Faraji is good, but these flighty thoroughbreds seem to respond better to you."

The excitement of a familiar challenge combined with someone actually wanting him lifted Gage's spirits. "Let me check my schedule to see if I can free up the afternoon."

"Is that the equine hospital?" Doc glared at him. "Tell them you're booked. All morning. Tell them you're booked the next two months."

Clenching his jaw, Gage muted his cell phone. "There's nothing on the books for the afternoon."

"Oh, there will be," Doc promised venomously.

They glared at each other amidst the raucous waiting room.

Doc stood on those skinny, unstable legs of his and tottered into the hallway, gesturing for Gage to follow. "I know you have a lot on your mind. But you can't burn the candle at both ends. You can't be here for these animals while you're a couple hundred miles away playing horse ob-gyn. One life isn't more important than another." The old man sighed. "These people...they're not just my friends and neighbors. They're my family. And those animals are their children. Harmony Valley needs someone who's going to respect that and be here for us, as promised." He lowered his voice. "And Shelby needs someone who'll be here for her, too."

Shelby. She wouldn't even talk to him. Frustration welled to flood stage. "Shelby doesn't want me to be here." Gage unmuted his phone. "Dr. Thomason? I'll be there after lunch."

"My life's work is trash," Mae moaned from a chair in the nearly empty shop.

Shelby balanced another load for the dumpster in her arms. "Your life's work was making women happy." But somewhere along the way, she'd begun hoarding the very items women adored. She hadn't learned to let go.

Shelby tossed her armload into the dumpster and took stock. Of dusty, musty dresses. Of bolts of lace that practically disintegrated in her hands. Of mismatched earrings, shoes in the oddest sizes, stained wedding planners, warped, empty photo albums. And how could she forget the boxes of hangers, piles of display hooks, stacks of racks, bags of blank price tags.

The one surprise had been Mae's insistence on saving the window display dress. Shelby had to promise to take it to a specialty shop in Cloverdale for restoration. Instead of undressing Conchita and risking damaging the dress further, Shelby decided to transport it mannequin and all.

Mae may have closed the store and moved her precious inventory into storage, but she'd clearly been hopeful that Dream Day Bridal would reopen one day, that love and weddings would return to Harmony Valley.

Love. Weddings. Much as Shelby didn't want to, she relived the events leading up to Gage's kiss.

Had he known she thought he was dying? It was both comical and embarrassing. Not the kissing part. No. There was power in his kiss. Heat in his touch. An intensity of emotions she didn't want to name.

Shelby sighed, leaning against the edge of the dumpster. It was her emotions that were hard to ignore. The longing to be close to someone, to be important to someone, to be in love with someone.

Who was she kidding? Insert Gage's name for someone. No other man interested her.

Mae called, her voice thin until the coughing struck.

Shelby came inside, Lucky trotting next to her. She'd shed her jacket an hour before, placing it over Mae's lap to keep her warm. "Are you ready for the dress boxes?"

Mae nodded and stood. Shelby steadied her. The old woman didn't have the rolling gait of Grandpa, but she didn't have the sturdiest pair of legs in town either.

Shelby dragged Mae's chair to the storage room and made sure she was settled before she turned to the hardest task of the day—the expensive dresses. She would've thought cleaning out the shop to be an impersonal task, but Mae made each item seem like a misfit in need of love. These last boxes were going to be tough.

Wardrobe boxes six foot high stood like a modern day Stonehenge. Shelby dragged one away from the wall and pointed out how the cardboard had been chewed on the bottom. "I don't think there'll be anything to salvage here."

Lucky dropped to the ground at Mae's feet with a grunt.

Mae cursed rats. "Open it. I have to see. There are five or six dresses in each one."

Shelby hesitated. "Shouldn't we let sleeping rats lie?" They'd been fortunate not to see any so far.

"I can't let them go without knowing." She looked on the edge of tears.

"Mae. This could take all day." Rats. Shelby didn't want to disturb the rats.

"And how many days do I have left? Look at me." Mae held up a fist that was mostly skin and bone. "I used to swing a mean softball bat. Now I can barely wield my cane. Open the box. Open all the boxes."

Heart breaking a little, Shelby complied.

The first dress she pulled out was a drop-waisted ivory gown. Zipped in plastic it was still beautiful and looked intact.

"That's a good one." Mae loosened her grip on her cane.

Shelby shifted the heavy dress around, crinkling plastic. The bottom of the storage bag had holes in it. The train of lace eaten.

Mae cursed the rats again. Shelby thanked them for having moved elsewhere.

Three boxes later, they hadn't found a dress that was salvageable. With each disappointing discovery, Mae grew quieter. She began staring at the front door, mumbling to herself. Occasionally, Shelby heard her mutter something to Oliver.

Shelby was hoping for a miracle. And then she opened the fourth box.

"Mae." Shelby laughed with relief. "Oh, Mae. These are untouched."

All the dresses were cocktail length. A robin's-egg blue mother of the bride dress. A variety of bridesmaids dresses. And a short ivory sheath wedding gown with a removable four-foot train. The train was on the hanger, which had probably saved it from being eaten by rats.

"Try on that wedding dress," Mae commanded as if they were in battle and only wearing the ivory dress would save them.

"No." Shelby hung the dress back in the box. "It wouldn't be right. I'm married."

"You're widowed," Mae snapped, her mood turning as quickly as a model on a catwalk. "Does your heart still beat? Do your lips ever smile? Do you lie in bed at night missing a warm body next to you?"

"Mae, I—"

"You'll get married again. If I have my way, it'll be in that dress."

"No." Shelby felt sick. She wanted to leave, but she couldn't abandon the old woman. They should have had so much in common, but Mae was the braver of the two.

"I know what you're thinking." Mae pounded her cane on the floor. "It hurt too much the first time. You girls today are soft, avoiding the pain. Pain makes life worth living. It makes you appreciate pain-free times." Her cane pounded the floorboards again. "Put on that dress."

"I'm not like you, Mae." Shelby's voice felt high enough to crack crystal.

They glared at each other in silence. Lucky lowered his head between his paws.

And then the silence was broken by the meekest of meows.

Chapter Nineteen

G age escorted the last of the morning patients back to the waiting room. In only a few hours, he'd been bitten, scratched, and vomited on. Who said horses were more dangerous than small animals?

"I'm going to the equine hospital." Gage tossed a file on the desk in front of Doc. "Schedule any new appointments for tomorrow morning."

"Maybe you shouldn't come back." Doc's voice was a drawn out, disapproving growl. "You're not giving anything here a chance. Not the practice. And not my granddaughter."

"Giving a chance runs both ways."

Old War had nothing to say to that.

Gage's cell phone rang.

"I have kittens in the walls at Mae's shop," Shelby said breathlessly. "Who knows how long they've been in here."

Shelby was asking for his help? When was the last time that had happened?

Sure, sure. He was good enough for a call when she was in trouble...

The clock on the wall ticked.

Time. It had always been Gage's enemy. He'd taken too long to ask Shelby out. He hadn't had enough time with Nick. And there was never enough time in the day to do everything he wanted or felt obligated to do.

If Gage left now, he'd be in Davis by midafternoon. Plenty of time to make the equine delivery and give Leo cause to frown. And if he didn't go? He'd be putting his goals second to a love that might never pan out.

"Gage? Could you…" Shelby paused, as if finally noting his silence. "Could you tell me what to do?"

"You'll need… You'll need to…" He hung up. On Shelby. It took a moment for that to sink in.

What was he doing? He loved her.

"Where are you going?" Doc called before Gage realized he was moving toward the door. "When will you be back?"

Gage didn't answer. He couldn't. He got in his truck and started the engine. The sun had warmed the cab to near stifling. He shed his jacket and put the truck in gear.

He wasn't sure where he was going—to Davis or to Shelby—until he turned down King. He parked in front of Dream Day Bridal but didn't shut off the ignition. He could still leave. Delivering horses was what he lived for.

So what if he'd kissed Shelby? She clearly viewed that kiss as a mistake since she'd avoided him ever since.

Kentucky was his future, not Shelby.

Kentucky.

Drive away.

Shelby appeared in the shop's doorway, wearing a plain black T-shirt, faded blue jeans and work boots, and looking like she could handle anything alone. And that's exactly what she'd been doing for two years. Handling things alone. Because he'd chosen to leave her.

Drive away.

She smiled at him with understanding, as if she expected him to choose horses over her. She'd already forgiven him so much, more than he'd ever hoped. She'd forgive him his choice if he drove away now.

But he could never forgive himself.

He shut off the engine and got out.

"Did you bring what we'll need?" she asked.

"I've got a hammer, a crowbar and a flashlight." While he dug into the small tool kit behind his front seat, Lucky ran out to meet him, putting his massive front paws on the bench seat and slobbering on Gage's arm. Unfazed, he wiped his arm on his jeans and told Lucky to get down.

The dog trotted inside happily, like a pony prancing in a parade.

"I'm glad you came." Shelby's gaze didn't waver when he approached. She'd always be strong and compassionate where others were concerned.

Strange, though, when it came to her own happiness, she didn't have the courage to reach out for the brass ring.

"What are those for?" Mae eyed his tools from a chair in the hallway. "You aren't damaging my walls."

"He is," Shelby said firmly. "Remember the kittens, Mae."

"Shelby cares more about a few stray cats than she does about her love life," Mae muttered. Lucky bounded over to her and rested his head on her knee. Mae stroked his broad forehead. "You're a beast."

"You're not fooling anyone, Mae." And neither was Shelby. She was blushing. "Even the dog can see through your façade." Shelby led Gage to a corner where the mirror and dais had stood a few days ago, dropping smoothly to her knees to press her ear to the wall. "I think they're here."

Gage knelt in front of her and set the tools down.

"Thank you for coming," Shelby whispered. "I didn't expect you to after... You know. Last night." The deepening blush in her cheeks unsteadied him.

Without thinking, he placed a hand on her leg for balance. It wasn't as if they'd never touched each other before, but she startled. "Get over it," he grumbled. "If we're not going to talk about it, you have to get over me touching you. I'll try not to." Because touching her made him want to kiss her again.

Her eyes widened, dilated, as her gaze dropped to his mouth. He may have been in love with her for years, but that didn't mean he had no experience with other women. He recognized she wasn't indifferent to him. Now that he had her attention, she knew how to interpret the signals he was sending.

"Yep," he said, feeling more confident than he had all morning. "You're reading me right." He wanted to kiss her.

She gulped but didn't argue or protest or draw away.

Everything's going to be all right.

Whether he stayed in Harmony Valley or left, whether he and Shelby were successful at rebuilding their friendship or not. For the first time in days, Gage didn't feel trapped.

"What are you two whispering about?" Mae demanded. "It's rude to whisper."

"Shelby shouldn't take Lucky without permission." Gage released Shelby, picking up the hammer. "Lucky is still under my care."

At the sound of his name, Lucky left Mae and came to sit next to Shelby.

She rubbed the ruff beneath Lucky's collar. "I... Can we talk about us later?"

He cocked an eyebrow. "I thought we'd talk about a lot of things last night. Or this morning."

"Later," Shelby whispered with a glance in Mae's direction. "I promise."

Something rustled in the walls, followed by a soft mew.

He'd make sure they talked later. For now, there were kittens in need of rescue. He tapped his hammer against the wallboard, trying to find a stud to the right or left of where he thought he'd heard a kitten. The sound of the hammer striking plaster must have worried the kittens because the mewling stopped instantly. He found a hollow point about two feet from the floor, high enough to be above any small cat. He swung the hammer through the lath and plaster. Dust, and debris heaved from the resulting hole, spewing onto him and the floor.

"They used to insulate the walls with newspaper and horsehair," Mae said. "Looks like it's disintegrated."

Shelby leaned in closer. "I can't see anything. Or hear anything."

"Give me a minute to make a bigger hole." Using his hammer, Gage yanked as much of the wood planking and plaster finish free as he could. "Flashlight," he requested using his doctor voice.

Lucky tried to poke his nose through the hole.

Gage nudged him away with an elbow. "Lucky, stay back."

Shelby handed Gage the flashlight. He could feel her anxiety to see what was in the wall, but he recalled seeing signs of rats upstairs. He pushed her gently back, as well. "There's a possibility that you've been hearing rats."

"There are kittens in there," Shelby said firmly.

"Acoustics can distort sound, Shel. If this is a rat's nest, I'd rather the mama rat leaped out on me than you."

"Oh." With a slight shudder, she gave him some space. "By all means, proceed."

He angled his head in and managed to see down to the floor with the light. There was debris, like a nest on the bottom. "They're not here." However, bits of fur edged the old posts, long, fluffy and orange. Not a rat-like color. "But they were. I can see the signs. There's some kind of hole in the beam, large enough for a kitten to crawl through." He knocked on the adjoining wall, presumably the sheriff's office.

A deep, unintelligible voice rumbled in answer.

"Those kittens are leading you on a game of cat and mouse." Mae chuckled. Her low laughter turned into a harsh cough.

Shelby went to the old woman's side, rubbing her back. "Are you okay? Do you want me to call Nate to come get you? We could use his help with these kittens."

"Nate?" Jealousy stabbed at Gage. What was happening to him?

Both women gave him a knowing nod, which only prodded at his ego.

"We don't need the sheriff. I've got this." *Easy, boy. No need to mark territory you've no right to after just one kiss.*

"I think the sheriff is just what we need." Mae smiled cryptically. "His office shares this wall. Perhaps he's seen these kittens. Perhaps Gage's looming hammer has sent them into Nate's arms."

"Don't torture him, Mae." Shelby turned to Gage. "Can we just save some kittens, please?"

The sheriff entered, looking hero-like in clean jeans and a pristine, tan sheriff's shirt. Even his badge had a shine. Gage brushed off some dust, but there was dog vomit on his work boots.

"This is better than my soaps." Mae sat up in her chair. "It's time I went home, Nate, and I'm taking a box full of dresses with me. I bet you can lift it all by yourself, you being such a big strong man."

Gage gritted his teeth. "I can help you with the box, Nate."

"I love it when men get ruffled." Mae stood, leaning heavily on her cane. "It only proves how serious they are about a woman."

"Now it really is time for you to leave," Shelby said with an apologetic look in Gage's direction. The blush was back in her cheeks.

After the sheriff and Mae left, Gage checked the time on his cell phone. If he didn't leave for Davis soon, he'd be stuck in traffic an additional hour.

"You're upset and I've interrupted your day. I owe you an explanation. About last night." Shelby's cheeks turned a deeper shade of pink. "The kiss was nice."

Gage thought he might sink to his knees to give thanks to the heavens.

Except the look on her face wasn't elation or joy. In fact, it threatened to rob him of any strength he had left. It was the let-you-down-easy face.

"The kiss was nice," she said again, unaware that he'd rationalized his way leaps and bounds ahead of her. "But I'm not looking for anything with anyone."

He put a hand on the wall for support. He should have driven to Davis after she called, then on to Kentucky.

"What you do is dangerous," she was saying. "Unsafe."

Safe? No one was safe.

He held up a hand. "You want someone who doesn't take chances?"

"I don't want anyone," she reiterated, staring at the floor.

"If I stayed here," he began as diplomatically as if he was discussing treatment options. "And practiced in Harmony Valley—"

"Gage." She came closer and gave his shoulder a gentle shove. "I'd never ask you to give up something as important as your dreams."

No. She'd never ask. But those were the conditions: *give up horse deliveries and treat small animals.* Because her work and her family were here.

Gage thought about the rush he experienced delivering foals and how people in the horse breeding industry sought out and accepted his advice. Their validation was important to him. "I won't give up Kentucky."

As far as he was concerned, the conversation was over. It was Nick laying claim to her all over again. He and Shelby weren't destined to be together. No matter how many times Gage circled the issue, the conclusion was always the same.

"So. On with the kitten rescue?" Shelby seemed to have come to the same conclusion he had. She blinked back tears.

Gage nodded. Now wasn't the time to lament lost opportunities.

He rose to his feet, taking stock of the situation. "We need to be as reassuring as possible to these kittens, which means ol' Captain here can't be part of the rescue unit." He shut Lucky in the storage room and opened up a hole in the wall by the front of the shop.

He refused to feel anything. He denied his disappointment, squashed the memory of Shelby in his arms, the taste of her lips, or the sunshine of her smile.

She crouched next to him and shoved a high-heeled shoe into the hole, preventing the kittens from escaping to another part of the wall. "It was destined for the trash," she explained. "If the kittens come this way, they'll be blocked."

"Good idea. You take the front." He returned to their original hole. Any more damage to the walls and the store would look as if it should have a little graffiti. "If I pound on sections, starting back here, and work my way to the front, that should flush them to you."

Gage began hammering in the corner. Pausing, he thought he heard the soft sounds of scrambling paws. "Don't let them see you." He moved forward and sent the hammer through the wall a few feet up, prying out slats to make sure no kittens were hiding in the section below. Another few steps and he made another hole.

He'd made three holes in the wall before a scrawny, orange kitten tumbled out near the front of the shop. Shelby immediately snatched it up. "There's one more. It went back."

Gage sent the hammer through the wall above what he anticipated was the kitten's path. He reached into the small space, and it was as if he was reaching into a birth canal, only from this one came something small, dry, and furry.

He lifted out an orange and white tabby. The pair of felines looked to be three weeks old and nearly starved.

Shelby cradled the orange striped kitten, an expression of utter devotion on her face.

She'd make a good mother.

Once she realized love was safe, not the other way around.

And that would be when Gage was long gone to Kentucky.

Chapter Twenty

S helby held the two thin, trembling kittens in her lap while Gage drove them all to the clinic.

Bribed by a dog treat, Lucky sat in the middle of the bench seat, occasionally snuffling the kittens and drenching them in slobber.

"I'm a mess," Shelby admitted. "Dog drool, kitten fur, plaster, dust, sweat." The aftereffects of a kiss, the threat of another, followed by agreement that there would be no more kisses or threats thereof. And it was only lunchtime. "I must look scary."

"You look great," Gage said without so much as a sideways glance. "You always look great."

Shelby leaned against Lucky's solid shoulder, wishing it was Gage's. They drove the rest of the way in silence. Even the kittens were quiet.

Felix Libby, the town's number one cat lover, met them outside the clinic with feline formula and a take-charge attitude.

"How did you know we'd found them?" Shelby asked.

"Mae called." Felix took the orange tiger from the cradle of Shelby's arms, studying it through very thick glasses. The small cat nearly disappeared in the former fire chief's big hands. "And I called War. We'll need—"

"I'll get what we need after we do a preliminary exam." With a resigned smile, Gage handed off the orange and white kitten to Shelby before heading down the hall with Lucky at his side.

"I thought you were off to deliver another racehorse." Shelby's grandfather rocked back in his chair behind the front desk.

"Change of plans." Gage's voice held a defeated note.

Grandpa winked at Shelby, as if something significant had just occurred. She hurried after Gage, finding him in an exam room. Lucky was curled up in a corner. "Don't tell me you stayed in town when you should have been elsewhere."

He flashed that charmer smile at her, the one he used when he needed just a few extra minutes to finish a final exam or wanted a female bartender to bring them a free plate of nachos. "It's okay."

It wasn't. Her head was shaking. Her hands, too. "I should have talked to you last night. I should have said something to you this morning. Then you could have left without...without..." Without whatever their kiss might have meant had she been brave enough to face up to it.

"Shel," he said softly, coming forward to stroke the ear of the kitten. "It's just one delivery. There'll probably be another one in a few days and a slew of them in Kentucky. I was happy to help at Mae's."

He hadn't been. She'd seen his indecision when he'd pulled up to Dream Day Bridal.

"War tells me you're conducting the exam in here." Felix lumbered into the room, a challenge in his voice. "They're dehydrated and starved and may not make it if you don't hurry."

Despite Felix stating the obvious, Gage's smile never wavered. "It'll only take a few minutes." And it did. Gage performed a gentle exam—ears, eyes, nose, mouth—plus a gentle assessment of their bodies. "This one has a kink in its tail. Not too bad a mark when you consider what the little girl has been through."

Sure enough, the orange and white kitten's tail was bent near the tip.

"They're ready for their first feeding." Gage brought the chair from the second exam room so Shelby and Felix could both sit. He dug into Felix's bag of supplies.

Felix tried to order Gage about. "You need to—"

"I know." Gage prepped two bottles of formula.

The orange tabby gave a loud meow in Felix's arms. "She's probably consti-pated. We'll need—"

"Damp gauze to wipe them down after they eat." Gage's smile was bright and softened the older man's objections. "The wipe stimulates the anal glands. I've got this."

"I suppose you do," the older man admitted, settling back into his chair and feeding the kitten.

Grandpa leaned against the doorjamb. "How could a man who knows so much and cares so much about animals be a copper thief?"

"He couldn't." Felix glanced up at Gage and gave him a nod of respect.

The orange and white kitten in Shelby's arms burped, then began purring, kneading her arms with its small, sharp claws.

Gage handed Shelby a piece of damp gauze. "I'll prep a box." As he left the room, his phone rang. His voice became distant as he walked along the hallway. "I'm sorry, Dr. Thomason. There was an emergency here. I can be there."

Shelby's gaze fell to the kitten, whose eyes had closed. Then she spied Lucky, and his big brown eyes stared soulfully at her, as if he wasn't fooled by Gage's smile either.

He regretted staying.

When Gage spoke again, his voice was a mix of apology, disappointment, and anger. "Dr. Faraji did the right thing. I'm sure there was nothing more that could have been done."

There was silence in the clinic. And then the back door banged shut.

"The foal died," Gage said when he heard Shelby's footsteps behind him.

He'd been staring at Bea's goat, who was still grazing her way through the paddock. Another day and all the wild grass would be gone.

Lucky bumped affectionately against his leg, bringing his head beneath Gage's hand. His fur was soft and silky.

"I'm sorry." Shelby came to the other side of him, slipping her arm around his waist. "I shouldn't have asked you for help."

"Don't say that. Don't ever say that." Even as he spoke, his words seemed to heave with sadness. Over lost foals and lost loves. He wrapped his arms around her shoulders and laid his cheek on top of her head.

"Could you have saved the foal?"

Gage's jaw seemed wired shut. He'd promised to be there and when he hadn't shown up, there'd been a death. An image of Nick in the water flashed through his mind.

"Can you tell me what happened?"

"There were complications." Would he have known had he been there? Gage liked to think so. "The outer placental membrane ruptured too soon, which began depriving the foal of oxygen. The mare was agitated and hit her head against the stall and stumbled." He shouldn't be telling her any of this. It was more ammunition as to why she couldn't love him. "The attending veterinarian was tossed against a wall. The time they spent attending to him was time the foal needed to survive."

Shelby's other arm came around him until her hands clasped about his waist.

"I know Dr. Faraji. He doesn't see the value in trying to read a patient's personality or mood." Having been raised around livestock, Gage viewed animals differently. They had feelings and anxieties the same as people, and that required care and treatment, too. "I would have tried soothing the mare's nerves before things got intense. I wouldn't have been a bystander or observer as she transitioned into different phases of the delivery."

"I think I understand a little better why you do what you do." Her arms around him were truly comforting.

Lucky rubbed his jowls on Gage's pants, leaving a large wet streak.

"You shouldn't have come to Harmony Valley. Your work means the world to you. My grandfather will understand if you don't stay." She tilted her head up to look at him. "I'll understand if you don't stay."

He caressed her cheek with the back of his hand, wishing there were no complications between them—no fears, no differing goals. Wishing he could kiss her. "How can I leave when there's this?" And then because he couldn't stand not kissing Shelby any longer, he lowered his head and claimed her lips.

Their kiss began tenderly, their breath mingling upon a sigh. Their lips softly greeting each other.

Her arms crept around his neck. His hands settled at the base of her spine. She raised onto her tiptoes. He pulled her closer.

His heart was soon pounding. His brain had switched off. And—

"Dogs, all mighty! It's the middle of the workday."

Shelby would have leaped back at her grandfather's intrusion, but Gage kept her in his arms. "Don't run off."

Someone's cell phone was ringing. Hers.

She drew it from her back pocket. "I have to go." She took a step back from his embrace.

"We should talk," Gage stated woodenly.

"Tonight," she promised. And then she was gone, taking Lucky with her.

Shelby had paid Ryan twenty bucks to pick up pizza for her when he ran an errand in Cloverdale late in the day.

Pepperoni. Mushrooms. Fresh red pepper. Extra cheese. Dinner didn't get much better than that, especially when she was in charge of the kitchen.

Christine had called and asked Shelby to return to the winery because the Cabernet grapes were nearing their peak.

They'd be inviting everyone back to Harmony Valley for another night harvest soon, possibly giving the copper thief another chance to pick the empty businesses clean. Christine, Ryan and Shelby had spent the earlier part of the afternoon preparing. They transferred the Chardonnay juice from the fermentation tanks to smaller oak casks. Then they cleaned out the fermentation tanks in preparation for the Cabernet grapes that were to be harvested.

A quick call to Felix had reassured Shelby that the two orange kittens were doing well. He was feeding them formula every two hours and had promised Gage he'd bring them in for a checkup in the morning.

Shelby stretched her tense shoulders. She had no idea what she was going to say to Gage when she saw him later. She'd insisted she wasn't interested in a relationship and then kissed him. She thought her mind was made up, even if her lips had a different agenda.

The pizza was her peace offering.

Lucky and Mushu had been fed and were romping in the backyard. She was setting paper plates next to the pizza box when Gage and Grandpa came in.

Gage eyed the pizza box and threw open the lid. "You're my hero." Then he pressed a quick kiss to her forehead, took a slice and bit into it without bothering with a plate. His hip rested against the counter.

He always made things so easy.

Her tension eased. "Flattery will get you everywhere."

"I was afraid you'd bake that cardboard lasagna I saw in the freezer," Grandpa said, taking a slice and resting a hand on the back of a chair.

Why fight a trend? Shelby followed suit and ate standing up. "Would you rather I made something from scratch?"

They heartily reassured her they wouldn't. If she didn't own up to being a bad cook on a daily basis, she might have been offended.

Gage reached for another piece. He had a couple of thin, deep scratches on his hand.

"Where'd you get those?" she asked.

"Hazard of the job, hot shot," Grandpa said when Gage didn't answer. "Hazard of the job."

Gage studied his pizza. "How're those kittens?"

Shelby set her partially eaten pizza on a plate and poured a glass of milk for each of them. "Thankfully, Felix had some flea powder and dewormer."

"We need to stock our cabinets at the clinic," Grandpa said.

"I suppose you're going to adopt them, too? I bet they have names already." There was a glint in Gage's eye that made Shelby jittery. "Quite the family you're building here."

The irony wasn't lost on Shelby. She was creating a four-legged family when most women her age were having babies. Shelby should have felt demoralized. Mae's predictions were coming true sooner than expected. "I'm calling those two girls Sunny and Dusty. I'll expect a family discount when it comes time to neuter them."

The energy seemed to drain out of him. "You'll have to go to the clinic in Cloverdale. I haven't put enough hours in on small animal procedures."

"I could renew my license," Grandpa offered. "We could work together."

"Gage is leaving to work with racehorses, Grandpa. It's what he loves." Shelby was happy for Gage. Really, she was. That empty feeling inside her chest was just the fatigue of harvest season. Too many days started before dawn so she could be home to cook her grandfather—and Gage—dinner. "You can't make him give up what he loves."

"Don't say that," Grandpa muttered. "You two bail too quickly on everything."

"Meddler," Gage said.

"Procrastinator," Grandpa shot back. "Why can't you just—"

"I'll pack." Gage's pronouncement had Grandpa pressing his lips tightly together. "I promised to review your paper tonight. I won't do that if you meddle."

Grandpa made a frustrated noise. "Nobody likes a blackmailer."

Shelby was intrigued and amused. "Should I be concerned about the subtext of this conversation?"

"No," Gage said.

"Yes." Grandpa's gaze turned speculatively toward Shelby. "Good things never come to those who wait."

"What are we waiting for?" Shelby asked.

But neither man answered her.

Chapter Twenty-One

"I'm glad you support my hypothesis about equine musculature recovery post-delivery." Doc sat at a small desk in the master bedroom.

A brown log cabin quilt covered the bed. Dirty clothes covered the floor, except for a narrow trail, much like that in the living room. The room smelled stale.

Gage had opened the window over the desk while Doc's ancient computer booted up.

The old man had offered to show Gage his notes, but they were in a stack in the living room and Shelby had freaked out when Doc wanted to lead Gage into the maze that he called a library.

While they talked shop, Shelby had taken the dogs for a walk.

"If I could just collect more data," Doc was saying. "From someone respected in the equine community."

Gage glanced up from the printed draft of the article Dr. Wentworth had written, feeling the first click of a hidden trap.

"Do you keep records from your deliveries?" The old man drew circles on his screen with the mouse, ever so careful not to look at Gage.

"I don't keep records like this." Gage shook his head. "At this stage in my career, I'm more interested in the practical aspects of my specialty."

"Could you keep records like this?" Doc's voice rasped with urgency.

And there it was. The jaws of Doc's trap snapped closed, with almost no wiggle room. "Could I send you data via email from Kentucky?"

"I prefer paper record keeping."

"Meaning you don't have email."

"What's wrong with the postal service?" Doc shot Gage a cagey look beneath a lock of unkempt white hair. "Of course, if we shared an office and a file cabinet and—"

"No." A rush of frustration stiffened his shoulders. If Gage could have been in two places at once, he'd do it. But the events of the day proved he had to make a choice. "We'll be pen pals."

"At least I'll have enough data come June." Dr. Wentworth sat back, sending his computer chair creaking.

Gage dropped the article on the desk. "Why are you doing this? At your age, you don't need to work this hard."

Doc snorted. "When you retire, the brain doesn't shut down. I still need a challenge."

"You could lecture. Travel the world." Although with his mobility issues, that probably wasn't wise.

"But I wouldn't feel relevant." In the light of the computer monitor, Doc's skin appeared sallow. He looked less the old ornery vet, and more...just plain old. "I know it's hard for a rising star like you to understand, but I want to feel...not so much important as—"

"Valued." Gage knew exactly what he meant.

"Precisely." Doc slapped his thigh. "It's not just the mental challenge or the boredom, but the fact that your opinion counts for something. That sounds a bit egotistical, doesn't it?"

"I understand." More than the good doctor realized.

"I guess someone needs to do a load of laundry." Shelby stood in the doorway, tapping her foot, having come back from her walk.

"I'll get to it," Doc grumped. "My house, my rules."

Shelby made a frustrated noise that Gage completely related to. "I'm going over to the bridal shop to finish cleaning things out before the demo team shows up tomorrow morning."

"I'll come with you." Even though Gage wasn't staying, they had unfinished business between them.

The sun was setting as they walked across town. Every so often, Gage's gaze collided with hers.

I wish, his eyes seemed to say.

Was that what she really saw, or was that what she wanted to see? She couldn't deny the sense of longing that grew stronger with each step she took. Until she practically stumbled over Lucky.

"I told you the leash was a bad idea." Shelby focused on the asphalt beneath her clumsy feet. "He's a free spirit."

"And that's why he's a stray." She felt the smile in his words, the warm sensation reached all the way down to her toes.

"He's not a stray. He's mine."

"It hasn't been a week, Shel."

"He feels like mine." She patted Lucky's back. "There's a distinctive smell to his fur. I can't resist the soulful look in his eyes. And he knows me, too. He can tell when I'm nervous or upset."

"I can do that."

"But you're leaving." They turned a corner and the wind whipped against them.

"Yes," Gage said. "And we'll still be friends."

"Don't say it like it's a bad thing." They approached the town square. In the center was a huge oak tree. Beneath it was a wrought iron bench. It was the location of decades' worth of marriage proposals, including her own. "I was always Nick's princess, not his friend." She hadn't realized it was true until she'd spoken the words.

Gage didn't refute her, which meant he'd known it to be true. "Does that bother you?"

"I loved him. Of course it bothers me, just like you being jealous of his always being the leader bothered you." She wrapped her arms around herself and walked faster. But there was no walking away from the truth. "I thought Nick and I would have time to grow beyond that. But I feared—"

"It doesn't matter if you were his princess. You were his everything. You two wouldn't have divorced." His certainty comforted her.

She reached for Gage's hand. They continued in silence.

It was odd that Gage had let the conversation drop. And it kept dropping. Across the town square. Down King Street. He hadn't said another word even when she pulled the store key from her pocket.

Instead of opening the door, she faced him. "What's wrong?"

"You've always known what you wanted, despite your fears and whatever obstacles were in your path." He spoke slowly, as if choosing his words carefully. "You've always pushed forward, whether it was moving here or marrying Nick. Why are you letting fear hold you back now?"

She could have asked what he thought fear stood in the way of, but she knew. "Can you blame me?"

"Yes."

The air left her lungs in a rush.

He didn't stop to let her catch her breath. "You say you were afraid Nick would never take you off a pedestal. It didn't stop you from not only dating him but marrying him."

"You're comparing apples to oranges. Overwhelming heartbreak doesn't come close to the princess treatment."

"I think you need to listen to Mae. I'm all for a black shirt when things are going to get dirty. But every day?"

"Oh, do go on." She crossed her arms.

"Fears, Shel. You kiss me like I mean something to you and then you run away."

Shelby opened her mouth to refute him but shut it again.

"Fears," he said again. This time the bitterness in the word was so sharp she could almost taste it on her tongue. "You're willing to invest more in a dog or a pair of orphaned kittens than in..." At her raised eyebrow, he conceded. "All right. I'll say it. You're willing to invest in animals more than you are in me." And then he added on a softer note, "Or in love."

"This has nothing to do with you." When had she become such a liar? "I don't want to love a man who might die before his time. You practically paint a target on yourself every time you step into that birthing stall."

Lucky crouched low, resting his massive head between his massive paws and staring up at them.

Gage's eyes blazed in the streetlight. "People get hit by cars. They choke on chicken bones. They get shot out of the sky in passenger planes. How can anybody be safe?"

"No one can," Shelby said, not recognizing her own voice. It sounded so small.

"That's right. Nobody can." Gage edged closer, cupping her face in his hands. He was going to kiss her again.

Such a wonderfully bad idea.

They shouldn't kiss in the middle of a fight. They shouldn't kiss at all.

She waited for his lips to connect with hers.

She waited and waited.

"Someday, Shelby, when I'm long gone to Kentucky, you'll understand that love isn't risky. Love is safe. Love is what gets you out of bed in the morning. It's what keeps you going on the bad days." He stroked her cheeks with his thumbs. "Love is—"

"Shut up and kiss me already." She tugged his head to hers, disregarding the fear in her heart.

One brief touch of his lips to hers, and then he trailed kisses along her jawline. "Stop thinking, Shel. Please, stop thinking."

"Two people with our IQs? That's an impossibility."

He silenced her with a kiss that brooked no argument, bringing her tightly against him as if they were on a crowded street corner.

Except they weren't on a crowded street corner.

This was Harmony Valley. And many of the town's residents were already tucked in for the night.

Her hand drifted beneath his jacket, beneath his T-shirt until she touched the smooth skin of his chest.

She'd missed having someone to confide in. She'd missed being held. She'd missed kissing.

"Can I help you two find a room?" Sheriff Nate exited his office.

Shelby fell back against the door frame of the bridal shop. "We were just...just..."

"He knows what we were doing, Shel," Gage said quietly.

"Well, I don't." Her heart clambered as if trying to get out of her chest, as if trying to make her come to her senses and realize this kiss-littered path dead-ended long before Kentucky.

Thirty minutes before the volunteers were expected to arrive, it was standing room only beneath the propane heaters on the winery's patio. Volunteers didn't fill the seats. Harmony Valley's elderly residents did.

There was no wind. The air was thick and humid. Gage maneuvered his way through walkers and wheelchairs to Doc's side, doubting the harvest would go off as planned.

"This is ridiculous," Doc grumbled. "None of the people who show up tonight will be the copper thief. Everyone's told their kids and grandkids. No one is that stupid."

"But that's why everyone's here, to solve the mystery." Gage ran a hand through his hair. "Even you."

"Dogs, all mighty. I'm here to make sure no one makes a fool of themselves." Doc scanned the crowd. "Heaven help us if somebody's grandchild pulls up in a four door silver sedan and some idiot draws his gun."

"I think the sheriff is more than capable of handling this crowd." Gage nodded toward the local lawman.

Mae sat across from Doc, swaddled in a purple coat and matching scarf. "I've had enough of this tomfoolery." She pushed herself to her feet and used her raspy outdoor voice. "This isn't what Harmony Valley is about. We don't show up to watch people fail. We gather to celebrate our successes." She wobbled a little and gripped the edge of the table for support.

Shelby appeared behind her, slipping a hand to her waist for support. Gage stepped nearer the pair as Mae reached back to clasp Shelby's hand.

Mae lifted her chin. "Would Flynn's grandfather, Edwin, have sat here, waiting like a vulture for one of our own to show up? Would he have taken pleasure in knowing it was someone else's grandchild, not his own?"

"No." Flynn separated himself from the crowd. "He would have told everyone who wasn't here to celebrate and support our harvest. He would have told us to ask first why someone needed that copper before we threw them in jail."

"Here, here," Doc said.

Almost as one, the crowd's gazes dropped to hands and tabletops.

"Well? What are you waiting for?" Mae's stare was hard. "If you're not waiting for a child or grandchild, vamoose!" She looked up at Shelby. "I guess I need to go home, as well. Just give me a minute to catch my breath." She sat back down.

"Bravo," Shelby murmured as more than half the crowd heeded Mae's command and made to leave. She glanced at Gage, absently reaching to smooth his cowlick.

He caught her hand. It had been a few days since they'd kissed. She tugged her hand, a token effort to free herself. Gage had to step closer to clear a path for Mildred and her walker. "You're going to have to stop touching my hair."

Her blue eyes widened. "Why?"

"Because it makes him want to kiss you." Mae chuckled, and then coughed.

Shelby's gaze drifted to Mae, then back to Gage, a wrinkle to her brow. "I've always done that."

His thumb worked slow, gentle circles in her palm.

"So I should stop?" Her gaze slipped to his lips. Immediately, she raised it once more. "I should stop."

"We're friends." Gage sighed and released her hand. The truth had to be faced. "If it's such a big temptation, I'll cut my hair."

"I'm sorry. I...I should be more aware." She swallowed and looked everywhere but at him. "You're going to Kentucky."

Mae shook her head. "Have you ever seen two people more clueless about love than these two?"

"Nope," Doc said.

Shelby ignored them. "No more kisses."

Gage nodded. Because they both knew where kisses led. To distraction.

Him being Kentucky-bound, Gage didn't need distractions. It was almost enough—almost—that he knew there actually was chemistry between them, that it wasn't one-sided and merely a hypothetical in his head.

Many of the same people from the first harvest showed up within the next hour. Gage didn't fail to notice there wasn't a small older model silver sedan in the parking lot. The sheriff drifted from one group to the next, trying to subtly reduce his list of copper thief suspects. From the serious slant to his brows, Gage didn't think he was succeeding.

Christine provided music this time. It blasted out of the second story office, filling the vineyard with a beat that had everyone moving. He supposed that was the point—to keep everyone's energy up, and their minds off suspecting their co-workers of theft.

As they were finishing in the wee hours of the morning, when Gage was feeling cold and numb and ready for a respite from dance music, his phone rang. It was his new boss from Kentucky.

"Dr. Jamero, we were wondering if you could start in a few weeks. Dr. Timmons has decided to retire earlier than expected to enjoy the holidays with his family."

"I don't know, Oscar." Gage lowered his voice. He'd seen Shelby's back stiffen. "I've taken on a temporary commitment."

A couple feet away from him, Shelby frowned at him over her shoulder.

"Check your calendar and let us know. We can contract someone to temporarily fill in, but we'd prefer to get you on board as soon as possible."

When the call ended, Shelby's expression was pure barnacle. "You promised my grandfather two months."

"I didn't say I'd be there tomorrow, did I?" Gage was tired and lonely and wanting to slip his arms around Shelby. But that would cross the line.

Shelby held up a hand. "I know you'll do the right thing. You always do."

Gage wasn't so sure anymore. He only knew what he was meant to do.

And that was to deliver racehorses in Kentucky.

Chapter Twenty-Two

Twenty-four hours after the harvest was finished, Gage was still dragging.

He poured himself a cup of coffee and sat at Doc's kitchen table. He was wiped out and couldn't work up the enthusiasm to adequately face the day with his trademark smile. That was saying a lot, considering bacon was frying and Shelby had entered the kitchen barefoot, finger combing her short blond hair. She dropped her work boots near her chair. He wished she'd drop a kiss on his cheek.

Kentucky, man. Kentucky.

"I used to be the king of all-night study sessions." Gage yawned. "What happened to me?"

"Old age." Shelby softened her remark by patting his shoulder on her way to the coffeemaker.

The house phone rang, saving Gage from further comment. Doc grabbed the receiver from its corded mount on the wall. After his initial hello, he listened intently.

Shelby poured herself a large cup of coffee in a travel mug and doctored it up with a lot of milk and sugar.

"Yes. That is good news." Doc stretched the twisted phone cord so that he could talk and turn the bacon in the pan. "I heard his parents fell on bad times." He tsked. "Such a shame. Thanks for letting me know, Felix. Uh-huh. I'll tell her."

Rather than telling Shelby anything, Doc hung up the phone and returned his attention to the bacon.

Much as Gage liked bacon, it sounded like there was big news in town.

"I've got this one," Shelby reassured Gage as she sat at the table. "Who was on the phone, Grandpa?"

"Felix. He said to tell you those kittens are thriving."

Shelby undoubtedly knew that. She made time to visit the two kittens every day. Gage's curiosity was piqued.

With the patience of a saint, she sipped her coffee, cradling the mug between her hands. "What else did he say, Grandpa?"

"Dogs, all mighty!" Doc speared bacon from the pan with a fork. "I have a lot on my mind today. I had an epiphany about my latest research paper and there's a lot to do at the clinic. Mondays are the busiest day of the week."

Shelby set down her fork. "Really? You're that busy?"

Gage nodded. "You wouldn't believe how many people haven't taken their pets in for their annual shots because they'd have to drive to Cloverdale. We ran out of both rabies and feline distemper vaccine Friday."

"But the phone... Grandpa... What did Felix have to say?"

Doc turned off the burner and dished up plates for them. "The sheriff arrested Carl Quedoba while he was trying to break into Nick's old house. The one he and his family used to live in. Nate found a trunkful of copper pipe. I guess Carl suspected you saw him drive away that morning and brought his mother's car this time." Doc tottered into his seat. "This'll kill Clementine. She used to think her grandson could do no wrong."

"Case closed." Gage dug into a steaming plate of eggs and bacon. "I'm going to miss your home cooking when I'm in Kentucky."

"Mine?" Shelby's blue eyes twinkled.

Gage suppressed a smile. He didn't have to answer. Last night's overly salted pork chops did it for him.

Doc peppered his eggs. "After breakfast, I'll make some calls. If this is Carl's first offense, we should ask for lenience. Maybe take up a collection."

"He didn't just rob one place," Gage said.

"You'd have him go to jail?" Doc's bushy eyebrows disappeared into his shaggy white hair. "Your friend? Without knowing if he was in need first?"

"Well, I—"

"He wouldn't." The look in Shelby's eyes almost convinced him of it. "I wouldn't either. That's not how we do things in Harmony Valley."

Doc grinned approvingly. "And that's why you're staying. You're one of us."

Shelby beamed.

Gage looked hesitant.

"You're going to Kentucky." The light had gone out of Shelby's eyes. "They want you to go early."

"They can't have him." Doc held his fork like a weapon.

"I told them I made a commitment."

Doc wasn't listening. "We have something good going on here."

"It'll be a good practice for someone," Gage agreed.

Doc pointed his fork at Gage. "You bet it will. Some lucky vet will come along and love that clinic."

"And the people," Shelby said with a straight face. "He has to love the people."

"Darn right he does." Doc stabbed a bite of egg.

Shelby started to smile. "This town deserves a vet who gets out among the residents. Not someone who sits at a desk all day writing papers."

"Hey!" Doc nearly spit out his eggs in protest.

Balance was restored. At least for Shelby and Doc.

For Gage, things seemed rather grim.

It wasn't long before Shelby and Lucky were out the door and off to the vineyard.

Doc and Gage moved a bit slower. For the first time since he'd been back in Harmony Valley, Gage's breath created small white puffs in the morning air.

As he and Doc approached the truck, there was a large crate next to it and something inside was moving.

"Wait." Gage blocked Doc with his arm. He knelt to see inside the crate. "What the... It's a goose."

"I don't know anyone in town that has geese." Leaning on Gage's truck for balance, Doc gazed thoughtfully down the street, as if reviewing the occupants and pets of each household.

The goose tried to walk, made a plaintive noise, and fell over.

"Easy now," Gage crooned. "There's something wrong with its leg. Someone might have hit it and brought it here for care."

"We'll take it to the clinic." Doc resumed his seafaring steps. "Load it into the truck."

"Have you ever splinted a fowl's leg?"

"Nope. But there's always a first time for everything, isn't there?"

The goose did indeed need a leg splint. Gage accessed the university website for rudimentary instruction, and then placed a quick call to a friend of his practicing in a farming community. By the time he was done, they received a delivery of vaccine and folks accompanied by their animals started rolling in.

"Who's next?" Gage said midmorning to Doc, belatedly noticing the lobby was empty.

"Grab your bag. We're making a house call." Doc flipped the open sign to Closed.

Gage's interest perked. "What is it? A horse? A steer? Sheep?" It had to be something larger than Bea's milk goats. She'd taken Sissy home yesterday.

"You'll see," was all the old man would say. Once they were in the truck, they drove toward Parish Hill. At the base of the hill, Doc directed Gage to pull into an oak shaded driveway.

The one story ranch house had a handicapped ramp leading to the front door. There were no corrals. No barbed wire. No fences to keep in a large animal. Gage's enthusiasm began to wane.

The front door swung open, revealing a woman in a wheelchair. The lower half of her face was disfigured. Her gray hair was pulled into a loose bun at her neck. Her magenta flowered blouse was slightly askew, as if in her haste to get to the door she'd knocked it off her shoulder. "Thank you for coming. It's Ramsey. I can't get him to come out and eat." She backed up and did a U-turn in the foyer. "Please come in."

Gage turned to Dr. Wentworth and whispered, "And Ramsey is...?"

But the older man seemed not to have heard him. He stepped inside ahead of Gage. "Deborah, this is Dr. Jamero."

"I remember him from high school." Her smile transposed over an old memory. "You were in my English classes."

"Mrs. Hobson?"

"Don't apologize for not recognizing me. I was in an accident several years ago." She waved toward her face, speaking in the same matter-of-fact way she'd taught. "Had to give up my Victorian downtown. My children want to put me in a facility near San Francisco. But Harmony Valley is my home." She rolled down a wide hallway to the rear of the house.

They entered a large open kitchen with butcher block counters, a farmer sink and planked floors. In the far corner was a wood-and-chicken-wire hutch. A black-and-white bunny stood on its hind legs and slapped its foot on the cage floor.

"Rabbits?" Gage's spirits sank.

The mighty had fallen. And fallen hard.

Mrs. Hobson nodded. "I have a pair of Mini Lops. Brothers. Ramsey and Riley." She pointed toward a shoe box with a hole cut out in the back of the hutch. A small white rabbit with black spots twitched its nose at them. "That's Riley. Ramsey hasn't come out all morning. I'm afraid I can't reach that far back into the cage. There's a tray at the bottom that I can remove for cleaning and a small opening where I replenish their food and water, but it isn't like Ramsey to hide from me."

Gage lifted the lid of the hutch. Dr. Wentworth stood next to him peering over his shoulder. "You sure he didn't escape?"

"I can hear him in there every once in a while." Mrs. Hobson hooked her fingers in the wire and gave Gage a worried look that made him feel guilty about thinking of his reputation, instead of his veterinary oath. "Ramsey loves his food. He wouldn't miss breakfast if there wasn't something wrong."

Riley stomped his back foot once in warning and scampered to the corner near the water feeder. Gage lifted the small box at the back. There was Ramsey, also white with black spots, nose twitching, ears wobbling, crouching awkwardly.

Something moved underneath the bunny. Something pink and...

Doc chuckled. "Congratulations, Deborah. Ramsey's had a litter."

"That can't be." She leaned closer. "Both rabbits are males."

"It's hard to tell with young rabbits sometimes." Gage carefully returned the shoe box to its original location. "A common mistake."

"I only wanted two rabbits for company. They're barely four months old." Mrs. Hobson looked up at Gage. "Can you neuter him? I mean, her?"

"You could neuter either one," Gage said carefully, mentally cataloging what kind of surgery equipment they had at the clinic.

"Ramsey's a girl." Mrs. Hobson rubbed her forehead. "That'll take some getting used to."

"She seems to have embraced her gender." Doc was grinning. "Well, if there's nothing more, we'll be off. Call me later to schedule the procedure."

"We're not performing surgery on Peter Rabbit," Gage said, once they were driving back toward the clinic.

Doc nodded slowly. "I know someone in Cloverdale who specializes in very small animal care. You should at least observe the procedure. You never know when small animal skills will come in handy."

"Meddler."

"You're destined to stay."

Gage thought about Secretariat. "I'm destined for Kentucky."

Chapter Twenty-Three

The sheriff's truck pulled up next to Mae.

Nate rolled down the passenger side window. "Need a lift?"

She'd been out to get milk, and hoping she'd have enough energy left to walk around the block and see what had been done to Dream Day Bridal. But the wind was picking up, she hadn't yet reached the town square, and her legs felt like bags of compost left out in the rain.

"If you're going to El Rosal, Nate, I'd be grateful."

Nate put the truck in Park and came around to help her into the vehicle. "You need to eat more, Mae, you're dwindling."

"You shouldn't talk to a woman about her weight." She clutched her purse in her lap. "Is that why she left you?"

Nate stiffened behind the wheel. When he spoke, it was in a cool, prideful tone. "No one's ever left me."

Mae fought back a triumphant smile. "Ah, you're one of *those* men."

"Mae," he said warningly.

She didn't care about Nate's pride or his warnings. "You left her at the altar."

He opened his mouth to deny it, but nothing came out.

She chuckled. It was a comfort to know she hadn't lost her ability to read people. "It festers inside you. I'm surprised no one else noticed. Is that why you came here? To bury your head in the sand?"

"Were you planning on eating lunch at El Rosal or buying something?"

"I need milk." She reached over and poked his shoulder with one finger. "And answers to my questions. Why Harmony Valley? Did she grow up here?"

Again with the silent treatment. The sheriff pulled into the red zone in front of the restaurant. Nate never did anything against the law. She must have really struck a sore spot.

He came around to help her down from the truck. "Now, sheriff. You still love her. So it's not too late. You need to propose to that girl again, making sure you apologize first. Actually, the apology might require several weeks for her to accept. I'd never forgive a man who jilted me unless he groveled, but good."

Nate's jaw ticked. "Will there be anything else?"

"Yes. I have the perfect wedding dress for your bride. Don't disappoint me." She walked slowly across the patio outside El Rosal. "I've written you into my will, but you don't want a woman's broken heart on your conscience."

The sheriff pulled away from the curb with a squeal of tires, leaving Mae chuckling.

Chapter Twenty-Four

S helby sat on the bench in front of Dream Day Bridal feeling sick to her stomach. She had one arm slung across Lucky's broad shoulders, the other wrapped around her midsection.

The place had been gutted. Gone were the dressing rooms downstairs. Gone was the appointment and checkout counter. Gone were the windows, the bathroom, the stairs. It was an empty shell.

The demolition was supposed to depersonalize the shop. Instead, it'd taken away everything that made it the unique and hopeful place it'd once been.

"I'm glad Mae isn't here to see this," Shelby whispered to Lucky.

The big dog made a snuffling noise and lifted his head, gazing up the street toward the town square. Mae stood at the corner, leaning against a brick store front. She carried a paper bag, and wore a purple velour tracksuit, which wasn't nearly warm enough for the nip that hung in the air. Summer was giving way to autumn without a fight.

Shelby bolted into action. She'd do anything to protect Mae from seeing her store as it was now. She yanked opened the back door of her SUV for Lucky and tossed in a dog treat. Then she quickly got behind the wheel and drove to the corner, parking across several vertical slots to pull up to the curb. "Mae, you look like you could use a ride." She hurried to the old woman's side, intending to load her into the SUV and take her home.

"I want to see the shop." There were tears in Mae's eyes. "There's something purple sticking out of the dumpster. The only thing purple in there were my walls upstairs. Did they tear down my walls?"

"Mildew damage." Shelby nodded. "The sales rep for the cooling unit came by and measured yesterday. We had to move the stairs and the downstairs bathroom. I'm so sorry, Mae."

"I want to see." Mae seemed to sag deeper against the wall.

Shelby clutched her arm. The purple velour was cold to the touch. "I don't think you do. Let me take you home."

"I will not be weak." Mae might have tried to pound her cane on the sidewalk, but she only managed to give it a shake. "I have never been weak."

"Okay. All right. How about we get into my SUV, and I'll drive you past the shop?" Hopefully Mae's eyesight hadn't improved, and she wouldn't see the complete devastation.

Mae nodded and walked on shaky legs in the direction of the SUV. Lucky had taken the front seat. Seeing Mae, he hopped in the back.

Once Mae was settled, Shelby made a slow U-turn and drove back toward Dream Day Bridal. She stopped in the middle of the street instead of parking nose first in front of Mae's shop, hoping to dilute the impact.

It didn't work.

"There's nothing left. Nothing." Mae hung her head and let out a heartbreaking moan. Lucky leaned over the backseat and nudged Mae's cheek, drooling on her shoulder. "Take me home."

A few minutes later, Shelby pulled up in front of Mae's purple house.

Mae hadn't lifted her head during the entire drive. "And to think, I was teasing the sheriff about his love life. What right have I to cast stones at anyone when my life is in ruins?"

Shelby rubbed Mae's arm. "Let's get you inside." All that purple would cheer her up.

"The beast can't come in," Mae said, opening the door and stretching her purple sneakered feet toward the sidewalk.

"I thought you liked Lucky."

"He's a tolerable soul, as dogs go." Mae turned to pat Lucky's head through the open rear window. "But I have dresses everywhere. The last thing a bride wants is a muddy footprint on her train or a drool mark on her bodice."

Shelby gave Lucky the stay command and followed Mae inside. "You weren't kidding about the dresses."

Dresses hung from curtain rods, were draped over the purple furniture and dining room chairs. Matching shoes were on display beneath each dress. Dyed satin pumps, ivory sandals, white crystal-decorated heels.

"You've been busy."

Mae nodded. "Nate took the dresses out of the storage boxes for me, and I had some in the guest room closet. I like to appreciate a beautiful dress." She closed the door and worked her way slowly to her plum-colored velour recliner, which was the only piece of furniture not being used as a mannequin. "Dresses are like husbands. There's something special to appreciate about each one."

Shelby wandered through the living room fingering satin, taffeta, and lace. "They're all beautiful. And each one shines in its own way."

"The way you dress expresses your mood. Just like every man a woman loves changes her. Every time I fell in love, I felt renewed." Mae coughed thickly. "The way you dress is an expression of your inner self and your love. I see you're still wearing black."

"I told you. Black hides stains." Shelby approached a side table with Mae's six wedding photos. "You were married in a blue dress?"

"Once. It was the palest royal blue. The silver beadwork was exquisite. I'd just lost my fourth husband and was feeling delicate. Soft colored bridal gowns were in fashion for a time." Mae sighed. "They should never have gone out of style. Colors are a wonderful way to set yourself apart."

"Which one is Oliver?" The husband Mae mentioned most often.

"The man with the broken nose." Mae's smoker's voice smoothed like fine grain sandpaper. "I wore a tea length dress when we were married."

Shelby studied the photo. Oliver had bright green eyes, a big bump in his nose, and a smile that rivaled Gage's. "He's very handsome."

"And you're a very good liar. He wasn't handsome in the traditional sense. His personality made it hard to look away from him." Mae gave a short, wheezy laugh. She held a hand toward Shelby and gestured she come closer. "I need to show you something."

"Does this have anything to do with Oliver?"

"Yes and no." Mae reached into a drawer in a coffee table next to her recliner. "I want you to have this." She handed Shelby a small notebook.

Shelby jammed her hands into her coat pockets. "It looks like a diary." She wasn't touching it.

"It's my widow's journal." Mae continued to wave the book at Shelby. "I was never a believer in diaries, but a friend of mine who was widowed at a young age told me about it. You write all your depressing, dark thoughts in here after you lose someone. And then at the end of each day, you record one thing that made you smile or gave you joy."

Shelby tucked her hands behind her back.

Mae didn't seem to notice. She rested her elbow on the recliner's arm and kept holding the journal up to her. The old woman's gaze turned distant. "I used it through my divorces, too. It's a means to expunge your worst worries and your fears. It helped me rediscover love. Take it."

Shelby shook her head.

Gage would call her a coward. Christine would urge her to be supportive.

Shelby couldn't move.

"I had body image problems when Stan left me." Mae made a disparaging noise. "I'd just given birth to my two girls in the span of three years. Who wouldn't feel as if they were a swaybacked brood mare? I didn't feel the least bit attractive."

Shelby would add this conversation to the uncomfortable file, along with the time her father tried to explain the birds and the bees.

"You know." Mae wheezed, and then caught her breath. "I felt guilty when I started dating Raymond, because I couldn't stop thinking about kissing him."

That struck a chord. She thought about kissing Gage all the time.

"I kept looking at his lips and thinking my mother would call me a hussy, but I never would have wanted to kiss him if I hadn't been falling in love with him." Mae let the book drift down to her lap. "Oh, it was a turbulent romance, but that short time we had together before he died...I wouldn't trade it." Her gaze sharpened on Shelby. "In fact, I wouldn't trade a moment of happiness or upset with any of my husbands. It was love and it was a journey and it made me who I am today." She thrust the book in Shelby's direction once more. "I want you to read it."

"No. Something like that needs to go to your daughters."

"And it will. Humor me and read it." Mae didn't speak with annoyance or anger. She spoke as if she was inviting Shelby to tea. "I don't care if you skim through it. Bring it back sometime in the next week. I bet you shed that stain-hiding black."

Shelby's mouth was dry. She didn't want to read her way through someone else's darkest hours. She'd lived through her own. But what she was offering... It was hope. "You're not going to let this go, are you?"

"No, because you're young and that Gage fellow is a keeper."

Shelby glanced again at the six different wedding photos, then back to Mae's journal.

"Such a martyr. When was the last time you laughed with a man?"

"This morning." Okay, maybe she hadn't laughed out loud when Gage silently disparaged her cooking, but she'd been laughing on the inside.

"Ah, with the keeper you're throwing back."

"Mae—"

"He's reeling you in. Let him." Mae coughed again. "First impressions are everything. I think the white knee-length sheath will suit you perfectly. You don't need to wear the train for a courthouse wedding." She gestured a pale, mottled hand toward a dress hanging from the living room curtain rod. The same one she'd tried to coerce Shelby into trying at the shop. "It says you're young, modern, confident, and open to love. Why don't you try it on?"

Gage's bruised back. Hormonal horses. Funeral homes.

The purple walls closed in. "I can't."

"You can. You will. I'm leaving you that dress in my will. And that dress..." She pointed to a pale rose satin gown with a sweetheart neckline and a mermaid skirt hanging over a dining room chair. "That goes to Nate."

"It's not exactly the sheriff's style."

Mae smiled. "It's for the woman he jilted at the altar."

"What? When did this happen?" Grandpa was plugged into all the gossip and he hadn't said a word.

Mae settled into her recliner. Her eyes drifted closed. The thick black coats of mascara gave her face a bluish cast. "I don't know."

"He must have told you."

"He told me nothing. I guessed. I guessed it all, but he, of course, said nothing."

"So this is all conjecture?"

"Mark my words. The truth will come out someday and he'll need this dress." Mae opened her eyes. "The woman who wears that dress will need to be bold and strong, yet gentle. Strengths to counter the darkness in Nate."

It was all truly interesting, but about as believable as a fairy tale. "How do you know all this?"

"I watch people. They have the most incredible tells." Mae's eyes drifted open. "I could have been a world-class poker player. For example, you scrunch your face when things don't go your way. And that vet of yours tugs his hair when you frustrate him."

Shelby caught herself before she got all barnacled.

"And that man of yours gets silent every time he offers you his heart and you elbow it back."

Now she knew Mae was wrong. "Nick was never silent." He was always moving, always talking.

"Not your husband. Your man." Mae coughed. "The vet. Gage. He loves you. And you love him. But all that black you wear." She tsked. "It's in your way. Read my widow's journal and you'll see."

Shelby knew she loved Gage, but in a lonely, emotional transference way. Gage didn't love her. Not like that. He couldn't. Not if he planned to leave.

But then she recalled his touch. His hand so tender on her cheek. Those kisses. His vulnerable expression.

It couldn't be...It couldn't... It...

"Do you want a haircut?" Phil, the barber lowered his newspaper and squinted at Gage.

Gage took in the shaking hands, the slightly rheumy eyes, the dust on every flat surface in the barber shop.

Maybe this isn't such a good idea.

Phil levered himself out of the chair, crumpling the paper in the process. "Come on, then. It's not like you're the first young man to come in here and have second thoughts. I cut Mayor Larry's hair once. He didn't always have that ponytail."

"I...uh..."

Phil snapped a drape. "Don't lose your nerve. Terrible trait in a man. Once you make a decision, go with it."

Gage liked his hair. He liked the way it curled up disobediently, and the way Shelby ran her fingers through it. But there was Kentucky and a man had to take a stand.

He stepped forward.

"That's it." Phil nodded. "I don't have all day."

Gage sat in the chair and allowed Phil to settle the plastic drape over him. *Kentucky. Secretariat.*

Only when Phil's hands shook so badly he couldn't snap the drape at the back of his neck did Gage have second thoughts. Finally, Phil got it fastened, but it was so tight Gage felt choked every time he swallowed.

"Why I remember the first time I cut your hair. Had to use the booster seat." Phil rummaged in one drawer and then another. "Almost forgot to ask. What are we doing here? A little trim or should I get out the clippers?"

Gage had come in with a trim in mind, but those hands...

"That's all right. You don't need to say a word. I know just what you need." Phil held up the scissors, opening and closing them with a definitive snip-snip.

"Lucky? Is Lucky here?" Shelby hurtled into the clinic, panicked and breathless.

Gage had been back in the kennel area checking on the goose.

Lucky, currently acting as Gage's assistant, blinked up at him, then loped toward the front of the clinic and, presumably, Shelby. The sound of his paws scrambling over worn linoleum and the surprised gasps in the lobby drifted down the hallway, followed by reassurances from Doc that Lucky was fine.

"Lucky! Where have you been?" Shelby's relief was palpable.

The goose honked and waddled down the hallway before Gage could stop her. She was a spry gal, that goose, despite her splint. And she'd taken a liking to Lucky.

Running a hand over his short hair, Gage trotted after her, entering the lobby as Doc was explaining, "He showed up here a few minutes ago. I thought you'd dropped him off."

"Why would I drop him off and not come inside?" Shelby patted Lucky's big barrel chest. "What's this?"

The goose hesitated for a moment as she reached Lucky's side. And then she did the strangest thing. She limped to Shelby, looked up and honked.

Right there. In the middle of yowling cats and whining dogs, Shelby fell in love. Her blue eyes softened. Her mouth formed a gentle O. And Gage wanted to hug her.

"She wants you to touch her," Gage said, resigned to the fact that Shelby had become the Pied Piper of the animal kingdom. "Just to acknowledge that you're aware she's interested in you."

"On the shoulders," Doc mumbled. "I'll be darned if that goose isn't as motherly as a hen. Thinks we're all in need of watching over."

Shelby gingerly patted the goose's white feathered shoulders. "Whose is she?"

"Yours," Gage said before Doc could reply. "Someone abandoned her this morning. She's particularly fond of those kittens of yours. Frank dropped them by. He said they're ready to go home with you."

"That goose isn't coming in my house," Doc said, before answering the phone.

Gage knelt to pick up the goose, tucking her beneath his arm. "She shouldn't be rushing around on that splint." He returned to the back room and put her in a cage next to the two orange kittens. Shelby followed. "I told you Lucky needs to be on a leash."

Shelby hesitated in the doorway, Lucky at her side. "Gage, I... You cut your hair?"

He was not having this discussion within hearing distance of Doc. "Having animals is a responsibility, Shel. A dog, two kittens, and a goose." But not him. His gaze touched everything in the room but her. "The goose will need a small wading pool and—"

"Gage?"

He stared at a scuff mark on the faded brick linoleum.

"Thank you."

He sighed, trying his hardest not to look at her. "For what?"

"For not giving up on me." Her hand stole across his shorn hair. Smoothing. Soothing.

He didn't dare move.

"It's been more than a week since we found Lucky."

Gage made a noise of assent, risking a glance at her.

Shelby's eyes were watery. "We made a deal, remember? After a week, we'd consider him mine and you'd set me up on a date with someone." She swallowed thickly, whispering, "I'm ready."

He wasn't. Set her up on a date? What a colossally stupid idea! His choices were limited to Leo or the sheriff. "Shelby, I—"

"I'll always love Nick," she rushed on in that whisper-like fragile voice. "But lately...things have happened...and I...maybe Mae's right. Maybe it's time I stopped wearing black." She tugged at the hem of her T-shirt. "It hides stains, but it hides other things, too. Like my fears."

He didn't know what to say. The sheriff or Leo? If he chose Leo, she might never date again. And if he chose the sheriff, she might fall in love with Nate.

"The things you and Nick did always scared me." Her gaze drifted to his booted feet. "Heights, cliffs, white water. It always scared me."

"Sometimes I was scared, too. But I had Nick there to lean on." Gage removed her hand from his hair.

The bell over the clinic's front door rang.

She drew herself up, gulping a deep breath. "About that date—"

"Do we have to talk about that now?" Gage glanced at the clock on the wall. He had patients waiting.

"I want to settle things between us." She'd gone extreme barnacles on him—her face, her voice, her stance. She was a scrunched up ball of tension, tears no longer threatening. "I'm trying to settle things between us."

"Okay, I'll set you up with someone." It hurt to say the words. They even made it hard for him to hold on to his smile.

"But Gage...I don't want just anybody to take me out. I want you."

Gage felt as if he was on a ledge looking down. Way, way down. "On a date?"

"Well, yeah. We've kissed a couple of times. It makes sense." She searched his face, adding, "Doesn't it?"

"Yes, Shel. Yes." He tried not to shout hallelujah. He tried not to tug her into his arms with all the finesse of a tuna fisherman dragging his prize on board. He tried to compose himself and not kiss her. He tweaked her nose instead. But she grinned and blushed and he laughed. "All I ask is we give each other a chance.

I'm leaving soon and I wouldn't feel right if we didn't at least see if this is going to lead anywhere. Come with me to Davis when I get the next call to deliver. We'll have dinner and you'll see what I do isn't as dangerous as you imagine."

Her features began to twist with tension, but then she smiled. Too brightly. "It's a date."

Chapter Twenty-Five

L ife had a way of changing your course without you being aware of it.

A few weeks ago, Shelby had been alone and lonely. And then she'd blinked.

Now she had a community, tentative friendships, a date on the horizon, and a collection of animals depending upon her. Her life was beginning to feel full and normal.

Although it scared her, she was committed to going with the flow where Gage was concerned. Perhaps it was easier now since there was an expiration date on his time in Harmony Valley. His future was with racehorses. Hers was with wine.

Shelby was reviewing the safety procedure document she'd been preparing to submit to the state when Gage appeared on the stairs to the winery office. His features were somber. The happiness on his face when they'd agreed to a date that morning seemed a distant memory.

The bottom dropped out of Shelby's stomach. "Is Grandpa okay?"

"Yes."

Lucky scrambled to his feet, cocked his head, and sniffed.

"Shel, I need you to come downstairs." Car doors slammed. Voices drifted up to them. It was too early for it to be Christine and Ryan, returning from a trip to Santa Rosa for supplies.

Lucky barked and charged the stairs.

"Come on, Shel." Gage held out a hand to her. They followed Lucky down the stairs, Shelby nearly stumbled on the last step. Gage's broad back blocked her view of the windows. Lucky stood barking on his hind legs, looking out the glass pane in the door. She couldn't see what grim thing faced her until Gage opened the door and Lucky bounded outside.

There was a minivan parked in front of the farmhouse. A harried brunette in rumpled sweats and a yellow T-shirt jiggled a chubby baby dressed in pink on her hip. Two little boys fidgeted next to her. When they saw Lucky, the boys whooped and ran forward, shouting, "Bucky! Bucky!"

Lucky skidded to a halt in front of them, and then twined between the boys, preening for pats of affection. The baby giggled and reached for the big dog. The woman carrying her smiled in relief.

"No. Oh, no." Shelby sagged against Gage. He put his arm around her.

"I can't thank you enough for taking care of Bucky." The woman bent to let the baby pat Lucky's broad head. "We thought we'd lost him. We were camping on the other side of Parish Hill. Bucky heard a noise and took off. We stayed an extra day, but when he didn't come back, we had to leave. I had to work. I called animal control in Santa Rosa, not thinking there was a branch farther north in Cloverdale. Finally, someone told me about Cloverdale and here we are." The joy in the woman's voice danced a cleated-jig on Shelby's goodwill.

She loved Lucky. He was the sweetest dog, highly intuitive to the moods of everyone around him. He deserved a good home. A safe home. A home where people didn't let him go astray.

Like I did this morning.

Shelby reached for Gage's hand and held on tight. "He...uh...likes other animals." Shelby's voice sounded distant and faint, as if it came from across the river. "Geese...kittens."

"Boys, settle down." The woman didn't acknowledge Shelby. Perhaps she hadn't even heard her.

Lucky didn't so much as glance Shelby's way.

"He's very patient with the elderly." They were going to take him. Something cracked inside her, something she'd held together for too long. "There's Mae..."

One of the boys produced a scuffed softball and threw it into the vineyard. Lucky ran after it, bringing it back with an excited bounce to his step. He danced around the boys and played keep-away. The baby laughed and clapped her hands.

Shelby's heart was in her throat. Lucky—*Bucky*—was so clearly theirs and so ecstatic to be reunited with them... She swallowed back the heartache.

"He didn't have any tags." Only a hint of reproach tinged Gage's voice. "We would have called if he did."

"He got a new collar for his birthday, before we went camping." The woman was too busy enjoying the reunion to pay Gage and Shelby much attention. "I didn't think to put his tags on it until it was too late. I have a hard enough time keeping up with the boys."

Lucky...*Bucky*...jumped into the back of the minivan without the enticement of dog treats and sat between the seats as if it was his usual spot. He kept touching the boys with his nose, as if to reassure himself they were really there. The poor thing must have been so devastated when he'd gotten lost. His boys...his family...

"Can we come visit?" Shelby's words weren't more than a whisper. She knew where Lucky belonged. A piece of her heart had been ripped out once more.

Shelby couldn't speak. She couldn't even bring herself to walk down the porch steps to say goodbye.

Too soon, Bucky and his family were gone.

In a blink, Shelby's life had changed again.

The goose didn't like Mushu, Doc's cocker spaniel, as much as it had Lucky.

Gage couldn't refer to the big dog by his proper name.

He sat at the kitchen table trying to eat a portion of the frozen lasagna Shelby had prepared for dinner. She'd barely eaten and was sitting on the grass in the backyard with the two kittens and the goose.

The goose, she'd named Fanny. Meanwhile, she had no idea Gage couldn't keep his eyes off her.

After Lucky had been taken away, Gage thought it best to give Shelby a distraction. He'd brought Fanny home as a result. The goose had limped a slow loop outside while Shelby ate. Afterward, she nestled next to Shelby in the grass, occasionally nudging a kitten over to Shelby with her beak or honking at Mushu when she came up for a friendly sniff.

"I miss that dog already," Gage mused.

"Best make sure no one comes claiming that goose," Doc said in a gravelly voice as he wandered from the kitchen to his library.

Gage agreed. "If someone shows up, I'll offer to buy it."

His cell phone rang. It was the equine hospital with a request he deliver a foal tonight. Gage considered turning it down. He wanted Shelby to come with him, but not when she was dealing with losing Lucky. But the last time he'd turned down a request, a foal had died.

"Don't tell me they want you again?" Doc's incredulous voice drifted to him from the living room. "They're having a baby boom over there in horses."

"It's several different breeding programs." Gage negotiated his way into the living room. The old man stood near the hearth. His balance had a pendulum quality that always made Gage nervous. "Steady there, Doc." Gage surveyed the space between the stacks and realized if he went any farther he might knock things over. "Why don't you bring whatever you're reading to the kitchen?"

"I'd just have to refile it later. It's easier to read in here."

"I'd be interested in reading whatever's got your attention," Gage lied as he glanced over his shoulder toward the backyard. Shelby still sat with her menagerie. Gaipan had joined the party, crouched in the grass a few feet away from the action.

"Leaving the stack messes up my entire filing system." Yet the old man tottered through the tall piles toward Gage.

When Doc made it out safely, Gage released a breath and led the old man into the kitchen. "Next time I go into Cloverdale I'll pick up some storage boxes."

Doc slapped a copy of Vet Med Magazine on the kitchen table in front of Gage. "Now don't you start. It's bad enough I have Shelby nagging me about change. This is my house and I like things just the way they are."

Shelby turned toward them, perhaps hearing her grandfather's outburst. Her features were barnacled, fighting against more tears. She didn't need an argument today with Doc about his safety and mobility.

Gage pushed the magazine toward the old man. When he spoke, his voice was as hard as metal. "You have the balance of a drunken sailor and at your age your bones are as fragile as fine china. If you want to sacrifice pride for being safe, that's your business. But if you fall and hurt yourself—*or die*—it'll break her heart." He pointed to Shelby outside. "And that's my business."

Staring at his granddaughter, Doc cleared his throat, but said nothing.

Gage ran a hand over his face. "I need to leave."

Shelby had insisted on going with Gage to the equine hospital.

She'd left the goose in her crate in the kitchen next to the crated kittens, which needed to be fed every four hours. Her grandfather had begun to grumble, but one look from Gage and he'd bit back whatever argument he'd considered making.

Neither she nor Gage had spoken much on the drive over. Gage had offered her his hand to hold, and she'd taken it.

The city of Davis was a mixture of small town, university facilities and suburbs. The parking lot at the equine hospital was large, nearly filled with trucks and horse trailers. They checked into what was the main building and continued through a rear exit to the birthing stables.

Shelby walked next to Gage, wide-eyed. "This place is huge." Larger than some people hospitals she'd seen.

"The biggest building in the back is a rehab center." Gage played tour guide. "It has a pool and the latest equipment for horses recovering from limb injuries." Gage pointed to a smaller building opposite the birthing center. "That's the ICU. On the other side of that is the boarding area."

"This is a huge operation. They must pay well."

Gage nodded.

"And yet you still drive that old beat-up truck."

"I don't need anything fancy. The engine works. The air-conditioning works. And it has sentimental value to me." His gaze was warm.

And yet, she'd noticed a difference in Gage as soon as he'd gotten out of his truck. There was more of a swagger to his walk.

She might have attributed his shift to a focus on work, except she was reminded of Nick—his swagger, his attitude, his confident laughter before he rappelled down a steep cliff. Gage may have held her hand, but once on the path to the birthing center, they didn't walk together. He charged ahead, she struggled to keep up.

It was wrong of her to come here. She'd known it, too.

She still wore black.

"Gage." Shelby drew Gage to a halt before they entered the stable. "We're just a couple of kids from Harmony Valley. You treated a goose this morning."

Gage frowned. "Is something wrong?"

He had no idea. This—the two of them—wasn't going to work. But now wasn't the time to tell him.

She stretched onto her tiptoes to kiss his cheek. "Never mind. Good luck."

He cast his arm over her shoulder and smiled. But it was the smile he gave to people to hide his feelings and get his way.

And there was a crowd milling about a stall ahead.

As they got closer, Shelby read the name on the placard attached to the wall. "Devil's Surprise Party?" She turned her wide-eyed gaze on Gage, a bitter taste in her mouth.

"Stall banger! Get outta there!" someone shouted.

Several people scrambled away from the stall door.

Shelby craned her neck to see inside. A black, very pregnant mare trotted past, then started kicking.

Bang!

"Thanks for coming, Dr. Jamero." A middle-aged man with silver-streaked hair greeted them. After he'd introduced himself as Dr. Thomason, the owner of the facility, he added unnecessarily, "She's one ticked off mother-to-be."

Gage watched the mare intently, almost eagerly.

Shelby's heels dug in. "Gage, don't go in there."

He looked down at her. His expression softened. "She's in pain, Shel."

"She's looking for blood." Shelby had to raise her voice to be heard over the noise of the mare kicking the stall again. "Please don't let it be yours."

Gage drew her into his arms. "Try to understand, Shel. She's in labor for the first time. It hurts and she doesn't know how to make the pain go away. The more hysterical she gets, the more frightened she becomes, the more danger her foal is in." He pressed a kiss to her forehead. "You can wait in the main building if it upsets you."

She buried her face in his chest, breathing in the scent that was distinctly Gage. "Please." Life wasn't fair. Disaster lurked around every corner waiting for you to blink. She was too weak to stop it, too helpless to protect him. Nick. Lucky. "I can't lose you, too."

"You're not going to lose me. I promise." He tilted her chin up and kissed her. His gentle press of lips promised shelter, hope...a future. She closed her eyes and tried to believe, tried to have faith, tried not to cling to him when the kiss ended.

Dr. Thomason touched her shoulder. "He'll be fine. He was born to do this."

She turned away.

Others began streaming into the barn to watch, pulling out cell phones to record the action. They jostled Shelby forward until she was pressed against the stall's observation window, facing Gage. She saw him unlatch the door and step inside.

In the corner, the mare breathed heavily, pawing the ground with her front hoof. Her nostrils flared. Her eyes darted from the quieting crowd to Gage.

And then she charged.

Chapter Twenty-Six

"Whoa!" Gage used his most dominant tone and threw up his arms as if signaling a touchdown.

The mare skidded to a stop in front of him. Her neck and flanks were dripping with sweat. A contraction clenched her bulging midsection.

He imagined it to be about as powerful as the adrenaline gripping him.

There was a towel hanging over the stall door. Gage reached for it slowly. "Easy, girl." He double folded it and stepped toward the mare, imagining the gasp in the crowd was Shelby's. "Easy, now." He ran the towel gently over the Devil's neck. "Pretty girl. I'm here now," he crooned. More patting of the mare's neck. "You've tired yourself out and it isn't even halftime."

Her ears twisted to listen to his voice.

He began whistling softly, so softly it was more like a breathy hum.

The Devil blew out a weary, shuddering sigh.

Gage kept rubbing her down, being careful to stay in front of her withers until he'd gained more of her trust. There was a thick liquid over her hindquarters. Her water had broken.

"It's time to lie down, girl." He eased his fingers into her bridle and drew her head down.

She made a chuffing noise, but soon settled into the straw. Resting on the ground, her stomach bulged with at least seventy pounds of foal. Just as quickly though, she lurched back to her feet, butting her head into his chest.

Gage took that as a request for another rubdown. This time he was able to gauge the tension in her belly, peeking beneath her wrapped tail to see if any tiny hooves were present. "Nothing yet, girl. Let's get you back on the ground." Where birthing would be easier on everyone.

The Devil complied, but once she relaxed her body, a contraction hit, and she staggered to her feet again. They repeated the process a few more times. Still no hooves in sight.

Gage retreated to where Shelby and Dr. Thomason stood.

"Let me through." It was Leo, looking as if he was ready to make hospital rounds in his pristine white coat. "No one called me. What's the status here? Get out, Dr. Jamero. This is my wing."

"I've asked Dr. Jamero for a consult," Dr. Thomason said crisply. "The Devil is high-strung. I thought it best to bring in a specialist." It was a nice way of saying Leo had messed up the last time and risked the equine hospital's reputation.

"Dr. Faraji..." Gage figured the least he could do to ease the sting of being replaced was to give the man an update. "She's going to deliver standing up. I can't get her to rest."

The mare paced the stall, nudging Gage's shoulder every time she passed by him. Gage gave Shelby his most reassuring smile.

She looked at Dr. Faraji.

"Get out." Leo edged his way along the door toward the latch.

The Devil kicked the stall with increasing force.

"Easy, girl," Gage crooned. "There's nothing bad going on here."

"Stay where you are, Dr. Jamero." Dr. Thomason's voice was sharp and decisive.

Leo's gaze turned thunderous.

Shelby was biting her lip. Her hold on the stall door was white-knuckled. This was not the scenario Gage had played out in his head when he'd asked her to join him. But he still had a job to do, a patient to attend to. This was what he was meant to do.

The Devil walked past him. Gage fell into step with her, running his hand from her withers to her rump, getting her used to his touch. Several minutes passed. Her pace slowed. The crowd was silent.

"She's almost there," Dr. Thomason said as Gage and the mare passed by the stall door.

The Devil grunted. Gage let her walk on. A pair of tiny hooves wrapped in the bluish-white amniotic fluid crested beneath her tail.

Gage opened the door latch. "I'll need help. One person." He didn't take his eyes off the mare as she continued her circuit.

Someone entered the stall. He spared a glance over his shoulder. Of course, it was Leo. He stepped forward too quickly, reaching for the mare's bridle. She kicked out, barely missing Gage's leg.

"Easy, Leo. Don't move until she gets used to you."

Leo huffed but stood still in the corner.

The next time the mare came around, Gage fell into step with her, draping an arm gently over the mare's haunches so he could keep an eye on the foal.

He felt the contraction build. Gage crooned meaningless words. The mare perked her ears to listen. "Now, Leo. Lockstep, and when she's used to you, take the bridle, and slow her down."

Amazingly, Leo did as instructed, waiting until the Devil had accepted him as a walking partner to take her bridle. The mare's muscles bunched. A nose appeared beneath her tail.

"That a girl. Almost there now." Gage kept talking softly as he slowed enough to walk even with her tail. He took the small hooves in hand and helped ease the foal out, inch by precious inch. "Stop her, Leo."

The mare kept moving.

"Leo." There was more tension in Gage's voice than he would have liked to use.

The mare didn't like it, either. She lashed out with a hoof Gage easily dodged, having sensed her muscles tense. Shelby cried out. The foal's chest was cradled precariously in his arms. Another push and the foal would be out. Another safe delivery.

He sensed rather than saw the mare toss her head, fighting Leo for control.

"If you don't stop her, Leo, she'll rupture the cord or the placenta." They could lose either mare or foal to excessive bleeding or infection. "I'm a little busy on this end."

Without stopping, the mare gave one last push. The foal's legs slipped free. Gage's arms filled with seventy pounds of slippery horseflesh still connected to fifteen hundred pounds of anxious mare. He couldn't walk behind her like this much longer. And the foal needed oxygen.

"Leo. Stop her."

The Devil bucked, missing her foal, but connecting with Gage's ribs instead. He fell to his knees as a haze dropped over his vision. Distantly, he heard voices and footsteps. Bodies surrounded him. The foal was lifted from his arms. And then everything went dark.

Every time Gage gasped for air, Shelby did, too.

"Shallow breaths," the EMT reminded him.

Shelby grimaced. She'd heard the crack of hoof against bone. She'd heard the speculation back at the birthing stall while they waited for an ambulance.

Broken ribs. Collapsed lung. Internal bleeding.

Gage could die.

The ambulance rocked over a pothole. She gripped Gage's hand tighter.

She'd wanted to live her life in a cocoon, but she'd let Lucky in. And then she'd let Gage in...

His eyes were scrunched closed. His skin pale. His hand in hers inert.

Unbidden, the image of Nick's face in the morgue rose in front of her. The room had been so cold she'd shivered, while the smell of antiseptic made her feel queasy, made worse when they showed her Nick's body. His blond hair was in a tangle. She'd smoothed it. Bruises replaced the smile she was used to seeing on his face. She'd kissed his cool forehead and turned to bury her face in Gage's warm chest.

Beneath the blanket on the gurney, Gage's chest was battered and swollen. His eyes were closed. His face was hidden behind an oxygen mask.

She couldn't stop hearing the crack when the mare had struck him. Couldn't stop seeing his body thrown against the wall. Couldn't stop the chant in her head.

Dead Gage. Dead Gage. Dead Gage.

Stupid, stupid nickname.

Her entire body fought the notion of losing him. Gage was here, with her, his chest rising and falling, if not deeply, at least regularly. He wasn't dead. He wasn't dead.

But he could've been.

Gage knew he wasn't dying by how slow his medical care was.

Concussion? Yes. His head pounded painfully, like a teenager with a new drum set. The hospital staff made sure he sat upright and instructed Shelby to keep him awake.

Ribs? Cracked, not broken. Shallow breaths and slow minimal moves were the way to go.

Collapsed lung? No. Internal bleeding? They were running tests and monitoring him for shock.

It was Shelby who looked to be in shock. The color had left her face. And when she spoke to the nursing staff there was a distant hollowness to her voice that did nothing to reassure him.

They'd transferred him from the emergency ward to a room with putty green walls and a picture of the windswept California coast.

He preferred Secretariat.

Had Leo done this on purpose? Gage found that hard to believe. As hard to believe as Leo being unable to control the mare's head.

"I'm okay," he whispered hoarsely after several unsuccessful attempts to speak.

From her chair at his side, Shelby nodded tightly. "I called Grandpa so he wouldn't worry. And I told Christine I'd be in late tomorrow. If I come in at all."

Although she touched a patch of short hair on his forehead, he couldn't stop the feeling that she was drifting away from him. Not the quick way that he'd lost Nick, but with the slow pace of the Harmony River, drifting around the bend and out of sight forever. Fear of losing her made him tense up, made him breathe too deeply.

He gasped and writhed as if he was dying. He just might be if the look on Shelby's face was any indication.

"Don't," he said finally, when he could form words without his ribs cutting off air. "Don't. Give up. On me."

Her eyes widened. And she shook her head. "I'll be right here."

He knew she wouldn't lie to him.

Still, he couldn't help but think: For how long?

Gage was released late the next morning. They took a rideshare to the equine hospital to pick up his truck.

Shelby was thankful for the stick shift. Working the gears kept her mind off of other things.

As she drove them to Harmony Valley, Gage dozed in the passenger seat, occasionally breathing too deeply, and awakening with a gasp of pain. Each time, he reached over to pat her hand and ask, "Are you okay?"

How could he ask her that and not realize what a stupid thing it was to step into a stall with a raged, hormonal horse?

Shelby wanted to wail in agony. Instead, she nodded when he asked, and kept her eyes on the road.

When they arrived at her grandfather's house, Shelby helped Gage into bed. She tugged off his boots, got him a glass of water, and carefully propped him up with extra pillows.

Grandpa fussed. "It's a fluke. Happens now and then. But your color's good." He pushed his glasses up his narrow nose. "When do you think we can re-open the clinic?"

Shelby herded Grandpa out of the bedroom with instructions to feed the kittens and check Fanny's splint.

"I did that already," Grandpa complained.

"Then do it again." She closed Gage's door in his face.

Gage had a soldier's grin that told her he was in pain, but not dying. Not this time anyway.

She didn't believe in anything anymore.

Shelby sat on the edge of his bed, took his hand in hers and closed her eyes against the tide of emotions that threatened her—fear, regret, heartache.

I will not cry.

"I'm okay," Gage murmured, squeezing her fingers.

"You can train someone to go in there with you. Someone better than Leo. Train someone who cares about animals." *Train me!*

It was a dumb idea. So dumb, she couldn't even say it out loud, because she was afraid. Afraid he'd reject her offer almost as much as she was afraid he wouldn't.

Disgusted with her cowardice, she left him and walked out.

"Well, look what the cat fought and dragged in," Mae said when she opened the door.

Shelby wrapped her arms around Mae's skin-and-bones frame and began to sob. Mae let her. Mae really didn't have much choice, since Shelby couldn't seem to let go.

When the tears were spent, she and Mae went to the couch, moved skirts of satin and lace aside, and sat down. She handed Shelby a box of tissues.

"What on earth is wrong?" Somehow, one of Mae's penciled-in eyebrows had rubbed off, probably on Shelby's black T-shirt. Who could tell? Black hid stains.

After recounting what had happened to Gage, Shelby blurted, "Why do these guys need to test the limits? Why can't loving me be enough?"

If she'd been expecting sympathy, she should have gone to her grandfather. "A man can't define himself by who he loves," Mae scoffed. "Men need a purpose in life outside the home. You said Gage was good with horses."

"He's been kicked twice in a month's time. If I was his insurance company, I'd cancel his policy."

"And how many times has he been kicked in his whole career?"

Shelby shrugged. She didn't want to imagine his bruised flesh, his pained, belabored breathing.

"Never mind." Mae held up a hand. "You want safe? Doesn't exist. No one can promise you'll be safe. There are cancers and drunk drivers and earthquakes. All kinds of things you can't predict, not even here in Harmony Valley. Home of predictability."

"It's different than running *to* danger."

"My third husband, Marvin, was the exact same. He ran to danger. But he was a fireman, and he was trained. I worried about him until the day he retired, but that was his job and he loved it. How many of us have that? Or a man who's happy and fulfilled and comes home to you every night? Perhaps a little battered, but in need of some kindness, some tenderness."

Shelby glanced at the pictures of Mae's husbands on the mantle. Mae was talking about Marvin as if he was still alive. "So you divorced Marvin?"

"I... He..." Mae frowned. "It seems like he's still here with me. But he's not. And Oliver isn't..." Mae blinked, staring at the room in confusion. "Who are you?"

A new fear raced through her veins. "I'm Shelby."

Mae laughed awkwardly. "I remember you. You're my...my..."

"Friend." Shelby stood. "I'm going to call the doctor. Is his number by the phone?"

"If you're my friend, you'll realize I don't want the doctor. I'm going to die here. At home, where I belong."

"But—"

"No doctor." That was the first thing she'd said with any clarity since Shelby had asked about Marvin.

Shelby got out her cell phone. "Then I'm calling Sheriff Nate."

Chapter Twenty-Seven

"You really mucked things up with Shelby." Doc dragged a kitchen chair into Gage's bedroom.

"I'm fine, thanks," Gage whispered, whispering being less likely to aggravate his rib cage.

"Since Nick died, Shelby's been playing it safe." Doc's gruff voice filled the room, comforting in its familiarity. "It'll take a lot to get past this."

Tell me something I don't know.

Gage stared at the picture of Secretariat leaning against the closet door. "She can't get past who I am."

"You don't define yourself by what you do." Doc gestured at him. "Young people and their dreams. Give me a break. Relationships are about give-and-take, compromise and being happy with a path taken with your spouse, regardless of whether or not it was the path you thought you'd take when you were a kid."

"I'm not ancient. Shelby just started a job here." Gage sucked in a shallow breath. "With the potential to make a difference and a name for herself. From the ground up. That doesn't happen often."

"Love doesn't happen often," Doc retorted hotly. "Why is it Shelby has to be the one to compromise? She might be right. You don't seem to have a good track record with horses."

"You'd like to see me stay." Gage gasped in pain, both physical and emotional. "That was your plan all along."

"I have no plan, son. I want you two to be happy." The gruffness turned into a grandfatherly tone. "Now, the way I see it, you can wish Shelby well and go to Kentucky. And the work there will be fulfilling—when you're working—but those nights when you're home? Those will be lonely. And Shelby will be out here throwing herself into her work, occasionally adopting another animal. Oh, she'll tell herself she's happy. She'll visit Nick's grave. But she won't venture out, not out of this house and not out of her comfort zone."

"It's what she wants," Gage rasped.

"In the two years since Nick passed, you're the only thing she talked about."

Gage listed toward the wall. Pushing himself upright was agonizing. "*Dead Gage.*"

"You were top-of-mind. Then you came back, and I watched her watch you." Doc removed his glasses and cleaned the lenses with his flannel shirttail. "If you think Kentucky is more important than Shelby, by all means, leave tomorrow. I want her to have a full and happy life, but it'll be a long time before she ventures out for any man."

"Your hypothesis doesn't include one important factor. Shelby isn't sitting here nursing me to health. She left. That's what she does. She runs and hides."

Doc doled out a pain pill and handed Gage the water bottle from the night-stand. "Even a timid rabbit has to take a stand sometime, son. Put your faith in her. You won't be disappointed."

Mae pointed at the cocktail wedding dress hanging from the light fixture. "If you want to make me feel better, go try that on. The shoes, too."

Shelby had called the sheriff and told him her concerns. He was in Cloverdale and couldn't get back for another thirty minutes. "Mae, I—"

"Those are my terms, girlie." She coughed for a full minute. "I'm so tired. Too tired to go to the hospital. What an undignified place. Everyone wants a look-see... I'm just not going." Her smudged brows drew down. "Try on the dress or go."

Shelby thought it best not to argue. She took the dress and the shoes and ran down the hall to the bathroom. Mae's house was the same floor plan as her grandfather's, so she knew the way.

The wedding dress was a sheath. It was just her size.

Mae was right. The dress suited her. She slipped into the shoes.

She thought of Gage's smile when she presented him with her bad cooking. Of the tender expression on his face after he kissed her. Of how right he felt in her arms.

I love him. Desperately.

She loved his humor and his patience with her. She loved how he had a way with animals. She even loved how he was willing to risk his life to help them. When she was with him he made her feel smart and attractive and alive.

Not safe.

Could she be like Mae? Could she think of Gage as if he was a fireman or a policeman? Someone trained to handle a dangerous situation?

She didn't want to be safe anymore. She wanted to live.

It meant leaving this job and moving to Kentucky. Since that's where Gage was going to be.

Her hands were shaking as bad as Mae's had been.

She opened the door and rushed into the living room. "Mae, you're right. I love Gage and—"

Mae was silent, slumped in her chair.

"Mae?" Shelby reached for Mae's wrist, trying to find her pulse. There was none. "Oh, Mae."

She hurried back to the bathroom, retrieving her cell phone from the pocket of her jeans. She punched in Sheriff Nate's number and told him what had happened. Shelby then returned to Mae's side and held the woman's hand. Mae hadn't wanted to die alone. She'd also wanted to die with dignity. And she had. When Sheriff Nate arrived, he looked at Shelby, at her fancy dress and shoes, at the room full of fancy dresses and fancy shoes but said nothing.

"She wanted you to have the rose-colored one." Shelby pointed to the dress over a kitchen chair.

Nate swore.

Shelby stayed and waited for a medical person to pronounce Mae dead. She stayed until the mortuary arrived to take Mae away. She told them about the wedding dress. They told her Mae had come in a few days ago to make her funeral arrangements.

Shelby cried then because Mae was one of the strongest women she'd ever known. And because she hadn't listened to her sooner. Could she now?

"How are you feeling?" Shelby stood in the doorway to Gage's bedroom looking like a dream—a young bride, his young bride.

"Like you left." Shallow wheeze. "And I couldn't follow."

There was something wrong with Shelby's face. She looked like she'd been crying. But that dress... It was a wedding dress.

"I'll go with you," she told him.

Gage was confused, possibly due to the pain meds. "To the doctor?" He had a follow-up visit planned for next week.

She shook her head. "You were going to ask me to go with you to Kentucky, weren't you?"

"Yes." It couldn't be that simple, but in the rising joy, he couldn't figure out what was going on. There was a chance he was hallucinating.

"I'll go with you," Shelby said. And then she was gone.

What did it mean? Did she want to move out there as friends? His heart couldn't take that scenario. Was this her way of letting him know that she wanted their relationship to go to the next level? Was this a pain-killer induced hallucination?

Gage dragged himself out of bed with care, taking slow steps to Shelby's room. He knocked gently on the door. No one answered, but he could hear noises in the room. Had she rescued another stray?

Gage opened the door.

Shelby lay curled up on the bed in that wedding dress, clutching her pillow. He went over to the bed and sat on the edge of the mattress.

Her face sobered, and then she climbed into his lap, wrapping her arms around him. "Am I hurting you?"

"No. Are you upset because of Kentucky?"

"Mae died. One minute she was talking to me." She gulped a deep breath. "And the next, she was gone."

Now the reason for her going with him made sense. Shelby didn't want to lose anyone else. First Nick, then Lucky, then Mae. And someday, Doc. "You can't save everyone." But it would be nice if she could, just once.

"Maybe if I go to Kentucky, I can save you." She tilted her head up so that she could see his face. "I could train to be your birthing assistant. Nothing bad would happen if we're together. You want to be together, don't you?"

More than anything. But not like this. She was clinging to a false hope, rather than accepting the reality. The notion that she could protect what and who she cared for, 24/7, starting with Gage, a dog, some kittens and a motherly goose was not going to do anyone any good. She'd offered to train to be his birthing assistant. No way was he letting her inside a stall with flighty mares.

"Tomorrow," he said slowly. "We'll talk."

The news spread like wildfire through Harmony Valley. They'd lost another of their ranks.

Agnes was at Rose's house for a potluck dinner when the call came in. She looked at her friends and said, "I know exactly what we're naming our boutique. Mae's Pretty Things."

The cocktail wedding dress was the first thing Shelby saw the next morning, draped over one of her wardrobe boxes. Whatever the day brought, whatever the future brought, she'd be forever changed because of Mae. But the pain of another loss chilled her.

Shelby dug in some boxes for clean clothes, grateful that Grandpa had made coffee. The aroma filled the house. When she stumbled into the kitchen, her grandfather was reading the paper. "Isn't it time for you to open the clinic?"

"I fed your animals. The kittens are sleeping, and that goose is outside." Grandpa studied Shelby's face. "Gage and I are taking a day. Why don't you take one, too?"

She nodded. "I texted Christine last night."

"Hey, look who's here." Walking like a man with cracked ribs, with small steps and shallow breaths, Gage led Agnes, Rose, and Mildred into the kitchen. "I heard them drive up and had to make sure they didn't come through the living room obstacle course."

"That's my research and I'll thank you not to make fun of it," Grandpa grumped.

The visitors ignored him. One by one, they hugged Shelby. Each embrace made Shelby feel a little better, a little warmer.

Gage pulled a chair close to hers and took her hand. His touch chased away most of the chill that remained. She needed to find someone to keep an eye on Grandpa after she left. She hadn't thought about him last night when she'd told Gage she'd go with him. She hadn't thought about the special opportunities she was losing at Harmony Valley Vineyards. She hadn't been able to think past the emptiness of loss.

"Normally, we visit the family the morning after with Rose's triple chocolate treats." Agnes uncovered a tray of chocolate chip cookies and brownies. "But her family won't be in until tomorrow and Mae had grown fond of you, Shelby."

"Between the chocolate chip cookies, brownies and hot chocolate, we'll all feel better soon." Rose sniffed as she opened a thermos.

Shelby brought down mugs and passed around napkins. At Rose's urging, they each took a treat. Shelby worked the chocolate chips from her cookie to nibble on, having no appetite. The kitchen seemed overwhelmingly cheerful this morning, no place for the somber discussions death necessitated. Mae would have scoffed at the mood in the room.

"Mae wouldn't appreciate black at her funeral." Shelby plucked at the sky-blue T-shirt she'd dug from the bottom of a wardrobe box. She couldn't remember the last time she'd worn it. One of Nick's blue bandanas had lain on top of it. "I need to put a rush order on Conchita's dress restoration."

Everyone in the room seemed perplexed.

"She called the mannequin in the window Conchita." Shelby managed a small smile. "She wanted to be buried in that wedding dress."

Rose gasped. Mildred blew her nose.

Agnes nodded. "That's exactly how she would have wanted to go."

"I was thinking of dying my hair red for the funeral," Rose said.

"What a fitting tribute." Mildred blew her nose. "I hope I can still fit into the dress she picked out for me for my niece's wedding."

"We'll get it out of your closet today," Agnes promised.

"It's...purple," Mildred squeaked before shedding a tear.

They all agreed the color was very fitting.

When the ladies left, Shelby drifted outside, drawn by the fog-filtered rays of the sun on the lawn. With an excited honk, Fanny waddled up to her, dancing on webbed feet in a ploy for attention.

"Silly goose." Shelby patted her. "I hope you enjoy long car rides."

Gage came up behind her, wrapping his arms gently around her, being just as careful of his physical injuries as he was her emotional wounds. "We'll get through this."

There was a loud, elongated crash from the house.

"Grandpa?" Shelby spun around, elbowing Gage's ribs in the process. "I'm sorry, but... Grandpa?"

"Shelby?" Her grandfather's voice. Conspicuously absent was his bite. "I need help."

The living room stacks had tumbled like dominos. The mounds of books and magazines were largest by the fireplace. A hand moved weakly between two thick volumes.

"Grandpa! Gage, call the sheriff. He's knocked over the piles and is buried by the fireplace." She stepped over the fringe of disaster and rooted her foot through an opening to the avocado shag. "Grandpa? Talk to me."

He didn't.

She began tossing books and magazines into a far corner. In her urgency, they smacked against the wall so hard a picture fell.

Gage helped, but he moved slowly, hindered by his injuries.

Finally, she reached her grandfather, sprawled on the brick hearth and in obvious pain.

For the second time in forty-eight hours, Shelby found herself in the emergency room.

"There's no chance I could have broken my hip," Grandpa grumbled, in a much better mood since they'd given him pain meds in his IV bag.

"Are you saying X-rays lie?" Shelby had lost her patience a while ago. "Are you saying the doctor lied?"

"I didn't break my hip." So mule-headed. She wanted to shake him.

"Get up. And dance." Gage sat stiffly in the only chair in the room, looking like he was trying not to breathe.

She'd have to get Gage home soon. They hadn't brought any of his pain meds, and Grandpa was staying in the hospital until they could schedule his surgery. "That's right. If you can dance out the door, Grandpa, I'll take you home."

Her grandfather moved his legs as if to get out of bed, and then froze, his face contorted in pain.

Shelby softened. "Don't argue anymore. Please."

"A broken hip is the kiss of death," Grandpa whispered. "Six months, tops."

"I'll be here with you every minute." And by the time he came home, she'd have the living room cleared. She'd said she wanted to leave Harmony Valley; run to a place where no one got hurt. Her gaze caught Gage's. She couldn't go with him to Kentucky now.

Gage nodded, as if understanding.

"How can I?" she said out loud, feeling the need to explain herself. "My mom can't come for more than a week. She's got an important business pitch."

Gage nodded. He understood.

That didn't stop Shelby's heart from breaking. "Maybe in six months…"

Gage shook his head.

Realistically, Shelby knew that her grandfather could no longer live alone. His balance had been precarious before this. He hadn't been taking care of himself. She'd allowed him to bully her into ignoring what shouldn't have been ignored.

"Go to Kentucky," Grandpa grumbled. "I can fade into the twilight on my own."

"No. You can't." She'd just lost Mae. She wasn't losing him so soon. "I'm going to keep you safe."

Safe. Was there such a thing?

As she drove Gage back to the house, she didn't think there was. "I'm sorry. About Kentucky."

"I wouldn't have let you come anyway. You'd hate it."

Shelby took her eyes off the road long enough to glance at him. His face was in shadow. His eyes closed. "But I thought—"

He made a chopping motion with his hand, grunting at the effort. "I want you to be with me because you love me." He winced. "Not because of some misplaced sense of duty to try and keep you safe."

She wanted to tell Gage she loved him. But what would be the point? She couldn't leave Grandpa here alone. And she knew the old man wouldn't move to Kentucky.

Gage nearly cracked another rib loading his suitcase in the truck. He hadn't slept much at all last night. He hadn't taken any pain medication, wanting to be clearheaded when he left the next morning.

Shelby cradled the orange tabby in her arms, watching him. Fanny watched him, too, honking sadly.

After his second and final suitcase was taken care of, he returned to the kitchen. "Look after the old man."

She nodded. "I will."

"If you raise them right, those two cats will be good mousers."

She tried to smile, struggling not to cry.

The back of his hand brushed over her cheek. He'd always remember her like this—the sun catching the highlights in her sunflower hair, her eyes the color of the clear blue sky, the slight waver in her brave smile. She'd been right all along. It hurt to lose someone. There was too much risk in loving someone. "Look after yourself."

She nodded again. "Can I call you?"

He hesitated too long before answering.

"Never mind," she mumbled.

Talking to her would be hard. He knew the taste of her lips, the feel of her in his arms, the smell of her hair. Talking to her would bring all that back, all that he'd lost, all that he'd traded to be a racehorse vet.

It was past time to go. He held out his arms.

She hugged him gingerly but didn't let go for a long time.

"I love you, Shelby. I always have. Since the day you walked into science class." He wasn't sure if he had said it out loud or if he was testing the words in his head. His arms tightened around her, despite his brain telling him to leave. He had to leave before his heart broke completely.

"Oh, Gage." She stepped free of his embrace. "I wish... It doesn't matter what I wish. Just know that I love you."

But she didn't love him like they should spend the rest of their lives sharing a house, a mortgage and a bed. She didn't love him like she wanted to have his children and laugh with him into old age. She loved him like her friend.

His heart knew it wasn't enough.

Gage was gone.

Shelby ferried stacks of books and periodicals into the garage. She arranged them in her grandfather's dusty, cobwebbed truck bed. She fed the kittens, Mushu and Gaipan, and Fanny. She washed her grandfather's sheets, which smelled as if they hadn't been washed since Easter.

Gage was gone.

She called Christine and told her she wouldn't be working today. She called the hospital to see when her grandfather's surgery was scheduled. She called Nate to find out the day and time of Mae's funeral.

Gage was gone.

The house was too empty. She walked down the street. Stopped and peered up at the clouds. A car passed by and honked at her. Shelby waved.

Gage's house was shut up tight. They'd fought over hypotheses and theorems in that house. They'd watched movies with his kid sister. And she'd never known he loved her.

Nick had leaped into her path that first week of school. He'd been exciting. A daredevil. She admired that in him. She, who wasn't at all like her risk-taking mother.

Rounding the corner to Nick's house, she noticed the bungalow's windows were broken. He'd asked her to prom on that front porch. Gage had been there. They'd all hugged afterward. Later, when she and Gage were walking home, she'd joked that someday when she and Nick got married she wanted Gage to be her maid of honor.

How blind she'd been. Unwittingly hurtful.

She'd loved Nick with an innocent devotion. She'd assumed he'd grow out of his need for speed. She assumed they'd become closer and grow old together. Now she couldn't imagine him aging. He'd be forever young in her memories.

Gage was careful. He'd protected that foal, taking the hit from the mare himself. He helped with high-risk deliveries because of his desire to protect life. He wasn't like Nick.

She'd told Gage she loved him, and he'd still walked away. She couldn't hold it against him. He had a dream.

She wouldn't think of him as Dead Gage any longer.

She'd think of him as Gage, the man who'd risked everything for her heart. Won it. And then let her go.

Gage couldn't seem to lift his foot from the brake.

His truck remained at the crossroads leading west to the highway and Cloverdale.

Still, he couldn't go.

His ribs hurt badly. His heart hurt worse.

She said she loved me.

In her kiss, Gage knew there was a promise of reciprocal love. If he was patient, if he put his dream on hold, he could wait for her to love him like a husband rather than a friend.

Kentucky, with all its wild green grass and excitement, beckoned.

Shelby's face seemed superimposed in the clouds drifting past.

What good was a dream if you couldn't share them with the one you loved?

She said she loved me.

She wanted to save the world.

He wanted her to save him, but to do so, he'd have to give up everything he'd worked for.

Shelby sat on the curb in front of Mae's purple house, having read some of Mae's widow journal and needing a moment to process before heading back home.

A vehicle pulled around the corner. She glanced up to see Gage's truck moving down the street toward her.

He parked and turned the engine off. With deliberate steps, Gage left the truck and headed for her. "I thought I might find you here."

Her heart started to pound. "Gage?" She stood, uncertain. "Did you forget something?"

"Yes," he said with purpose. "I forgot I shouldn't leave you. Not ever again." He framed her face with his hands, and then he kissed her.

Here was love, injured, kind, powerful.

Here was love, ready to catch her when she fell and be supported in return.

Here was love, in the man who knew her best. Gage.

Shelby sank against him, accepting his kiss and all the unspoken promises that went along with it. Her life was changing again. Not in a blink and not because of disaster. But because of the love of the man in her arms.

"I can follow you to Kentucky later," she breathed, love giving her strength to let him go, if only for a short time. "After Grandpa is walking again."

"Not a chance." Gage rested his forehead on hers. "He needs you. He needs *us*. You'll keep him safe. I'll keep his brain occupied at the clinic."

Shelby shook her head. "But what about racehorses? What about delivering the next Secretariat? I won't stand in the way of your dream."

"You are my dream." Gage's arms tightened around her. "Maybe I can consult with the equine hospital, or I could build a birthing stall in back of Doc's clinic. It's a compromise but you're worth it."

"I love you," she whispered for the second time that day. "The way you want me to love you."

"Shel, I don't want to rush you—"

"It's not a rush. I was talking to Mae the day…"

Gage brushed a tear from her cheek.

She lifted her face, staring into his eyes. "And I knew that I loved you. Desperately. But that didn't mean I had the right to stand in the way of your dream."

"You should have told me." His breathing was labored. They'd been standing too long.

Shelby eased him down to the curb. "I have the day off. We should get married. I have a wedding dress. We can use my grandmother's wedding ring."

Gage groaned but that may have been because he couldn't seem to get comfortable sitting on the curb. "What about our families? Your parents?"

She knew they'd ask questions and advise her to wait. She wasn't going to miss out on another minute of love. "I have something blue." Nick's bandana. "I think the dress and shoes are both old and new—they've never been worn. I just need something borrowed." Inspiration struck. "And I know just who to ask."

"Why do I feel as if I'm being barnacled?"

"Gage, I love you." She twined her arms around his neck. "I know you don't like Brussels sprouts and you're allergic to peaches. I know you're smart and gentle and kind. You have just as strong a protective instinct as I do." She pulled him closer until their lips were almost touching. "But more importantly, we both know how precious life is and how short it can be. There is no time to waste."

"No regrets," Gage murmured.

"Marry me today, Gage Jamero. If it makes you feel better, we can break my grandfather out of the hospital for a few hours to be a witness."

He didn't answer. He kissed her instead.

And that was answer enough.

In the end, they weren't married that day. But they were married the next day.

Gage called his parents, who were ecstatic to witness his and Shelby's vows in the county clerk's office in Cloverdale. His sister drove home from college and acted as Shelby's flower girl. Shelby made a live connection to her parents overseas via a cell phone app so they could be present. They checked Grandpa out of the hospital to be the best man. He was wheeled about and fussed over by Agnes, Rose and Mildred. Christine and Slade came down with Ryan for the event.

There was no pomp. There was no glitz. But they were together, surrounded by friends and family, and in love, and nothing else mattered.

"Do you have everything covered, Shelby?" Agnes fluffed Shelby's short train as they stood on the steps in the crisp late morning sunshine. "Something old?"

"My dress." Whereas before there'd been emptiness, Shelby felt filled with love and happiness.

Rose snapped a picture. "Something new?"

"I bought these earrings. I've never worn them." Small pearl studs.

"Something borrowed?" Perched above them on the landing, Mildred was using the seat on her walker to conserve her strength.

"My mom loaned her my grandmother's pearls." Gage's sister, Penny, gave Shelby a hug. She'd been smiling since they'd had an all-girl breakfast together earlier. "She'd love being part of your special day with Gage."

"All you need is something blue," Agnes said.

"I have that, too." Shelby patted her shoulder strap. She'd tucked Nick's folded blue bandana there.

"It's time," Ryan called from the doorway. He wore a blue button-down with a beautiful black silk tie, borrowed from Slade, who apparently had an abundant supply of ties from his Wall Street days.

"Your flowers are pretty," Penny said as they climbed the steps slowly, letting the older women go in first. "I love purple and red."

"Me, too." Shelby paused on the landing to glance heavenward, sending a silent thank-you to Mae.

Once inside, Shelby followed Penny into the clerk's office. Just inside the door, Christine stood beneath Slade's arm, her hand on his bright red tie. Nearby, Grandpa sat in his wheelchair. He held out his hand to Shelby. She took it, leaning in to kiss his cheek.

And then there was Gage, standing tall and proud at the counter waiting for her. He wore a black suit and purple tie. His dark hair may have been short, but a few tufts at his forehead were already starting to curl. His dark gaze met hers with a deep and lasting promise of love.

"I love you," she said, unable to resist standing on tiptoe to kiss him.

"Dogs, all mighty. Wait to make it official, hot shot."

Gage smiled. His expression didn't try to bamboozle or charm. It was an honest smile, a joyful smile, a smile that said you are my everything. "I love you, too." He pressed a kiss to her forehead.

In a blink, they were married, and Shelby's life was changed once more.

Together, they returned Grandpa to the hospital. Together, they walked into the dry-cleaning shop that was restoring Mae's dress. It was ready and they delivered it to the funeral home in Harmony Valley. Together, they visited Nick's grave. Shelby laid her wedding bouquet at the base of his tombstone.

With Gage's arms around her, she felt safe and adventurous at the same time. And loved, so very deeply loved.

And according to Mae, that's the way life was meant to be lived.

The End

Read on for a sneak peek at Book 5 in the series: *Forever Family in a Small Town.*

Forever Family in a Small Town

Excerpt

When Kathy Harris was a teenager, she'd dreamed of being a fashion designer, a professional basketball player and an airline pilot—anything to get out of her small hometown.

So much for dreams.

She shoveled another pile of manure into the wheelbarrow.

She was back in Harmony Valley, the smallest of small towns in the remotest of remote corners of Sonoma County, California.

She made a clucking noise with her tongue and gave Sugar Lips a gentle shove in her chestnut haunches. The former racehorse turned brood mare nickered softly and ambled to the other corner of the paddock. Kathy scooped her manure-filled shovel again, beginning to feel warm in her jacket despite the brisk breeze that had the last reddish-gold leaves of fall swirling around her feet.

"You must be Kathy." An unfamiliar, masculine voice.

Kathy looked toward the veterinary clinic where she worked, trying to identify the source of the voice, but the afternoon sun was in her eyes and all she could see was a silhouette of a man—tall, broad-shouldered, a baseball cap on his head.

"I'm Dylan." His voice was smooth as molasses, sweet as honey to a fly. It drew her closer. "I'm here to help with the horses. Dr. Jamero said you'd be back here."

Dr. Gage Jamero was Kathy's boss. He ran a small-animal clinic for the locals and a horse obstetrics unit at the rear of the property. Kathy hadn't seen Gage in action yet, but she imagined him to be an equestrian midwife, high-strung mares being his specialty, although his tales of Sugar Lips hadn't lived up to her reputation. The mare may have been a hellcat during her first pregnancy, but most of the time she was more like a tired kitten.

Gage had hired Kathy despite her just getting out of rehab. She kept the animals, big and small, fed and watered, and cleaned the clinic, inside and out. Out being her preference. That was where the horses were and where she felt she could breathe.

The fifteen-hundred-pound kitten nudged Kathy forward, causing her to drop the shovel. "Knock it off, Sugar."

Dylan, whose face she still couldn't make out with the sun in her eyes, laughed. It was a friendly laugh. An I-don't-know-you're-an-alcoholic laugh. Whoever Dylan was, Kathy dreaded telling him the truth, as she did with anyone. And she was blunt about the truth nowadays. She'd hid her addiction too long. She hid very little lately, only her most painful of secrets.

Kathy hefted the shovel and walked toward Dylan. The mare trailed behind her. They both stopped in the shadow of a sixty-foot-tall eucalyptus tree near the paddock gate. Its silver-green leaves rustled like tissue paper in a gift box on Christmas morning.

Dylan's appearance didn't match his voice or his laugh. His silhouette was deceptive, too. Who'd seen those cowboy boots coming? Broad shoulders, yeah, but he was linebacker-solid beneath that navy vest jacket and those blue flannel sleeves. His laugh might have been friendly, but his scrutiny of her was not. A fringe of soft brown hair beneath his red ball cap contrasted with sharp gray eyes, a strong nose that looked as if it'd been broken at least once and a firm slash of a mouth.

Someone had already told him who she was—*what* she was.

Kathy swallowed back the sudden bitterness in her throat, tugged off a work glove and extended her hand. "Hi, I'm Kathy, and I'm an alcoholic. Four months sober."

She expected his mouth to turn down. She expected his eyes to drift away from hers. Instead, he smiled. The smile transformed his face from intimidating to accepting to handsome. "Good to meet you, Kathy." His grip was warm and firm, almost too firm.

She retrieved her hand, resisting the urge to shake the bones back into place. "Are you delivering another mare to us? Gage didn't tell me we were expecting a new guest." The veterinary clinic made most of its money from their high-end racehorse breeding clientele.

Dylan hooked his arms over the metal paddock rail, still smiling at her. "No, I didn't bring any horses. I came to assess the ones here and work with them a few days a week. If things work out."

Suddenly, she remembered Gage mentioning him. "Oh, shoot. You're the miracle worker."

"Horse trainer," he corrected, gaze dropping to his scuffed and stained cowboy boots.

Sugar rubbed her long, elegant chin back and forth over Kathy's shoulder. Kathy resisted the urge to check for slobber streaks on her pink jacket. "Go on, have your fun, Sugar. Your spa days are over. This man's going to save Chance and put you through your paces."

Sugar blew a raspberry at Dylan.

"Never mind her." Kathy patted Sugar's cheek. "She's a tease."

Dylan blew a raspberry of his own, smiling not at Kathy but at the horse. The mare sniffed the brisk air, then stretched her head toward Dylan, bumping Kathy out of the way.

"Careful," Kathy warned Dylan as Sugar gummed the navy flannel sleeve of his shirt. "Sugar prides herself on being unpredictable." She'd already chewed the finger off one of Kathy's gloves. Good thing Kathy's finger hadn't been in it at the time. "Her papers say she's a Thoroughbred, but I think she's part mule."

"It's okay. She and I understand each other." Dylan scratched beneath the crown of Sugar's halter. "Dr. Jamero is busy with a patient. He said you could show me around."

"Of course. You'll be wanting to see Chance." Kathy put the shovel into the wheelbarrow and pushed it outside the paddock, thanking Dylan for opening and closing the gate. "We've got two pregnant mares stabled, plus Sugar and her colt, Chance. We have room for eight horses back here, pregnant or otherwise, and expect to be booked up come spring."

Dylan walked with a slight limp, but with a gracefulness that reminded her of Sugar when she trotted around the paddock. Another contradiction in a man so big and muscular.

The stables were up a gentle incline from the clinic. The walk was quiet except for their cowboy boots on pavement. Dylan stopped in the stable's entry and breathed in deeply, as if reveling in the smells of home. It smelled of hay and manure. Kathy was growing used to those aromas, but she still spritzed herself with perfume every morning.

"I thought Dr. Jamero only took in mares ready to deliver," he said in that honeyed voice.

"Chance is Sugar's." When Dylan didn't say anything, Kathy's suspicion sensor went off—like a finger tap-tap-tapping her temple. She cast a quick glance his way. "Didn't Gage tell you about Chance?"

Dylan quirked one eyebrow, as if to say, *What? You doubt me?* "I'm here to evaluate. I like to see for myself."

Two equine heads poked over stall doors.

"This is Trixie." Kathy pointed to the tall gray mare who nickered a welcome. "And that's Isabo." A tired-looking bay who seemed too long in the tooth to be having babies. The mare stretched her nose toward Kathy.

"They like you." Dylan sounded surprised.

His reaction pressed her pause button. Was it surprising because she was an alcoholic? A woman? Or...

There was a loud thud in one of the rear stalls.

"That would be Chance." Kathy hurried to the stall. "I hear you, baby." She slipped inside, moving slowly, surveying the stitches and bandages on the chestnut colt's lower neck and chest. He pranced nervously through the straw, eyeing Kathy as if he'd never seen her before. The stitches beneath his round cheek were oozing and needed attention. "What's up with you, baby? Are you lonely?"

Despite the long gashes, Chance was beautiful. He was only a few months old, his head barely reached Kathy's, and yet he held himself with the proud dignity of a long line of racing Thoroughbreds.

Chance froze, staring at the stall door. A moment later, he began kicking, striking out at anything within range—imaginary foes, walls, Kathy.

A large hand gripped Kathy's shoulder and yanked her out of the stall.

"Let me go. I can calm him down." Kathy struggled to free herself as Dylan dragged her back several feet.

In the paddock outside, Sugar whinnied.

"You're not going back in there." Dylan's voice became clipped and seemed to harden until his words hit her like gravel spitting from beneath a semi's tires. "That. Colt's. A. Killer."

Kathy twisted free of his hold. "That colt is why you're here." She was shaking. Shaking with anger and fear and adrenaline. She was shaking and it wasn't because she needed a drink. She and Chance had a lot in common—social handicaps. He by his appearance and outbursts. She by her reputation as a drinker and parental failure.

She tugged Dylan out of Chance's line of sight. Sugar trotted back and forth along the paddock fence.

"I heard about this colt, but not from Gage." Dylan raised his voice to be heard above the huffing and hoof strikes Chance was making. "Mountain-lion attack."

Kathy nodded. "Since the drought, they've been coming closer to civilization looking for food. Chance and Sugar were in a remote pasture at Far Turn Farms. They moved them here a few weeks ago." She pitched her voice high, as if she was talking to a baby, taking a few steps back until Chance could see her again. "He's just a scared lamb."

At the sight of her and the sound of her voice, Chance's outburst seemed to lose some steam, just like when her son, Truman, would throw a tantrum as a toddler. A bit of gentle reassurance and everything would be okay.

"He's not a lamb. He's nearly as large as you are." Dylan's face was set in hard, disapproving planes, a cookie cutter of most people's reaction to her past mistakes. She didn't want to admit how disappointing it was to see that familiar expression on his face, especially since she'd just met the man. "I've seen that look before. Don't go in there. He's a lost cause."

The stall latch was cold beneath her fingers as she prepared to rejoin Chance. "That's what some people say about me."

Make sure you check out the *Love in Harmony Valley* series, including Book 5: *Forever Family in a Small Town!*

About the Author

USA Today bestselling author Melinda Curtis has written and sold over 70 titles, mostly contemporary romance, but including two writing craft books. Working both traditionally and as an indie, Melinda writes sweet romance, women's fiction, and sweet romantic comedies. One of her romances – *Dandelion Wishes* – was made into a TV movie – *Love in Harmony Valley* – starring Amber Marshall. Melinda is married to her college sweetheart, has three children, and currently lives in Oregon. When she's not writing, Melinda enjoys brief stints of gardening (if it's sunny) or catches up on cleaning and laundry (begrudgingly), all done efficiently so she can get to her to-be-read pile and list of shows to binge.

Check out Melinda's Shopify Store for autographed books, bundles, and sales: ShopMelindaCurtis.MyShopify.com

Other Sweet Books/Series by Melinda Curtis:
A Cowboy Worth Waiting For, Book 1 in the Cowboy Academy romance series
A Kiss is Just a Kiss, Book 1 in the Summer Kisses (Grandma Dotty) romcom series
Can't Hurry Love, Book 1 in the small town Sunshine Valley romcom series
Kissed by the Country Doc, Book 1 in the small town Mountain Monroe series
Her Alaskan Valentine's Day Matchmaker, Book 1 in the bearded, Alaskan Matchmaker series

A Son for the Mountain Firefighter, Book 1 in the emotional, action-packed Mountain Firefighter series

Christmas, Actually, Book 1 in the long-running Heartwarming Christmas Town series

Christmas at the Sleigh Café, a 1st person romcom from the Christmas Mountain series

Discover more titles and a reading guide at:
https://www.melindacurtis.net

Happy reading!
Melinda Curtis

Made in the USA
Las Vegas, NV
27 February 2025

18773100R00134